MW00711597

SILENCE
OF THE
BONES

THE MADISON MCKENZIE FILES
(BOOK 1)

BEV FREEMAN

Jan-Carol
Publishing, Inc
"every story needs a book"

SILENCE OF THE BONES
Bev Freeman

Published September 2016
Little Creek Books
Imprint of Jan-Carol Publishing, Inc
All rights reserved
Copyright © 2016 by Bev Freeman
Front Cover Illustration: Robert L. Conway

ISBN: 978-1-945619-07-6
Library of Congress Control Number: 2016954762

You may contact the publisher:
Jan-Carol Publishing, Inc
PO Box 701
Johnson City, TN 37605
publisher@jancarolpublishing.com
jancarolpublishing.com

To Margaret DeCastro-Nelson, who first encouraged me to write.
And to my loving family who allowed me to ignore them

DEAR READER

Thank you for choosing my first published novel. I trust it will not take you as long to read this book as it took me to create my characters and tell their story. The process spanned a period of twelve years. I've never been known for giving up, however, I've been sidetracked at times. Eventually I learned and applied the craft of writing to my ideas. Together the combination became my third novel. The other two are still hiding from the eyes of the public, for the moment at least.

Now that Silence of the Bones has been adopted by the kind people from Jan-Carol Publishing, I will edit my first two stories to follow Madison McKenzie as she evolves in life's choices.

So if you enjoy reading *Silence of the Bones*, I hope you will look for *Where Lady Slippers Grow* in the future.

With humble appreciation,
Bev

ACKNOWLEDGMENTS

To my family and friends who encouraged me to reach for the stars, thanks for being my sounding board. To Nada Kirby, who told me if I wanted to be a writer I needed to surround myself with writers, SO I DID, beginning with Janice Hornburg, my personal spell-check and grammar guru. Thanks to Mom, who paid for my first big conference, and encouraged me to keep writing. To my older brother Greg, resident authority on Alaska and flying, thanks for helping me get the info correct. Thank you, Michael, my younger brother who keeps me in a working computer, all the way from Florida. You make the world a lot smaller and less threatening for your dummy sister. And lastly, thank you to my husband, Bill, who slept many nights alone while I created strangers on the page. We have more room in our bed now with them locked away in this novel.

Thank you "Bob" Conway, Sultan, WA. Your artwork on my cover is perfect. I love you, my friend!

Thanks to Abbi Kincade and Judi Hopson, editors. And a special thanks to Janice Hornburg for your devotion to perfection. As my critique partner—you went above and beyond the duty in final inspection. Your expertise is irreplaceable. Your friendship is priceless.

CHAPTER 1

Madison and her dog Bud hit the trail before sunbeams penetrated the hollows of Eagle Ridge. She jogged effortlessly, filling her lungs with pure mountain air, and exhaled the bitterness of resentments stored away like files in the cabinet of her soul. She couldn't shake the feeling that *this* March 17th, her twenty-first birthday, might be the most important of her life.

Running, her only escape, brought an independence she'd never known before. In these woods she felt free: in control of her muscles and her mind. In real life, everyone else thought they knew what was best for her.

The slap of a low sweeping white pine branch jarred Madison back to the moment. She looked for the black and tan dog. Bud streaked along with the natural exuberance of a half-grown blue heeler pup. A mass of energy on four legs, he sometimes lagged behind to investigate a scent, or charged ahead after rabbits or deer, until she feared he'd get lost.

She called him to her side, prepared to scold him. He melted her heart with his adoring brown-eyed gaze, so she dismissed the thought of putting him on a leash. She flung her arms around Bud's neck, inhaling the piney scent of his dark coat. "You're my best bud, aren't you, boy?"

He grabbed the heavy braid that fell across her shoulder.

"No, we aren't playing tug of war. That was cute when you weighed four pounds; now you can drag me down the mountain." She flung her hair behind her back and stood. "Today is special. Aunt Denny let me off from work because I wanted to hike this trail. We ran this far. Now let's slow our pace and enjoy the sights." She drew her hand through mid-air as though illustrating a picture. "Bud, this is the famous, historic Appalachian Trail."

Then she had to laugh at the strange look on the dog's face. Even though she didn't feel silly talking to Bud like she would a human, she knew he didn't understand *all* she said. Or did he? It was enough for her that he was on a new trail, a birthday present to herself. Bud was enjoying their adventure, and that's all that mattered.

Shards of light pierced the shadows of hardwood trees looming over ground cluttered with sprouts of lacy ferns, colorful mushrooms, and red spruce seedlings. The trail snaked through the underbrush, yielding to thick clumps of mountain laurel. Smells of damp earth and rotting vegetation filled Madison's nostrils. Her cheeks stung, but she loved the chill in the air; soon enough, spring's warmth would awaken buds and replace the leaves winter tore from the branches.

Bud ran ahead and then back, making sure she followed. At a washout in the trail, he stopped to sniff and paw at something.

She picked up a small, yellowish object, examining a root formation. *It's an upper molar.*

Nose to the ground, Bud left the trail to follow the wash up an embankment.

"Hey, come back." Madison chased after him.

At last he stopped, and dug so furiously that a plume of dirt sprayed out between his back legs.

As Madison approached, a grayish white object rolled out of the hole and came to rest at her feet. Empty eye sockets stared up at her. She stumbled backward and sat down hard.

Bud lunged toward the ball-like object and clamped his jaws around it, wagging his tail in anticipation of a game of fetch.

"NO!" Madison shrieked.

Bud dropped the thing, tucked his tail, and slunk to her side.

She grabbed his collar, holding it like a lifeline.

After a few moments, curiosity overcame shock. Releasing Bud's collar, she struggled to her feet and picked up the bleached, bony orb.

"Where did you come from?" She rotated the small skull in her hands. There were wisdom teeth, which meant the person was late teens to mid-twenties. It was old and fleshless: scoured by the elements, stained by the earth, and completely out of place.

Madison felt overwhelming sympathy for the pitiful, abandoned remains. She knew what it's like to be thrown out like garbage. As a baby, her mom vanished like smoke—leaving nothing, not even a memory.

She replaced the skull in the spot where it had slumbered for so long. Her fingers lingered for a moment as she stared at the disturbed earth. It was time to notify Sheriff Perry; he'd' know what to do.

Madison retreated along the trail, carefully observing landmarks so she could find her way back with the sheriff. She had no choice but to return to Cold Creek, a half-hour drive down the mountain. It was probably the smallest town in East Tennessee, and her home.

Her vehicle left a trail of dust in her rear view mirror as she steered the four-wheel-drive Blazer from the gravel road onto the main highway for the final couple of miles into town.

The pit of Madison's stomach tightened when she pulled up in front of the sheriff's office.

"Here we are." She took her time snapping a leash on Bud's collar before opening the car door. She let him lead the way inside the open door to Sheriff Drew Perry, sitting behind a long desk.

He stood as they came in the room. A smile spread across Perry's tanned face. "Hey, Madison. What are you and Bud up to?"

"Sheriff, we were hiking, Eagle..." She tried to answer, but her mouth was as dry as a cob.

Sheriff Perry settled his six-foot frame onto the corner of his desk. "Take a breath. Now, what's wrong?"

"Bud found a skull."

Perry's blue eyes widened. "A human skull?"

She nodded. "First he found a molar, which was odd enough. Then he dug up the skull..."

Perry threw up his hands. "Whoa, slow down. Let me get this straight." He crossed his arms and stood again.

"You and Bud were hiking." He took a long breath. "Okay, tell me about the skull."

Madison began, "I drove up to Eagle Ridge before daylight, and it was great fun until Bud ran off the trail and dug up a skull."

"Can you show me?" He stepped away from his desk and called out to his deputy in the adjoining office. "Come on, Franks."

Madison and Bud moved toward the door. A pudgy man in a khaki uniform approached them.

"Good boy." Deputy Franks reached a hand toward Bud.

Bud let out a low growl as the hair on his back rose. His normally fast-wagging tail slowed to a standstill.

"Quiet, Bud." She pulled him close to her side. "I'm sorry; I've never seen him do that."

"Aw, that's okay. Maybe he's already spooked from the skull." The deputy slapped a cap over his prematurely receding hairline and followed them out the door.

Five years behind a desk had made his already wide girth even wider than when he and Madison had gone to school together.

She felt a twinge in her gut. It's odd for Bud to show aggression. Did he sense something in the deputy that she could not?

CHAPTER 2

When they reached the turnaround at the end of Eagle Ridge Road, Sheriff Perry parked the vehicle and opened the back door. Bud hopped out as Madison emerged on the other side.

Deputy Franks pulled in next to them, exiting his cruiser with a camera swinging from a strap on his neck. He carried a short-handled shovel in one hand, and a small pickax in the other.

"Today *is* your birthday, isn't it, Madison?" The deputy laughed. "I mean, it isn't Thanksgiving or Christmas. Can't think of any other reason Denny would give you a Friday off."

She snapped a leash on Bud's collar and pointed to dense evergreens. "We go that way." She took off, her long, athletic legs striding up the inclined trail, leaving the deputy huffing and puffing in her wake.

"I was right!" Franks yelled.

"Shut up, Franks!" Sheriff Perry caught up with Madison. "I'm sorry, he can be rude."

"Don't apologize for him. I'm used to Willy Franks; known him all my life."

Her muscles tensed as she approached the area where she'd seen the skull; she raised her hand and pointed. "Just up that incline is where Bud dug it up. Guess that's the crime scene."

"I wouldn't call it a crime scene yet," Sheriff Perry said. "You keep Bud down here."

The sheriff climbed the hill, locating the skull immediately. After a while, the deputy arrived and joined Perry. Madison and Bud watched from below. She strained to hear their conversation, but stayed on the trail like she was told.

The two law officers soon rejoined her. "Franks will take you home. I'm going to nose around here for a while longer." The sheriff stood looking up the hill. "We only found a couple more bones. They're old, all bleached out. Probably from an old family cemetery." Then he turned to face Madison. "You okay?"

She nodded, turned to go back down the trail with Franks, then stopped and said, "You will find out who she is, won't you, Sheriff?"

"I'll do whatever I can. Try not to worry."

Franks moved down the trail with the speed of a slug. Madison pulled the leash to stop Bud so the overweight deputy could catch his breath.

Franks leaned on his shovel. He studied her as if he were deciding how to pose one of those taxidermy mounts he made as a hobby.

"I'm surprised Jess lets you wear those sweat pants."

"What do you mean?"

"Women in your church aren't allowed to wear the family pants." He sneered. "But I guess old Jess must be catching up with the times. Took him ten years to realize you're not much of a runner in petticoats."

Madison's stomach tumbled as she remembered her humiliation in the eighth grade. She'd gotten tangled up in her dress trying to tag home plate, and failed to score the tying run. Willy Franks, then a senior and team captain, razzed her for weeks, tripping over imaginary skirts as he stumbled down the hall. She'd begged Jess for jeans, but he'd quoted a Bible verse about how women shouldn't wear man's clothing. She'd obeyed, because one girl's opinion didn't count for much against Jess and the Bible.

Madison looked at her shoes. "If you must know, Aunt Denny finally convinced him pants are more modest than skirts when I run."

Franks grinned. "Bet that hair's never been cut. You don't wear makeup. You pleasing God, or Jess?"

"How could you—" She felt dizzy and her ears burned. But she remembered how after that ball game, she'd watched from the bleachers. How different she was from the other girls, who wore makeup and pretty clothes that showed off their figures. She'd hated her mousy looks and dowdy clothes. Even more, she'd hated that she didn't have the nerve to tell Jess how she felt. But that was disrespect, and she'd never be disrespectful to any adult—especially her adopted father, whom she loved.

In spite of his strict rules, he'd been a good daddy to her. She didn't always understand his ways, but she loved him for the tenderness he displayed for her and Momma Shirley. Everyone liked Jess and respected his strengths. She thought he could do anything; he was her hero.

Although half a head taller than Franks, Madison felt diminished under his scrutiny.

"Why does it matter to you how I was raised, Willy?"

Franks lurched forward. "Don't call me Willy! My name's Franks—just Franks."

Bud growled. Madison reeled in his leash. "It's okay, boy."

She pulled Bud and retreated down the trail. "I'm sorry, Franks."

Franks followed at a safe distance. "I'm just saying, what's a twenty-one-year-old woman doing living at home, letting her folks run her life? Jess ain't your real father anyhow. Everybody knows your real dad died before you were born."

"Well, at least Jess has his right mind, which is more than you can say for your father."

Franks glared at her when he caught up with her at the road. "Get in the car!"

Madison wished she could shrink into the earth. She remembered Jess had said once that some kids are just plain mean, and never outgrow it. She dreaded the long ride home.

Franks jammed the cruiser in gear and goosed the gas, fishtailing down the gravel road.

"Unlike that mealy-mouthed Perry, *my* father was the best, most respected, longest serving sheriff this county has ever had. When he got sick, I was too young to run for sheriff. You just wait; I'll be the sheriff of this county next election."

You're not sheriff material. You're just dreaming.

"Where was your mother? I don't remember her at all." She stared at Franks.

"I didn't have a mother. Dad raised me."

"Everybody has a mother. *Somebody* gave birth to you." She tried not to grin,

7

but it didn't work. After a few minutes of silence, she said, "Listen, Franks, let's call a truce. I was wrong to say that about your father. He can't help having Alzheimer's. I apologize."

"Okay, truce. As for my mother, she didn't want me or my dad." His voice dropped to a whisper.

"There was a lot of that going around." She looked away again, not wanting to make eye contact.

"We didn't need anybody! Dad and I got along just fine without any help." Franks rested his arm in the open window. His body odor wafted to Madison's nose.

"Do you mind putting up the window? I'm cold." Madison pulled her windbreaker snug. She felt sick from hunger, and his odor compounded the problem. She hadn't eaten since her early breakfast.

Franks cranked up the window. "One more thing, stay away from the crime scene."

"Sheriff Perry said it's not a crime scene," she argued.

"What does he know? I bet he won't even bother to put up yellow tape. Just stay away from there, if you know what's good for you."

"I've got a splitting headache," she said. She looked out the passenger window and hoped he'd just shut up. Franks had always been a bully, but this was way over the top.

"I mean it. You stay out of this!" He pounded his fist on the steering wheel.

His tone chilled her. "Are you threatening me?"

"Just looking out for your best interest," he said.

It felt like a long time before they reached town. Today's birthday hike should have been peaceful, but Bud dug up someone's daughter, or wife, or mother. Who knew who this could be? She felt sicker as different scenarios spun in her head. The skull could've been someone's mother. *Who was my mother? What would she think of me now?* Her hand felt the half-heart pendant under her shirt. Aunt Denny said her mom had placed it around her neck at birth. The feeling of the cold metal channeled Denny's cold words from her memory of her sixth birthday party.

"Child, you're old enough to know the truth. Your birth mother abandoned you as an infant, so Shirley and Jess adopted you."

At the young age of six, Madison slipped into a cloak of caution and mistrust. She strived to please everyone around her, and earned the nickname Mousy Maddy at school.

Finally, she realized the car had stopped moving. "Thanks for the ride." She and Bud got out of the cruiser.

"No problem," Franks said. "Be careful going home."

Madison pushed open the front door of Jess's house. Her folks were still at their restaurant, Shirley's Home Cooking, the only eating establishment in Cold Creek. On Fridays Shirley's stayed open late, so they'd be a couple of hours. She felt relieved to be home alone for a while. There were so many things to sort out.

Madison dropped into a rocker as Bud made his way to his food bowl in the kitchen. She pushed her shoes off without untying them, and sat a long time in the dim light of the living room. Her body ached worse than when she'd had the flu back in winter. All she wanted was to pull the covers over her head and go to sleep, thinking perhaps this was all a bad dream.

Bud emptied his food bowl and curled up on the rug below Madison's chair.

After a while, she went to the refrigerator and peered in. Then she remembered Franks' squinty eyes appraising her body and walked away empty-handed. She slumped against the wall in her bedroom, removed her clothes, and left them in a pile on the floor.

She stepped into the shower and spilled herbal shampoo onto her head. It drizzled down her body. She lathered into a mummy of bubbles, then stood motionless while the warmth rinsed away the scent of Franks—and hopefully the mood of the day. She dried off and wrapped her hair with the towel, put on her pajamas, and walked into the living room.

Why were the bones haunting her? Normally, she'd go to the restaurant to eat on Friday evenings. But tonight, there was no way. Franks' rude words had shaken her more deeply than she realized.

She'd always felt like a misfit in school, and even now she didn't fit in. It was more than Jess's rules that made her different; she didn't even know what she wanted out of life.

The phone rang, causing Madison to jump. She stared at the ringing object for a moment before she reached for the receiver and read *Henry and Holly Jacobs* on the caller ID.

"Hi Holly, I'm glad to hear from you."

The voice on the line sounded jovial. "Happy birthday!"

"Thanks." Madison listened for a while, then sat on the couch with her bare feet tucked underneath her. Holly had been her best friend since they were in first grade. Even though Holly married Henry, her high school sweetheart, who by all reasoning was one step away from abuse. Madison treasured Holly's friendship.

"So, what did you do to celebrate?" Holly asked.

"Nothing much. Bud and I started up the Eagle Ridge trail, but we came back early."

"Too cold for you on the mountain?" Holly asked.

"Something like that." Madison was quiet for a few minutes. "I need to ask you something. You have to promise to tell me the truth."

"What is it, Madison?"

"When we were in school, did the kids talk behind my back?'

"They didn't dare if I was around."

"That sounds like 'yes' to me. What did they say?" Madison persisted.

"Well, some called you Mousy Maddy. Others said you were a 'Holy Roller' because of the strict way you were raised. But hey, I was different, too, with my bleached hair and all that makeup. I thought I looked like Dolly Parton. But that's what influenced me to take cosmetology courses," Holly laughed.

Her high-pitched laughter reminded Madison of Dolly's voice. "You are shaped like Dolly. I've always envied how comfortable you seemed with your image. The boys all liked you. Hardly a week went by that Henry didn't fight for you. You remember?"

Holly sounded sad. "Henry's always had a hair trigger. He didn't need an excuse to fight."

The line was quiet for a few seconds. Then she said, "You and I are polar opposites: me with my pale colors, and you with your silky, dark chocolate hair and jade green eyes. And your eyelashes! My word, they're so long and curled, they look just like the false ones movie stars wear!"

"Oh, stop it." Madison felt a burn in her face. "Yeah, you Dolly, me Olive

Oyl. That's more like it."

"Maybe that's what made us best friends," Holly said.

Madison took a deep breath and let it out. "Up on the mountain, Bud dug up a human skull."

"What?!" Holly sounded as though she'd dropped the phone.

"I went to Sheriff Perry. He and that awful Willy Franks went back up there with me. I don't think they're very concerned about who she is. Perry thinks she washed out of an old grave."

Holly cleared her throat. "Well, there *are* graves all over these hills. Lots of the old home places had graves out back. That's the way folks have done for centuries, just burying their dead on the hill above the barn."

"Perry said not to tell anyone. You can't even tell Henry, understand?" Madison said.

"Okay, I promise. He'd laugh about it anyway, and agree with the sheriff."

"I have a feeling there's more to it."

"Feel it in your bones, huh?" Holly chuckled.

Madison ignored the attempt to cheer her mood. "She's so small, and all alone. I can't shake the image of her looking up at me, asking for help."

"Well, Sheriff Perry will find out who she is—err, was—and she can have a proper burial."

For a few moments the line was silent again. Then Holly said, "Okay, Madison now tell me what's really eating you."

Holly always could read Madison, even when she kept totally quiet. Holly was a smart girl, even though Madison thought marrying Henry had been the dumbest thing she ever did.

"Franks and I had words today," Madison said. "He made fun of how I dress and how I was raised. He even threatened me, saying I'd better not go back up there, because I might not like what I found. Can you imagine a deputy talking like that?"

"*That* deputy, yes." Holly tapped the phone with her fingernail. "Don't pay him no mind."

"Holly, he made me question my relationship with Jess. I know Jess loves me, but he runs my life. If I try to question anything, he quotes scripture. Says he's head of the family, and he knows what's best. He says it's time I joined the church, but I don't know what to believe anymore. A woman can run for president nowadays—but in their church, a woman can't even speak her mind in the business meeting."

"Madison dear, you've always had a hard time speaking up for yourself. The kids called you Mousy Maddy for a reason. You think if you don't do what people want, they won't love you. Maybe you're afraid someone else you love will leave you like your mother did. But don't worry, we all love you. We'll stick by you, no matter what."

"You're so right, Holly. All my life I've felt like a reject. To make up for it, I've tried to please everyone but myself. I guess I never looked at it that way 'til now."

"It's no big deal. You're the sweetest person I know. Everybody loves you, even my Henry, and that's saying a lot. 'Cause sometimes I'm not even sure he loves *me*." Holly giggled like she always did.

"Holly, will you help me change?"

"Wow! This don't sound like the Madison *I* know—but I like the way you're thinking."

"I'm twenty-one, and I need to stand up for myself. You going to help me?"

"'Course I will! I'd do anything for you."

The call concluded, and Madison replaced the phone on its charger.

She started to cross the living room when a noise at the door caused her to stop. Bud growled as the hair on his back rose. She held her breath to listen; hearing no other sound, she moved toward the door and switched on the porch light. Through the glass, she saw a dark figure jump off the porch and run into the shadows. Her hand went to the handle; the door was locked.

In Cold Creek, no one locks their doors. But she was glad it was locked this time. Then she thought of the back door. Her feet moved as though they were lead weighted. It too was locked, and the slide bolt was in place. Had she been so distraught when she came in that she'd locked the doors without realizing what she was doing?

Bud tilted his head and whined. Who had been on the porch, and why didn't he knock? She went to her bedroom, leaving the lights on and the doors locked. She thought of calling Jess, but decided against it. *Bud will bark if he hears anything out of the ordinary*, she thought. *Besides, everyone in town knows Jess will be home soon, and he is no man to trifle with.*

Bud made himself comfortable on the floor next to her nightstand.

"I'm so glad I have you, Bud." She scratched behind his ear. Dim light filtered into her room. Dreading the dreams that might come, she closed her eyes.

Today she'd made a decision on her own. The results may have been upsetting, but at the same time, she'd opened a door that might help someone else. Too restless to sleep, Madison swung her feet over the side of her bed.

"No, she's gone." *She'll never know I found her bones.* She shook her head. *But I will! I'll know who she was, where she was from, and maybe even who killed her.*

She patted the bed. Bud jumped up beside her and rested his head on her leg.

"What would I do without you, Bud?"

CHAPTER 3

It was Saturday, and Madison overslept. Although she usually left the door cracked for Bud to come back in, today she waited until he did his business and then locked it. She went to see if the sheriff had learned anything about the skull.

Perry poured a cup of coffee as she walked into his office. "Morning," he said. "Have a cup?" he lifted the pot again.

"No, thanks." She stood quietly for a minute, giving him a chance to sip the steaming brew. "Do you have news on the bones yet? Or identification?"

Perry shook his head. "This is going to take some time. But you also need to realize there's not much hope of learning a true identity."

"Well, you are going to try, right?" She edged closer.

"Those bones are probably a hundred years old. These hills are pocked with family cemeteries. I checked with the registrar of deeds in Erwin, and there's no property owner—but you can't rule out squatters. We didn't find a headstone. No marker at all, not even a rock."

"What will you do with her?" Madison asked.

"Seal the bones in a box and send them to Knoxville for forensic analysis. What else *can* I do? Like I said, no hope."

Madison stiffened at his response. She had to know who those bones belonged to; if he wouldn't or couldn't help, then she'd find out by herself.

"Sheriff, there's always hope! I've lived on hope since I was six." She stared him down and then turned to go. "Are you or Franks going back up there?"

"Don't plan to," he said. "And Franks isn't going to do anything without me prodding him along."

"Right." Madison closed the door, resisting the urge to slam it. She crossed the street and went into the restaurant. As she walked in, Jess poked his head over the swinging doors of the kitchen.

He said, "Lucky for me, I had my keys last night."

"Sorry, I thought I saw somebody on the porch."

She walked past him and sat at the counter next to Mr. Olsen, a longtime friend and the owner of the hardware store next to the jail. "Hey, Mr. Olsen. How's your arthritis today?"

He nodded to her with a friendly smile. "Been better, when I was young like you; but not too bad for an old man."

"At least you have a good attitude," she said. "That's more than some folks."

Shirley stood behind the counter, stacking clean mugs on a rack. She reached out and patted her daughter's hand. "Morning, birthday girl."

"That was yesterday." Madison smiled.

"But we didn't see you yesterday." Shirley leaned on the counter. "You must be starved, since you didn't come in for supper last night."

"No, not really." Madison tucked a long strand of hair behind her right ear.

"Someone saw you come out of the sheriff's office yesterday; what was that all about?" Shirley asked.

"The sheriff says it was nothing. I'll tell you about it later," Madison replied.

"You need to eat breakfast," Shirley said.

"Now Shirley, Madison is still growing up, not out yet. She'll eat when she gets hungry," said Mr. Olsen.

"I'm not hungry, and Bud is itching for our morning run."

Shirley shook her finger at Madison. "I know you haven't eaten anything this morning because there is nothing at home to eat, except maybe an apple. Madison, if you don't eat you'll make yourself sick."

"If I ate as much as you want me to, I'd be fat like Aunt Denny," Madison swung her feet to one side and slid off the stool.

"Denny's muscled out from wrestling those sled dogs, although I'll never understand why a professional woman would take up a pastime like that."

Shirley handed over a bottle of orange juice. "Here, this is better than no break-fast at all."

Madison took the bottle. "I'll see you later; I promise."

"Before you go, tell me about the skeleton you found," Shirley said.

Madison wheeled around. "What did you say?"

"I heard that someone in town discovered a skeleton up on the trail. Natu-rally, I assumed it was you," Shirley said calmly, but her eyes widened with excitement.

"I can't talk about it." Madison looked down at the floor.

"Well, you know Deputy Franks can't keep secrets. He's been talking up a storm, all over town." Mr. Olsen said, then tipped his glass of milk to his lips.

"It was just one skull. Been in the woods a long time," she told them. "Perry feels it's from an old cemetery, and he told me not to talk about it to anyone."

"As Mr. Olsen says, Franks is talking," Shirley replied. Before Madison could say anything Shirley called out, "Jess?"

"I'm coming," he answered, from somewhere back in the kitchen.

"We have a present for you." Shirley spoke softly again.

Jess stepped through the swinging doors holding a little box with a big or-ange ribbon. "This was my grandmother's, and I want you to have it."

Madison's eyes widened. "Oh, my!" She looked inside, and pulled a golden thimble shape from the box. "It looks like a thimble, but it's heavy."

"Not just any thimble; it's eighteen karat gold. Grandmother won it for a quilt she made when she was young. The price of gold nowadays, I'd say it's worth a lot. But I hope you might think of it as an heirloom and keep it." The smile on his face said he was proud of his heritage.

"I remember seeing her quilts in the county fair," Shirley said. "You might want to keep the tradition going. Generations of Appalachian women handed down the craft of quilting; it would be a shame to see it die."

Madison tightened both arms around the tall man. She felt his heart beat-ing against her cheek. Jess stood a head above her. His long arms wrapped around her slender frame as he kissed the top of her head. "I love you, Madi-son."

"I love you too, Jess. *Of course* I'll keep it!"

"Here, I have something for you, too," Shirley pulled an envelope from her apron pocket.

Inside Madison found a key and a folded piece of paper. She opened the parchment and skimmed the words.

Quitclaim Deed, on this date... The Grantor Shirley Chism McKenzie for and in consideration of: One Dollar ($1.00 and or other goods and viable consideration) conveys, releases and Quit Claims to the Grantee: Madison D. McKenzie the following described real estate situated in Cold Creek, in the county of Unicoi, and the state of Tennessee.

Legal Description: The historical dwelling and fifteen acres of property.

The oldest remaining dwelling in Cold Creek sits directly across the street from Shirley's Restaurant, maintained in recent years by Jess as a memorial to the past. Built in the seventeen hundreds, the entire community lovingly refers to it as "the shack." Since there is no hotel within miles, the shack has been used for overnight stays by commuters who find themselves stranded by weather, and even adventurers coming down from hiking the Appalachian Trail. Jess took great pride in preserving the historical house.

Madison looked up with tears welling in her eyes. "The shack—it's mine?"

Shirley walked from behind the counter and stood next to Jess. "It's yours, if you want it."

Madison flung herself into Shirley's open arms.

"This is absolutely unbelievable!" She dropped onto a stool. "Bring on the grits and eggs, Jess. I have to let Shirley know I'm not trying to starve myself."

Thirty minutes later, the screen door banged shut behind her as Madison left the restaurant. She eyed the tattered little shack, cutting through the yard behind it, across the land she now owned and onto Second Street, to her present home.

Bud met her at the door. "Ready?" She walked down the hall, expecting to hear his toenails tapping behind her—but he didn't follow. After changing into running clothes she returned to the living room. Bud's stare drew her attention to the kitchen door. She knew she had locked it earlier; now the deadbolt was undone, and the door stood open. As they left the house, she wondered about the unlocked door. She'd have to remember to ask Jess if he'd been home while she was in the sheriff's office. Or had someone else come in?

CHAPTER 4

Madison's five-mile run began at the meadow behind the play park every morning, rain or shine, a routine she rarely broke from. Bud led the way, scattering any birds hiding in the grass.

This morning, Madison didn't think of her pace. Her thoughts were of the woman who'd slept alone on the mountainside, until yesterday. She meant something to somebody, and Madison longed to find out who she was. If Sheriff Perry was finished with the case, then she was free to do all the investigating she wanted. Suddenly, she slid to a stop.

Bud looked back and waited for her to' catch up.

"Come on, we're going back." She turned and ran back the way they'd come.

The sun was high above the trees when she and Bud reached their porch. She stretched briefly and then went inside. She smeared mustard on whole-wheat bread, plopped on a spoonful of tuna, grabbed an apple and a treat for Bud, and put them in a paper bag. Then she grabbed her backpack and supplies she might need for the day, including her camera.

Patches of fog greeted the pair when they reached Eagle Ridge Trail. Bud ran ahead and she followed, jogging until they came to the site she had shown the sheriff. Pulling her camp shovel and other assorted tools from the backpack, she climbed the hill to the spot where evidence of the deputy's digging scarred the ground. Bud meandered up the embankment, not lingering long in any one spot. Franks had been right; there was no yellow tape identifying the area. She could make out the path of stream runoff—dry now, but its print was clear.

She looked up the hill, reasoning that if bones washed down this way, they'd started up there. Bud ran ahead, as she hoped he would. After a few minutes of sniffing, he dug with the same conviction he'd had when he unearthed the skull.

Madison waited until he stopped slinging dirt, and then moved in with gloved hands—sifting through loose soil, leaf fragments, small branches, and pine residue. Finally, she found a bone. She photographed what appeared to be a vertebra. Setting it aside, she continued sorting stones from sticks and occasionally, another bone—and then another. She carefully documented her finds with photos and marked the area with her own yellow tape.

With each step, Madison scrutinized the earth for signs of a grave marker, scraps of wood that might have come from a coffin, or more bones. She hoped to find some clue to the woman's identity—maybe traces of hair, or buttons, or jewelry. Even a coffin nail might help date the remains.

The trowel hit something that felt and sounded metallic. Picking it up, she scrubbed the dirt off the silver metal with her fingers. She fumbled for the chain around her neck. Her heartbeat quickened as trembling fingers fit the two pieces together. The tarnished half-heart was a match to the one her mother placed around her neck, the day she disappeared from Madison's life.

Madison and Bud returned to her vehicle parked at the turn around at the end of Eagle Ridge Road. She fumbled with the keys pulling them from her pocket, and they dropped to the ground. As she bent to pick them up, she noticed her left front tire was flat. When she walked to the back to get out the jack and the spare, she saw that the right rear was also flat. Fear gripped her. One flat tire could mean she'd picked up a nail; two was surely no accident. She unlocked the door and reached for her cell phone. There was no signal.

"Why am I not surprised?" She spoke as if to the clouds.

She looked at the winding road back toward Cold Creek. No way could she and Bud make it that way before night fell. Coming to a quick decision, she doubled back past the gravesite and onto the famous Appalachian Trail, heading east. Her best chance was to hike toward the interstate, where the trail ran along the ridge and crossed I-26 at the North Carolina/Tennessee state line.

From there, she could hitch to Cold Creek, if they were lucky.

They made good time. Bud enjoyed the fast pace, loping along beside her until something off the trail drew his attention. He disappeared into a laurel slick, and moments later, she heard ferocious, blood-curdling snarling and barking.

"Bud!" she screamed. Disregarding her own safety, Madison plowed into the thick underbrush. The commotion grew louder. She heard Bud yelp in pain. As she ran toward the sounds, one gunshot cracked overhead, and then a second. Madison froze; her heart pounded in her throat when the thick laurel shrubs shook. She stumbled back as an angry black bear ran past, nearly knocking her off her feet.

"Bud?" she cried out.

In the distance she heard a female voice say, "Come here, Boy. Are you hurt?"

Then Madison spied her dog, wiggling all over as if he'd met a friend. "Bud!" she shouted again.

"He's over here," the woman answered.

Madison ran toward her pup. "Lisa? What a relief to see a familiar face!"

"Hey, Madison, is this your dog?"

"Yeah, this is Bud," Madison said. "I'm really glad to see you!" She dropped to her knees and ruffed Bud's fur, feeling for claw marks. "Are you hurt?"

"She just swatted him away. I think she has a den around here and a couple of cubs." Lisa knelt beside Bud. She wore a bright orange UT shirt and carried a shotgun. "He's cute. Bud, huh? I was up on the ridge checking our trail-cam when I saw your dog charge that bear. I fired birdshot over her head to scare her off." Lisa paused and looked at Madison. "Where are you headed, without a pack?"

Madison relaxed her hold on her dog. She turned toward Lisa and explained. "I took Bud for a hike on Eagle Ridge. My Blazer has two flat tires, and I'm headed to the four-lane to hitch a ride home."

Lisa's eyes widened. "I can't let you do that! It's too dangerous! Come with me, our cabin is a half-mile down that way," Lisa rose and held her hand out. "Cole can drive you home after supper."

"I couldn't put him to that much trouble, but can I use your phone?"

"Nonsense, it's not any trouble. You'd do the same for me, if need be. Now, wouldn't you?" Lisa stared Madison down.

"You know I would." Madison took a shaky breath. "Thank you."

In a short time, Lisa led Madison and Bud to a clearing with a narrow, tumbling creek and charming cabin, with smoke billowing out of the chimney.

"Well, this is home." Lisa led the way to the porch. "Supper's in the oven. We'll eat as soon as Cole gets here."

"Thank you so much." Madison watched Bud step along the edge of the creek, drinking as he investigated bubbles from a low waterfall. "This place reminds me of a Thomas Kinkade painting. You and Cole are lucky to live so close with nature."

"We love it," she said with a secret-memory smile.

"There's a neat story behind *that* face. I hope to have something one of these days—a sweet memory, I mean." Madison looked at Bud. "You know, that really scared me, up there on the ridge. He always chases small animals and birds, but I had no idea he'd go after a bear." She dropped down onto the steps. "Then there's the thing about my tires, I know they didn't flatten themselves. It's..."

Lisa sat next to her and put a comforting arm around Madison's shoulders. "I read in the paper just the other day how vandals target cars parked at trailheads. You had some bad luck, that's all."

Madison shook her head, "No, it's more than that."

She filled Lisa in on the details of the last two days. "And that's why I think Weird Willy Franks had something to do with my tires."

Just as she finished her story, a red Jeep clattered across the creek. Brakes squealed, and a lanky man in bibbed overalls unfolded himself from the driver's seat. He bounded up the porch steps, kissed the top of Lisa's head, and exchanged greetings with Madison.

Lisa stood. "Madison found something in the woods, Cole. We were just going inside to clean it. Supper's in the oven, and will be on the table by the time you wash up."

Madison followed her into the house, telling Bud to stay on the porch.

"Let him come in. I have a puppy; they can play together." Lisa snapped her fingers.

Bud bounced into the house to be greeted by a floppy-eared hound with long spindly legs that looked a lot like a young colt. The two dogs rolled on the hardwood floor and across the rug in front of the fireplace.

"He's adorable—a coon hound, huh?" Madison asked.

"Yeah, same as UT's Smokey. Cole is a big UT fan, you know." Lisa took a jar from under the kitchen sink. She rubbed some paste on the blackened metal. As the tarnish faded, the letters became legible.

"What does it say?" Madison leaned in close.

"E, v... Why, it says 'Everlasting.' What does your half say?"

Madison handed over her pendant. "Mine says 'Love;' just 'Love.'"

Lisa placed the two halves together. "They fit; look at the extended line from the e in love. It runs over, into Everlasting. Looks to me like the heart was engraved before it was cut in half. That wasn't the original style. This one must have been special made." She turned it over to look at the back. "There's a tiny emblem, but it's too small to make out."

"I bet Mr. Dempsey can tell me about it. I'll take it to Johnson City and let him see it." Madison looked closely at the back of the heart she'd found. "That is small; my half doesn't have anything on the back."

They were sitting at the kitchen table staring at the heart when Cole came in. He petted the dogs and they both took off, running down the hall.

Lisa motioned for her husband to come closer. "We have a real mystery here. Look." She showed him the two hearts. "Madison found this one up on the mountain, near an old grave or something where she discovered some human bones yesterday. And this is the one her mother gave her when she was a baby."

A frown creased Cole's forehead. "You found the bones up there? They were talking about it at work." Cole dropped into his chair and downed a glass of iced tea. "Your mom died when you were young, didn't she?"

"Well, I don't know what actually happened to her. Aunt Denny said she just disappeared. Nobody knows for sure, they just never heard from her. I've always wondered why she turned her back on me, and I've held a tiny bit of hope that someday I'd find out."

"So you believe you hold a clue? Can't the sheriff get DNA from the bones? He *is* doing something to ID them, right?"

"I suppose the bone farm in Knoxville can, but that will take forever." Madison slipped the two metal hearts into her pocket. "She's up there, I just feel it. There are more bones. I found some today."

"Surely Perry will open an investigation. I mean, isn't that his job? To identify her and find the killer?" Cole sounded agitated. "No woman ventured up on that mountainside alone and then buried *herself*. I don't want to tell him his duty, but it only makes sense, doesn't it?"

CHAPTER 5

Late Sunday afternoon, Madison wrote detailed notes about the evidence she collected from the mountain. The next time she saw Sheriff Perry, she'd be ready, evidence in hand.

The cool evening air crept through the open windows. She closed them and went to her room for a long-sleeved shirt.

"Bud," she called, "let's go outside."

The dog stood, stretched his hind legs one at a time, and then followed Madison out the door. Shirley and Jess sat on the porch swing holding hands.

Shirley spoke softly from the darkness. "Are you alright, Madison? That was quite an ordeal you had yesterday. Please, promise me you won't go back up there anymore."

Madison let out a long sigh. "I'll admit I was scared, but I have a feeling something awful happened up there. I can't shake it—and I can't leave it alone, either."

"I just want you to be careful," Shirley scolded.

"Have you talked to Sheriff Perry again?" Jess asked.

"Not since he closed the case. He'll probably accuse me of grave-robbing anyway." Madison sat on the top step. Bud walked across the yard, sniffing out a special bush to water.

After a few minutes of silence, Madison cleared her throat. "All my life, this family has pretended my mother didn't exist. Even though I've asked, I've never even seen a photo of her, or heard a story about her. This is a small town—you must have known something about her. Please, tell me *anything*. I have to know."

Jess fumbled for his pocket watch. "Denny wanted us to keep it quiet."

"Keep what quiet?"

The watch clattered to the floor, and Jess leaned precariously out of the swing to pick it up. "Nothing in particular; she didn't want us to mention Tina. I guess she thought it would make you sad."

"Well, not knowing feels much worse at this point in my life. I know she was older than you, but didn't you ever see her around town?"

Jess carefully checked the watch for damage. "Yes, I saw her several times. She even talked to me about church a time or two. Since my grandfather was an ordained minister, and I'd grown up in the church, she figured I knew the Bible."

Excited, Madison jumped up and paced the length of the porch. "What did she ask you?"

"My dearest, Madison, Tina was a troubled woman. She followed the ways of the world. There were times she wanted to change, but the Devil always pulled her back."

Madison towered over the seated figures in front of her. "Do you mean to tell me that you knew my mother that well, and you never told me? I'm not six years old anymore! I want to know what she was like!"

Instantly, Madison wished she could withdraw the words that had come out so strong and harsh, but she couldn't. She was sure Jess would scold her. She waited in anticipation of his answer.

"She asked me if she was going to Hell," he said. "I gave her a Bible and hoped she would someday get right with God. That's all I'm going to say about it." Jess rose from the swing and shuffled into the house.

With Jess gone, she turned to Shirley. "If you knew all this, why didn't you tell me?"

Shirley twisted her hands in her apron and spoke softly, "Honey, I never actually met your mother; I didn't know Jess knew her—this is the first I've heard of it." Shirley followed her husband into the house.

Madison leaned over the porch rail and called for Bud. He came immediately to her side and looked up as if to ask, what's next?

"Where's your ball?" Bud raced around to the back yard.

She needed to ask old Sheriff Franks about Tina, since he did the investigation when she disappeared. *His mind comes and goes these days, but it's worth a try.* They say folks with dementia sometimes remember the past better than what they had for breakfast. The thought of running into Willie Franks made her shudder.

Bud returned with a bright yellow ball in his mouth, wagging his tail.

"Good boy." She walked down the steps, taking the ball as he dropped it. "Get your ball." She threw it as hard as she could across the yard, and he chased after it happily. They had not been for a run since she'd gone to church with her folks. The notes she made took up a long time, describing each photo she'd uploaded to the computer. So chasing the ball gave Bud a good workout. She'd let him walk in the shallow creek at the side of the property; he loved the cold running water and it cooled him down.

"Okay, now to the shower. If you're riding with me in the morning, you have to get a bath tonight."

No sooner had the words come out of her mouth than the dog ran from the creek and to the porch into a waiting towel. He loved the shower's warm water, and the blow dryer she used afterwards. This was a good thing, since the smell of herbal-shampoo agreed with her nose better than wet-doggy odor as he slept next to her bed.

Madison was scheduled to take her exam for the Dental Assisting Certification at ETSU on Monday morning in Johnson City. She knew the material well, because Denny had drilled it into her head over the three years she worked for her aunt. The test shouldn't take long; she'd have time to spend with Bud in the afternoon.

She chose to walk along the lake edge at Winged Deer Park. Few people came to enjoy the open fields with their dogs on weekdays, especially in the early afternoon, so they had the place to themselves. The March wind was living up to its reputation, whipping her hair across her face and eyes so that she couldn't see where she was going.

Searching her pockets, she discovered an elastic hair band. She twisted her hair and piled it atop her head, but one band wouldn't hold the weight of her long mane. In frustration, she tossed her head downward and sectioned it into three fat strands, braided them quickly, and secured the end with the elastic. Not a pretty sight, but it was out of her way.

Madison pulled Bud's collar and knelt beside him, all the time looking at the large bird circling overhead. "That's an eagle!" She stayed still and held Bud close. He caught sight of it and barked.

"Hush! You'll scare him." She hoped he'd land and reveal his nest. Instead, the mighty bird of prey swooped down and snatched a fish from the water, right in front of them. She had to hold tightly to Bud; he wanted to give chase.

Sure enough, the eagle flew to a tall pine tree on top of the hill above the lake. Madison could see another white head, in a nest midway up the tree. The male had taken the fish to his mate sitting on their nest.

She couldn't wait to get back home and tell Jess what she'd discovered. He'd read in the Johnson City newspaper that eagles were nesting in this area again; now she could tell him she knew where, and they could observe the pair as the young hatched and grew.

CHAPTER 6

Dr. Denson had not confirmed her patients' appointments for Tuesday, because she'd worked alone on Monday while Madison took her exam. Their 8:00 a.m. patient was late due to heavy fog, so she rescheduled him; the 8:45 patient didn't show up at all. She was frustrated, and blamed Madison because she'd taken Friday and Monday off from work.

"If you aren't going to be dependable, Madison McKenzie, I'll have to hire another girl just to handle the phones and scheduling." Dr. Denson slammed her fist on the instrument tray, scattering mirror, explorer, and cotton pliers onto the floor.

Madison quickly grabbed the soiled instruments, putting them in the sink. "I'm really sorry, Aunt Denny. I had to take my test. Maybe we could use a part-time person now; your practice has gotten busy in the last year."

"I'm the boss around this office; don't you forget that." Denny stormed toward the lab at the back of the building.

Madison called the remainder of the patients, hoping she could salvage their schedule for the rest of the day. She confirmed Wednesday's patients while Dr. Denson busied herself in the lab, doing work she normally did at night. Still, the day went slowly and Madison was easily distracted. She chattered nonstop about the pendant and quizzed Denny about the day her mother disappeared.

"I'd think you might want to concentrate a little on your job instead of letting your imagination lead you on some wild goose chase," Denny glared.

"But there's nothing to do until your next patient comes. Why don't you ever want to talk about my mother? I'm not that six-year-old girl anymore!"

"I've shielded you from the trauma of your early childhood, and this is the thanks I get." Denny's dark eyes widened as she stared at her niece.

Madison stared back. "Did she wear the necklace the day she left?"

"Don't get your hopes up," Denny said. "Those necklaces were a fad. I always thought they were silly. Everybody had them."

"That may be true, but I don't think this is a coincidence," Madison insisted.

"If you think you found your mother's remains on the mountain, you're wrong," Denny said. "I admit, poor Danny gave her the pendant for Christmas, but she wasn't the sentimental type where he was concerned. My guess is she sneaked over the mountain with some man, and tossed the necklace on her way out."

"Wasn't she still mourning my father?"

Denny snorted. "Enough; there's work to do."

Madison's mind spun faster and faster as she tried to assimilate the information. Dr. Denson became more and more irritated by questions directed both to her and to the patients. At lunchtime, she asked Madison to step into the lab.

"This personal conversation is not appropriate in front of our patients. Don't you think you should curb your appetite for gossip?"

Madison's jaw dropped. "I've known these people most of my life. They're interested in what's happened, and most of them started the conversation by asking about the bones."

Denny pulled off her gloves and tossed them into the trash as she brushed past Madison. "I don't care. I'm telling you to shut up. Do you understand me?"

"Yes, Ma'am." Madison was silent for a minute and then followed Denny into her office. "I'm hoping one of the patients might know something about my mother. It's your fault; you kept secrets all these years. In the last three days, I've learned a lot, and I plan to learn more, with or without your help or approval!" She peeled her gloves and tossed them in the trash, mimicking the way Denny had done in the lab. She turned her back, swallowed hard and left the room. *That was a bold move. Where is this newfound strength coming from?* Madison stopped shaking by the time she walked in the front door of the restaurant.

Denny entered shortly after Madison and sat at the counter reading the Johnson City Press. The headlines must have been too much for her. She threw the paper down and disappeared back out the front door.

Madison watched from the kitchen, where she always made their lunches. She felt at home because she'd been raised there. Besides, she didn't want Shirley to wait on them. Curiosity got the best of her, so she walked to where the paper lay on the floor, picked it up and read aloud, "Appalachian Trail littered with bones." A smile slipped across her face. She carried the paper into the kitchen and asked Jess, "Have you seen this?"

He nodded while tending the burgers and chicken breasts on the grill. Madison snatched a couple slices of turkey from a nearby table and stood reading the article to herself. "No wonder Denny got mad and left. She fussed at me for talking about the bones at the office, and now it's all over the front page. I wonder what she's worried about."

Jess kept his eye on the hamburger patties as he answered. "Me, too."

A loud voice sounded from the front of the restaurant. "I wanna see 'er—I know she eats lunch here!"

Jess and Madison rushed to the swinging doors to see a man stumbling toward them.

"Butch! You're drunk; you know you aren't supposed to be here when you're drinking," Shirley said to a shabbily dressed man, who swayed back and forth, barely able to stand.

"Outside, fellow." Jess pushed through the swinging doors. "Come on, I'll walk you home."

"*There* she is. You started this! If you hadn't messed around and found them bones, my Shelly wouldn't be all full of hopes of finding her little girl. She was doing good till you stirred up them memories." Butch Logan pointed a finger at Madison.

"She's done nothing wrong. Come on, Butch, ol' pal. Let's get you home," Jess said.

Butch jerked away from Jess's gentle grasp and nearly fell over himself. "She stirred it up again."

"What I did was what any normal person would have done, I told the sheriff and showed him where Bud found the skull. Then, after he took no action, I went back and found more bones and the other half to this necklace." Madison pulled the silver chain from under her scrubs. "So unless you put someone else up there, that might be my birth mother!"

"Me! Don't you try to blame me!" Butch lunged toward Madison.

Jess stepped between them. "Let's go, Butch. Give it up. No one thinks the skeleton is your girl. Shelly won't either, once the sheriff talks to her."

"Don't push me, big man. Tina didn't give me the time of day, but you—you she liked. Is that the reason you cared for her kid? You have an interest at stake here? Huh, big man?" Butch shook his finger in front of Jess's nose.

Jess snatched his hand out of the air and threw Butch like a wet noodle over his shoulder, walking out the door with him. Halfway across the street, he dropped him on his backside. By that time, Sheriff Perry was on the scene.

Madison watched as the two men picked up the drunk and escorted him toward the jail. She wondered what Butch meant: "You, she liked." Had Jess not told her all he knew about Tina Denson? Was this the reason Denny didn't want to talk about her sister-in-law? Had Madison's mother been the town tramp? Another name added to the list in her mind. She'd have to talk to Butch when he was sober. Maybe he would tell her something.

"I better go." Madison turned to Shirley. "Don't let Jess press charges."

"He won't. The sheriff will make Butch sleep it off and then let him out. Don't worry."

The remainder of the day was quiet—until Denny confronted Madison in the lab between patients.

"Your mind certainly isn't on work today. Are you still playing amateur sleuth?"

Madison turned to the sink and scrubbed the instruments for the sterilizer. "Right now, I'm thinking about something Butch Logan said."

"People will say anything to stir up a hornet's nest. Sometimes things are better left alone." Denny said in an unusually calm voice.

"I sometimes wonder how life would be different if I'd been raised by my real parents. They raised you, didn't they?" Madison said.

Denny ignored the comment. She motioned to one of the forceps. "You didn't get that clean. Watch what you're doing."

"Sorry." She rechecked the elevators and root tip picks she'd just washed.

"Danny took me in after our folks died," Denny said. "I'd always adored my big brother, but Tina never cottoned to me. She didn't want Danny's little sister competing for attention. You would have had a different life, all right." Denny turned the fill button on the autoclave to get it ready for the instruments, then added, "Jess is peculiar, but I think you're better off under his care."

"Maybe so, but I still want to know everything about my mother. If she died on the mountain, I want to bring her home and give her a proper burial."

"Put that romantic nonsense out of your mind. Had you rather imagine your mother is dead than face the fact she didn't want you? You'd have gone dirty and hungry if it wasn't for me. A cat is a better mother than she was." Denny stalked to the door and said, "Deputy Franks is right, it's against the law to dig up graves. If I hear of you messing around on the mountain, I'll tell Franks to arrest you."

Madison felt stunned and hurt. She hadn't meant to trigger Denny's temper again. She turned around to find water overflowing from the autoclave. "Oh shoot!" She closed the latch and set the timer and then grabbed a handful of towels to mop up the distilled water. As she walked to the front desk, she shook her head and wondered, what next?

Their last patient of the day was Mr. Stevenson, the pharmacist in Erwin. "That last filling you put in is hitting high. Can you adjust my bite?" He said as soon as Denny came in the room.

"I'll be the judge of that." Denny laughed and reached toward the drawer where she'd find the articulating paper.

Madison handed over a half strip of blue paper clipped between a pair of cotton pliers. She'd recognized the problem as soon as Mr. Stevenson called for the appointment.

Denny looked sternly at her over the top of her glasses, but did not comment. She placed the strip on the chewing surface of the teeth and said, "Bite down and rub your teeth together like you're chewing."

Mr. Stevenson complied and then opened his mouth. Madison adjusted the light so the upper molars were illuminated. Denny snatched the light away from her guidance and shined it on the lower arch.

"It's the upper," Madison said.

"Are you the doctor now?" She glared. "You can go and clean the rest of the instruments. I believe I can handle this minor adjustment." Denny shooed Madison with a flick of her hand.

Madison hesitated for a moment and then stepped out of the room, but waited just outside the door. She heard Mr. Stevenson say, "She's right, it was the upper."

"The upper restoration is perfect. The lower has to be the problem. It was too high before I touched the upper. I should have caught it then, but I didn't want to mess with an old filling." She used the slow speed hand piece, with a circular diamond disk. The grading sound of the tool could be heard throughout the office. "Hold still. This will only take a second." Dr. Denson replaced the blue paper strip and rechecked the bite. Then she smoothed the area with a rubber wheel she'd attached to the slow speed. "How does that feel?" She asked.

"It'll do." Stevenson reached for the cup of water to rinse his mouth. "Denny, are you taking your meds like they are prescribed?"

"Is that your business?" She snapped.

"As your pharmacist, it is my business to remind you how to take them." Mr. Stevenson sounded calm and polite. "You've been well-controlled for years, but have you forgotten what happens when you decide to stop taking your meds?"

Madison heard the hand piece clang as Denny slammed it onto the instrument tray. "You're not the only pharmacist around here, that's an easy fix."

Madison slipped into the lab and began scrubbing instruments as though she'd been there all the time. Moments later, Denny appeared in the lab.

"Were you lurking outside the door eavesdropping on my private conversation?"

Madison froze. Denny's pupils dilated, giving her a wild-eyed look. "I, I just wondered if that was going to work." She felt her lower jaw tremble.

"Are you serious?" Denny pressed closer. "I'm the dentist here, not you."

"I'm sorry. It will never happen again, I promise. Mr. Stevenson didn't even know I was there. No harm done. I was just curious, that's all." Madison babbled.

"It better never happen again, girl!" Then Denny left the office without another word.

Madison blew a sigh of relief as the door slammed behind Denny. She was up to her elbows in dirty instruments and surgical towels. At least now she could get the mess cleared without worry of her aunt watching over her shoulder, looking for something to squabble about.

She filed the charts and tidied up the front office while the sterilizer went through its cycles. The vacuum run and trash receptacles emptied, she returned to the lab for one last look, hoping her aunt would appreciate the extra effort and be in a better mood tomorrow. Although she'd ticked Denny off badly, Madison felt satisfied. Not that she was trying to make her mad, but Denny respected people more when they stood up for themselves. It was about time she earned her aunt's respect.

CHAPTER 7

Wednesday morning, Madison woke up with a headache. She called them weather headaches whenever rain came. She rolled over to face her roommate.

Bud came to her side and pushed on her leg with his paw.

"I'm calling in sick. Won't Denny love that?" She patted Bud's head and then gingerly righted herself. Moving slowly, she went to the bathroom medicine cabinet. She recognized Tylenol would not do the trick this morning. Snapping the lid off the Advil bottle, she popped a couple gel-tabs in her mouth. She opened the door for Bud to go out. "No running today; I can't stand the pounding."

After letting Bud back in the house, she stretched out on the couch as he curled up on the braided rug. She called Aunt Denny. "I'm not coming in this morning. I have an awful headache." She was surprised when Denny accepted her news well.

Denny sounded calm as she said, "I've asked Emily Watson to come in for the morning to reschedule my patients. I'm behind on lab work. If I'm satisfied with how she handles that job, I might hire her. I've given our conversation some thought. You're right; my practice is growing and I could use more help."

"Well, okay then, I'll see you tomorrow." Madison hung up the phone.

An hour or so passed before she awoke feeling a little washed out, but the pain in her head was gone.

"Bud, what do you think of making a trip to Asheville, since we didn't go on Monday? I need to talk with old man Franks. If I wait until after work, I might run into Willy. Today is my best chance. Something good came of the headache, after all."

When Bud saw Madison gather up her purse and keys, his pink tongue lolled out in a happy grin. He was always ready for a car ride.

On the drive toward Asheville, Bud sat next to her in the front seat, sporting a new harness connected to the seatbelt. He watched the landscape zoom past as they drove across Sam's Gap on I-26 eastbound.

"Look, Bud. There's a bobcat. He can't cross the highway or he'll end up as road-kill."

Bud's head turned as they drove past, and then he looked at Madison.

"I'd like to have seen that bobcat up close. That guy was as tall as you. You don't ever want to tangle with a cat like that. I need to teach you to avoid wild animals, like that momma bear!" She scratched Bud's ear and drove on.

The scenic drive over the mountain pass only took forty-five minutes. Approaching Tunnel Road exit, she drove east until she came to the VA Medical Center, where old Sheriff Franks was a resident.

Madison found a parking space next to a pond, where a number of ducks glided across the glassy surface. "I'm putting the windows down, Bud. You'll be cool in the shade of that weeping willow tree and the ducks can entertain you."

Bud hadn't taken his eyes off the ducks after his first sighting of them. He yapped once and attempted to stand on all fours. The harness held him tight as he watched the action through the windshield.

Ha, that's another good reason for the harness. You've never tried to get out of the window, but there's always that temptation. Madison ruffled Bud's coat, but the dog remained focused on the colorful ducks swimming in the pond.

Inside, Madison found the nurse's station and inquired about Willard Franks. Then she walked down the long hallway to a lounge, where she saw groups of residents sitting at game tables or on couches in front of vibrantly colored tropical fish. A well-groomed elderly lady approached her when she paused to gaze around the room.

"Hello, I'm Marge, the official resident greeter. Who are you here to visit?"

"Nice to meet you, Marge, I'm Madison. I'd like to see Will Franks, is he here?"

"Why, yes. Come along, I'll show you."

The stately woman led her toward a corner, where an old gentleman sat at a small table set up with checkers and a board. His fingers fluttered, moving random pieces and then moving them back to their original position. His frame looked thin and he was shorter than Madison remembered; he was not at all like the brawny man who wore the sheriff's badge when she was a little girl.

"Sheriff Franks, you have a guest." Marge waved her hand gracefully toward the girl who stood next to her. "This is Madison."

"Madison who?" The old man's voice sounded gruff; his eyes were locked on the checkerboard.

"Madison McKenzie, from Cold Creek," Madison answered. "I went to school with Willy, remember?"

"Do you play checkers?" The old man still did not look up.

Marge patted Madison's shoulder as if telling her to take a seat. "I'll be right over there by the fish tank, should he try getting fresh with you."

"Aw, go away, Sarge," he grumbled still staring at the checkers.

"I've played a few games," Madison said. "Shall we give it a go?"

"You'll lose, I'm warning you now," he said.

"Are you sure?" Madison teased.

Finally, he raised his eyes to meet hers. Madison noticed the cloudy haze edging the dark brown like a white halo.

"Oh, it's Madison, all grown up. But I'm warning you, no young whipper-snapper of a girl ever beat me," he snorted.

Madison smiled; she had played checkers with Jess since she was three, and knew the game inside out. The old Sheriff's reputation as a skilled player was well known, but she hoped she could give the old man a challenge. After a few moves, however, it was clear he had lost his edge as his pieces moved aimlessly around the board. To save his pride, Madison let him win.

"Sheriff Franks, I didn't come here just to play checkers. You were Sheriff in Cold Creek the year my father died and my mother disappeared. Aunt Denny has never talked about it, and still won't tell me anything about them. I'm hoping you can remember something about my parents." Madison leaned close to the old man.

He squirmed in his seat. Madison wondered if he was uncomfortable. Or was he trying to get away from her and the memories? She rose and rearranged the pillows at his back. "Do you remember my father, Danny Denson?"

Sheriff Franks' scratched his chin. "Yeah, I remember Danny. Had a nice woodworking shop, and I bought a fancy clock off him, back in the day."

Madison thought of the clock in Denny's office. "Aunt Denny has one. He must have made it for her. She prizes it so highly she won't let me even dust it." If Danny made that, wonder why she never bragged about it.

If old man Franks heard her comment, he didn't show it.

"Aunt Denny said he fell off a ladder and died. Can you tell me about the accident?"

Sheriff Franks narrowed his eyes and squinted in her direction. "Accident? Oh yes, I remember now. He fell into the stripping vat in the shop."

Madison clapped her hand over her mouth. "Oh, dear God! Did Denny see him?"

"She was there, alright; home from school, if I recollect. Had some trouble with her roommate and got suspended. Wasn't much meat left on his bones when I fished him out, and he wasn't in there long; he was just gone." The old man flipped his hand like tossing something away. "Never seen anything like that."

"Poor Denny. No wonder she doesn't want to talk about it," Madison said.

Sheriff Franks looked puzzled. "This is official business. Willy told me not to discuss business. You'd better go before he comes in."

Madison stood. "Sheriff Franks, do you remember Denny's roommate's name?"

"Victory Dance, or something like that. Yeah, sounded like victory dance." Alzheimer's disease hadn't completely erased his memory.

"Do you know where she was from?"

"Someplace outside of Asheville, north maybe. Her family was a big name in the political frontier generations ago—that's it: Vance. Victoria Vance." Then he looked back at the board. "Do you play checkers? I've never found a woman who can beat me. Wanna give it a try?"

"I think it's probably past time for your lunch. Maybe I can come back to visit with you again." She smiled, realizing his mind was taking a rest.

"You do that, Tina; you come back and see me again soon. I'd like that."

Madison walked out of the room, waving to Marge as she passed the fish tank. It wasn't until she got to her vehicle that she thought about what he'd said last: *"You do that, Tina." We were talking about Denny; did he confuse me with my mother?*

On the drive out of Asheville, Madison noticed the sign along the highway at Weaverville: Vance Birthplace. She took the exit and followed the signs to an historical site with old log cabins and outbuildings dating back to the 1830's, the home of Zebulon Baird Vance.

This has to be the family. I wonder if anyone working here knows Victoria. She turned her vehicle onto the gravel drive and followed it around in a circular direction to the main house. There, she spotted a young man sitting on the porch, whittling on a small stick.

"Hello," she said, in response to his greeting. "I'm doing investigative research on the Zebulon Baird Vance's descendants. Are you familiar with a Victoria Vance?"

"Victoria? Why sure. She's the main supporter keeping this display afloat. Works right over there." He pointed to a tall, narrow building with a shingle that read Law Office.

Madison thanked him with a smile and made her way across the parking lot. The office door stood open, so she walked in. A middle-aged woman sat at a heavy wooden desk, glasses hanging on the end of her nose, reading a thick leather-bound book. Without looking up she said, "This building isn't part of the display."

"I'm looking for Victoria Vance," Madison said.

"You found her." Ms. Vance looked up from her reading.

"Madison McKenzie." She offered her hand across the desk.

Ms. Vance shook with a grip like a man. "How can I help you, Ms. McKenzie?"

"I'd like to ask you a few questions about your college roommate, Denise Denson."

There was a long pause and then Ms. Vance nodded. "Why are you interested in Denise?"

"She's my aunt. It's a long story, but I just found out she probably witnessed her brother's—my father's—death. I understand now why she never talks about it, but I'm desperate to know about my parents. I was hoping you could help me."

The woman removed her glasses and put the book down. "Have a seat."

Madison sank into the worn leather chair next to the desk. "Did Aunt Denny tell you anything about her brother, Danny?"

"Denise was very close with her brother—didn't like to share him." A sly smile appeared when Victoria said, "But you probably already know that."

"No, I know nothing beyond the fact that my father died and my mother vanished when I was an infant."

"Really..." The woman's eyes narrowed. "Did Denise tell you that?"

"She did, and that I was left in her care, even though she was still in dental school. At some point, her dearest friend, Shirley, adopted me. I'm close with both of them."

Victoria Vance had a great poker face, which is an asset to an attorney; this was the face she allowed Madison to see. She picked up a pencil and twirled it between her fingers as she pondered the information Madison had shared. Then she sat forward and leaned her elbows on her desk.

"Before I say more, you need to understand something. Truth is not always pleasant. We look for it, but when we find it, we may discover it was better left alone. If you wish to continue your quest, I'll need a retainer."

Madison felt a quiver inside. "I was just thinking of a talk, not hiring an attorney."

"Do you have anything in your pockets?" Ms. Vance persisted.

Madison slipped her hand into her right front pocket. She came out with some coins and held them out.

Ms. Vance counted as she plucked them from her hand, "Twenty-five, fifty, sixty-five; that's perfect. Now I'm your attorney, so we can talk freely." Then she sat back and smiled.

"Oh, I see," Madison felt her body relax. "Officially, you can tell me what you feel is pertinent to me."

"I'll tell you what I know," she said with a solemn expression on her face, "But remember, your family may have good reasons for secrecy. Once the truth is out, you can't put the genie back in the bottle, so to speak."

Madison leaned forward in her chair. "Ms. Vance, I have to know."

Victoria Vance cleared her throat. "In her sophomore year, Denise fell in love with an older man. The guy dumped her when he found out she was pregnant. She scheduled an abortion twice, but cancelled both times. I was afraid she'd end up having the baby in a bathroom somewhere, so I called her brother. When she learned that I'd told her secret, she became enraged and tried to strangle me. If one of the other girls in the dorm hadn't broken it up, Denise may have succeeded."

"Security called the police, they contacted her family, and the Sheriff of Cold Creek came to take her home. She was upset at seeing him. I don't know why she'd think he was taking her to jail; I told her I wouldn't press charges."

Madison's chest burned like she'd been underwater too long. She couldn't remember holding her breath the whole time, but she might have.

"Were you badly hurt?" Madison asked.

"No, just shaken."

"When was that?"

"January of 1983."

Madison counted backward on her fingers, fearing the worst. "But it wasn't possible— " Madison felt dizzy. She tried to stand, but felt her body drop back to the chair in a dead faint. When she opened her eyes, Victoria held a wet cloth on her head.

"Are you all right?"

Ms. Vance's voice sounded far away. She offered Madison cool water from a paper cup.

"Drink slowly." The voice sounded concerned and sweet. "Have you eaten lunch?"

Madison shook her head.

"Neither have I; let's go to the main house."

Ms. Vance opened her desk drawer and pulled out a small pistol, which she stuck into her pocket. Madison could barely support her own weight at that point, so Victoria gave her the support she needed. Together, they walked slowly to the big house nearby.

"What is that for?" Madison nodded toward the pocket hiding the pistol.

Victoria smiled. "Nowadays women should know how to fire a gun, and have a license to carry. I haven't had to use mine for defense, but a few of my students have."

"Students?" Madison felt confused.

"Yes, I'm an attorney, but I'm also a state certified handgun instructor."

Madison felt a new excitement. "Sounds like a temptation I should indulge in."

"We can talk about that later. You need to eat. I have a couple of sandwiches in the icebox, if you're interested."

"I'd hate to impose, but you're right; I need to eat, and then you can tell me about the handgun classes. I'm interested in learning about self-defense," Madison said.

While they ate chicken salad sandwiches and munched on homemade seven-day pickles, Madison said. "I bet you're wondering about me fainting."

"Not really my business. I'm just glad you're better."

"Thanks, so am I. I admit that I have a habit of forgetting to eat. I get fussed at all the time for it. But I don't usually faint; guess my blood sugar dropped." She made eye contact with Ms. Vance, hoping to end the conversation.

Then Victoria politely asked, "Did you want to ask any more questions about your family?"

"Yes, do you know what happened to the baby?"

"I don't know. Rumors went around that she'd had a late term abortion. I'm sorry; I really can't tell you more than that."

"Did my aunt ever talk about Tina?"

"Rarely, and when she did it was with venom. She hated Tina. I guess it was because Danny was so in love with your mother. Eventually, Tina was a wedge between them," she said.

Madison's mind ran in different directions. The conversation lagged and they finished their lunch. "I need to let my dog out and get him some water."

Victoria walked Madison to her car. Bud sprawled out on the back seat, enjoying the breeze through the open windows.

"Thanks for lunch, and especially for talking to me about Denny. It seems each question answered leads to another." She opened her door. "Come on out, boy. You can get a drink from the creek." She started to put his leash on.

"No need for the leash, unless you fear he'll run off. Let him run, if he will."

"Thank you." She turned to Bud. "Run, go on, run." They laughed when he bounded toward the creek.

Victoria grew silent for a moment and said, "I hope I did the right thing telling you. I feel as if I've betrayed Denise twice now."

Madison smiled. "You did the right thing. At least this time you didn't get hurt. I won't tell her we've met."

"Thanks, Madison. I'd be grateful to you for that."

Madison extended her hand. "Thoughts of getting a gun for self-defense keep me awake at night, not only because of poisonous snakes but the two legged snakes in our woods."

"Yes, and you want to be legal, so the carry permit is a requirement." Victoria said. "I could recommend an instructor in Erwin. She took her classes from me and became a certified instructor. She'll help you choose the right gun; you should look her up, tell her I sent you."

"Oh, I will! Thanks. Erwin is just a few minutes' drive down the mountain from Cold Creek." Madison clapped her hands and Bud ran back to her. She pulled a blanket from the back of the Blazer to wrap him in. He had taken a plunge into the water, soaking himself from head to toe. "I can't eliminate that wet-dog smell, but at least you can sit on the blanket."

As soon as she had Bud situated in the harness and seat belt, she closed the door and walked to the drivers' side.

Victoria pulled her hand from her pocket. "Here's my card, if you ever need me."

"Thank you again for talking with me, and especially for lunch. If you're ever in Tennessee, I'll buy you lunch at Shirley's Restaurant. Just give me a call."

"Oh, is Shirley's still there?" Victoria asked.

"Yes, Shirley is my mom. She's the second Shirley. Her grandmother was the first."

"Of course." Victoria offered her firm handshake again. "Just be careful how you handle your aunt; remember, she can snap suddenly."

"I've experienced that already, but I'm out for blood." Madison climbed in and started her vehicle. "Bye, you take care."

Madison waved as she turned left from the gravel driveway, and sped onto the highway leading back to I-26. "Bud, this was a worthwhile trip! If you only knew what I've learned."

By the time they reached the interstate, rain was falling and black clouds loomed on the horizon toward home—a sign of things to come?

CHAPTER 8

Madison arrived early to spruce up the office and make sure everything was ready before Emily came the next morning. She walked in the door just as Madison switched on the lights. *Prompt; a really good sign.*

"Good to have you, Emily. We need an extra pair of hands," Madison said.

"Dr. Denson asked me to come in early, so you can work with me on proper phone etiquette." Emily giggled. "She thinks I don't know how to confirm appointments."

"I can assure you, Denny doesn't have a clue how to confirm appointments," Madison whispered. "I've got it down to a science. Be happy to share my secrets."

Emily's dad was youth minister at the First Baptist Church of Clear Springs, not far from Cold Creek. She and Madison met during Career Day at Erwin High School. Emily spent a long time at the dentistry booth. Later, Madison recommended hiring her part time at Dr. Denson's office, saying it could be a good investment for both parties, and Denny agreed.

Denny came in through the back door, humming a snappy tune. Hearing it, Madison sighed in relief. Denny greeted Emily with a smile, and suggested she shadow Madison. As soon as the dentist settled down with her first patient, Madison went to the front desk and asked her shadow to listen to her conversation with a couple of patients.

"Will you let me make the next call?" Emily asked.

"Sure, give it a whirl."

Emily left a message on the answering machine for her first call, and proceeded to the next.

Madison listened carefully as her apprentice moved smoothly through the next three calls. "Excellent," Madison said with a smile. "Come get me if you have any questions. From the lack of drilling sounds, I'd say the doctor is ready for my assistance."

Emily nodded with an air of confidence and returned to the phone, so Denny's right-hand gal dashed down the hall.

Dr. Denson spoke without looking up, saying, "How's she doing?"

"She catches on quickly," said Madison, pulling on a pair of latex gloves as she settled onto her stool.

"Good, I thought you'd be a better judge than me of her performance on the phone."

"Thank you for your confidence. I think you've made a good choice getting Emily in here to help," Madison whispered.

"She'll be on probation for two weeks. Teach her all you can in that time, will you?"

"She's smart; our receptionist job is a good fit for her." Madison lowered her protective shield as Denny placed the ultraviolet light on the restoration she applied to an anterior tooth. "I'd rather be here assisting you than talking on the phone anyway."

Denny raised her head saying, "You're that much like me. I don't like the phone either."

Madison walked on eggshells all that day, and kept her mouth shut. Her aunt controlled the conversation and answered all of the patient's questions.

Late in the afternoon, Denny praised Madison. "See how smoothly things go when I answer the patient's concerns?" She paused to look at Madison over the top of her glasses. "By the way, the office looked nice when I came in. You'd been slipping lately. I guess I *was* overworking you."

"Thanks, and yes, having someone up front *will* help." Madison watched the dentist walk into the lab. "Is there anything else you want done?"

"Check with Emily to see that charts are pulled and patients confirmed for tomorrow."

Madison could barely hear over the noise of the vibrator the dentist used to release the air bubbles in the plaster model she'd just poured.

"It's all done, and today's charts are posted and filed away," Madison said.

Denny shut off the vibrator. "Then it's quitting time."

"Aunt Denny, before we go, I'd like to talk to you."

Denny glanced at the wall clock. "Can it wait until tomorrow? I'd hoped to take advantage of the extra hour from daylight-savings time to exercise my team before dark. Can't let the dogs get soft, or I won't be running the Iditarod next spring."

Madison twisted her fingers together. "It won't take long."

Denny slumped in a flimsy chair, and it creaked under her weight. She stretched her legs straight out in front of her. "Okay, spit it out. I hope you're not still mooning over Tina, because if you are, I don't want to hear about it."

Madison sat and smoothed the fabric of her skirt over her lap. "I'm sorry about calling in sick yesterday. I ended up going to the optical place in the Mall in Asheville. He says my left eye is weak and that I need anti-glare reading glasses; they'll have a protective lens, and will double as safety glasses. I'll have them next week, so yesterday wasn't a total waste."

"That's what you wanted to talk to me about?" Denny scooted forward as if to get up.

"No, that wasn't all. I talked to Sheriff Franks, and I understand now why you can't talk about my father. It must have been terrible for you, the way he died."

Denny bolted upright. "What, do you mean you talked to Willard? I thought you were sick yesterday."

"Well, yes. I woke up sick, but when I felt better, I visited him in the nursing home and then went to see the ophthalmologist."

Denny shouted, "That old fool is not in his right mind! Don't believe a word he says! What did he tell you about me?"

While Madison told her what the old sheriff had said, her fingers moved nervously in her skirt, repeatedly pleating and smoothing the fabric. When she finished talking, Denny's face was white as her lab coat.

"I can't believe it!" Denny's voice lowered.

Madison sat quietly for a moment. "He said you were there, and saw your brother die. What happened?"

Denny stood up, towering above her niece, her eyes growing dark as she spoke. "How dare you go behind my back and snoop in my private life!" She moved closer, leaning toward Madison. "I've treated you like a daughter. First Tina ruined my life, and now *you're* ruining it!"

Madison drew back, cowering in her chair, convinced Denny was going to hit her. "I'm sorry... Why are you so mad? You won't talk to me about my parents."

"It's none of your business!" Denny wiped spittle from the corner of her mouth. "My relationship with my brother—that's none of your business," she yelled. "You're different since you found that skull. Get out of my office! I can't stand the sight of you!"

Madison stood. Her insides churned but she set her jaw and stood her ground. "No! You need to talk to me like an *adult*. I love you, and you *know* I appreciate everything you've done for me. Tell me *your* story. I need to hear it from you!"

Denny didn't speak, just shook her head.

Madison watched her turn to leave and then stop at the back door. "What have you done, Madison? Oh, what have you done?" She let the door slam behind her.

Madison let her go without saying another word. She'd never in her life raised her voice to an adult. Had finding the bones made this change in her? She wasn't sure how she got to this point. If this was a new side of her, it was uncomfortable and unfamiliar— but Madison felt it was necessary to get answers to newly raised questions.

Emily stood up when Madison approached the front desk. "Dr. Denson left? I heard the back door."

"Yes, she wants to take advantage of the extra hour of light to run her dog team." She didn't make eye contact with Emily. "Everything okay up here?"

Emily nodded and picked up a stack of charts. "Here's tomorrow's patients. Where do I put these?"

Madison directed her assistant to the file basket in the hallway. "We are all done for today then." She returned to the desk and shut down the computer, switched off the lights, and then turned to Emily. "You will be here tomorrow, won't you?"

"Oh, yes! Dr. Denson made sure I'm comfortable with the phone. She says she'll need me all week, and probably next week too. I hope I do a good job so she'll hire me." The young woman stood tall. "Do you think she will?"

"Pretty sure she will." Madison handed her key to Emily. "You'll need this in the morning in case you get here early. She likes it when the lights are all on by the time she arrives."

"I'll be here! You can count on me." Emily snatched the key, squeezing it with both hands.

"Goodnight, Emily, and thank you for what you're doing." Madison locked the door behind her as they left the office together. *Little does she know how much Denny needs her now.*

Madison took her time walking to the restaurant. She debated what had just happened. While she enjoyed helping people with their dental needs, how could she face Denny now? She considered her options: get a job in Johnson City—that would mean driving forty-five minutes each way, or move closer to the city. The very idea of moving caused butterflies in her stomach.

Shirley met her at the door, took one look at her and said, "What's she done today?"

"She didn't, it was me this time."

"*You!*" Surprised, Shirley said, "What did you do, talk back to her?"

"I don't even know how it got started." Madison stared at the floor, then said, "We argued, and she left the office in tears."

Hearing that comment, Jess came from the kitchen. "She *what?*"

Madison escorted her adoptive parents back through the swinging doors, where she hoped no customers could eavesdrop. She told them of her visit with old Sheriff Franks—that he'd said Denny was suspended from school, and she'd seen her brother die.

"Bet you didn't know all that did you? There's a lot you don't know about Dr. Denise Denson," she said.

Bristling, Jess said, "I know she treats her dogs better than her own blood kin." He took his apron off, tossed it across the room and went out the back door without another word.

Madison whirled around. "He won't confront her, will he?"

"No, Honey, he just needs to cool off. He's got a short fuse when it comes to his little girl."

"She's in no mood to trifle with anyway," Madison said.

"He'll be okay," Shirley told her.

But Madison wasn't so sure. She had never seen Jess lose his temper. Did he know something about Denny? Madison couldn't help but wonder what it was with those two.

Bud met her at the door when Madison went home alone. Instead of the usual romping on the braided rug, she dropped to the floor, pulling Bud onto her lap for a hug. She had mixed emotions about quarreling with Denny and wondered if they would ever be able to repair the relationship. She knew Denny hadn't been herself lately, and Madison worried about what Mr. Stevenson had said about her meds.

Needing answers to her questions, Madison turned to her computer, completely losing track of time. Shirley and Jess startled her when they came in.

"Glad you're here, Madison," Shirley said, and went straight down the hallway without stopping. "I'm going to take a quick shower; I'm beat."

Jess locked the door and went over and kissed the top of her head. "No need to check helpwanted.com," he said with a chuckle. "You'll always have a place at the restaurant with us."

"Thanks, but if I can't repair the damage between Denny and me, I'll be looking for a job in Johnson City. I'm certified now and can get higher pay there, but I don't want to go to that extreme if there's an alternative. First, I need to figure out what's going on with her. She's different lately. I guess we all are."

CHAPTER 9

On Thursday, Madison and Bud returned home from an early morning run; she showered and then dropped by the restaurant. The room was abuzz with local patrons getting their fill of Shirley's famous secret coffee blend and the latest gossip. Shirley was surprised when her daughter ordered one egg, over easy, and a piece of whole-wheat toast.

After eating her small breakfast, Madison was poring over the Johnson City Press want ads when a woman about her age, dressed in tailored brown slacks and jacket, walked in the door. Her attention returned to the ads, but she overheard the conversation between the woman and Shirley.

"I'm Nell Nielsen from WKXL News 3, in Knoxville." The woman said, "I'm looking for Madison McKenzie."

Shirley pointed to the back booth. "Right over there, Miss Nell. We country folk don't hold to formalities. I'm Shirley, and the girl you want to see is my daughter."

Madison inwardly groaned when the reporter approached the booth.

"I'm Nell. I'd like to ask you a few questions."

Madison couldn't help but notice Nell's smile exposed perfectly aligned and whitened teeth. "Yeah, have a seat, but I've nothing newsworthy."

Nell sat and folded her hands in front of her on the table. "Our mutual friend, Lisa Shelton, told me you found a skull while hiking up at Eagle Ridge. You went back later and found a locket that matched your mother's. I'd like to tell your story."

"There's no story to tell," Madison said. "Life would be a lot simpler if Bud had never found her. If you don't mind, I'd rather not talk about it."

Madison studied the woman. Her hair, a shiny chestnut brown, was cut in a stylish bob. Although her makeup was understated, it gave her skin a flawless glow, and her dark lashes were long and feathery. I wish I looked like that, Madison thought.

"Is Bud a friend?" Nell asked.

"He's my best friend, but he's also my dog."

"You're a brave soul; finding a skull would scare most women." Nell shifted and crossed one leg over the other at the knee.

"I'm a dental assistant, used to blood, bones and such. I felt sorry for her because she was alone, but I wasn't scared."

"Lisa said you might have discovered your mother's grave."

Madison looked over her shoulder aware that the room was suddenly quiet.

"Listen, Nell, we can't talk here; the details will be all over town by tomorrow."

Nell asked, "Would you feel more comfortable talking in private?"

Madison nodded, drew in her shoulders, and looked around the crowded room. "Yeah." She stood up. "I don't know why you want to know about me, but if we're going to talk, we need to go to my house."

The two women made their way outside and walked the short distance to the porch of Shirley and Jess's house in silence. Nell lingered at the flower boxes, smelling the different scents of spring blooms.

"I love your flowers; Siberian iris, aren't they?" Nell pointed to the tall purplish blooms next to the steps. "Isn't it early for them?"

"You know your flowers," Madison said. "One of the patrons at the restaurant has a greenhouse. He brings them to Shirley before anyone else's come back from the bulbs. Jess planted them for her, and he covers them to keep away frost."

"I wish I had a green thumb." Nell sighed.

"Come in." Madison opened the door. "This is Bud." She stretched out her hand, palm up, in his direction. "Bud, say hello to Nell." The dog sat and barked one time.

"Oh, how clever! Aren't you a cutie pie?" Nell dumped her purse and laptop onto the sofa and dropped to her knees on the braided rug. She placed her hands on either side of his neck and dug into his coat. "Oh, I just love dogs."

"Do you have a dog?"

Nell looked up and shook her head. Madison spotted the sparkle of a solitaire diamond on a chain hanging just above Nell's blouse opening. It looked to be at least a carat, the kind you'd like to have on your finger. She sat in the rocker and watched Nell and Bud bond.

"I wish I could keep a dog, but that's nearly as impossible as having flowers."

"Your schedule?" Madison asked, feeling sorry for anyone who couldn't have the two best things in life, a dog and live flowers growing around them.

"My schedule, my lifestyle... I can't even keep a boyfriend." Nell stood up and walked to the sofa. As she sat next to her stuff, she picked up the diamond at the end of the chain and rolled it between her fingers. "This was on my finger last year. It makes a lovely necklace, doesn't it?" She dropped it and opened the laptop. "Do you mind if I make a few notes as we talk?"

Madison shrugged her shoulders.

Nell began with routine questions, and soon Madison was speaking freely. After a few minutes, she paused. "What are you going to do with what I'm telling you? You're not going to put it all on the news, are you? I'd be glad for anything that would make Sheriff Perry take me seriously, but I don't want anything to get out that could hurt my family or the investigation."

"I won't mention anything you don't authorize, but don't back out on me now, Madison. You broke the silence of the bones, and it's too late to turn away."

Nell's words pierced the depths of Madison's soul. She felt a stir inside. *Broke the silence and now the bones haunt me; they've upset my life and yet, I feel I need to speak up for them.*

"We need to get to the bottom of this mystery," Madison added. "I hope you won't just write your story and leave me to pick up the pieces. I'm already in trouble with my aunt slash employer, and there are still lots of unanswered questions."

She stood and walked to the kitchen. "Can I offer you something to drink?

We have sweet tea." She looked back at Nell.

"Thanks, tea would be great." Nell set the laptop aside and moved to a stool at the bar. "You're a spokesperson for the skull, you know?"

"Yeah, I want to be her voice. I want to know who she was and how she died." Madison sounded as if she was talking only to herself.

Nell perched her elbows on the bar.

Madison threw a quick look at Nell. "Let's talk about you. Are you a crime reporter?" She filled two glasses with crushed ice and poured the golden liquid.

Nell accepted the beverage. "I write human interest stories."

"I like helping people, but I don't like attention focused on me," said Madison.

"So, tell me about Bud. How long have you had him?"

"Aunt Denny rescued him when he was tiny, and gave him to me. He's part Lab and part blue heeler. His feet are webbed, and he has a good sense of smell. We were walking the trail when he ran across a scent that led him to dig up the skull."

"Did you report it to authorities?" Nell asked.

"I went straight to Sheriff Perry, but like I told you, he's not interested."

"What did he say about the pendant?"

"So much has happened in the last couple of days, I haven't shown it to him. Come to think of it, my backpack is still in my Blazer, and there are more bones in it."

Nell's eyes sparkled, and her posture shifted. Although she remained poised, the subtle change reminded Madison of a bird about to take flight.

"Let's take the new evidence to the sheriff so I can see his reaction."

Madison got the knapsack from her vehicle and then she and Nell walked the short distance to Sheriff Perry's office. Madison knocked on the open door and the sheriff glanced up from a stack of paperwork.

"Hello, Madison. Come in."

Madison entered, with Nell following closely behind. She placed the knapsack on the desk, but he paid no attention to it. His gaze focused on Nell, reminding Madison of Bud begging at the table—an unhappy reminder that men never looked at her that way.

Perry stood. "Aren't you going to introduce me to your friend?"

After Madison's brief introduction, Nell handed one of her business cards to the sheriff. He studied it intently and then tucked it into his shirt pocket.

"A reporter... This is a surprise, although not necessarily an unpleasant one," he said.

Madison unzipped the pack. "I have more evidence to show you."

Perry winced at the word *evidence*. "Madison, you've been warned. If you can't stay away from the mountain, I'll have to charge you with something."

One by one Madison arranged the bones on his desk, dirt and bits of leaf mold dropping onto the white papers. She placed the silver pendant in the center and stepped back with a flourish.

"I found this pendant near the bones. It matches the one my mother put on me the day she disappeared. Sheriff Franks and the whole town assumed she ran away. I know you think I'm a troublemaker, but now that we have more bones, I think the case merits another look."

Nell leaned over the desk for a better view of the articles. "I agree with Madison, Sheriff, it's customary to reopen a cold case when new evidence is found."

Perry grinned. "I guess you smell a story."

"I have a good nose for stories, and if you reopen the case, I'll be right here to cover it."

Sheriff Perry had a hard time hiding his smile. He nodded and then said, "Okay."

Nell said, "If you turn up something big, the good publicity will help in the next election."

Perry stood. "Come on Franks, we're going back up on the mountain."

Franks almost fell through the adjoining door. It was obvious that he'd been eavesdropping.

"Go back? You said the case was closed. Are you going to let some girl reporter tell you how to do your job?" He glared at Nell. Then he took a step toward Madison. "You're the one stirring up trouble. She was up in Asheville bothering my father day before yesterday."

Madison had hoped Willy wouldn't find out about her visit—but he had, and here he was telling the sheriff. She felt a lecture brewing.

"That's right. I know everything you're up to. I'm watching you," Franks said.

Perry stepped between them. "Franks, go fetch the evidence pack. We'll need barricade tape, bags, and twine to lay out a grid. And step quickly; I want to get this wrapped up before dark."

Franks moved with deliberate slowness. "Go fetch," he muttered under his breath.

"Who *is* that man?" Nell asked as they walked out of earshot. "He's Barney Fife on steroids."

Madison laughed. "Oh, that's just Weird Willy. Don't mind him."

Nell said. "What a day! So much accomplished, and it's just now noon. Thanks for your time, Madison. The least I can do to show my appreciation is to buy your lunch."

Madison and Nell arrived at Shirley's with the lunch crowd. They sat in the back booth and chatted while waiting for their orders. Nell had been raised in Boston, but attended journalism school at UNC Chapel Hill. Madison was surprised to learn the school was ranked in the nation's top ten. After graduation, she'd taken the first available job, which was in Knoxville. Just a little older than Madison, Nell had lived on her own since she was eighteen.

"You have such an exciting life," Madison said.

"It's not as exciting as you think. Lots of the stories I cover are pretty dull—Junior League luncheons and things like that. I spend a lot of time alone in hotel rooms. Which reminds me, I need a hotel for the night. I'd like to stick around and see what Sheriff Perry uncovers."

Madison fluttered her eyelashes. "It's Drew to you, Honey."

They were still laughing when their plate lunches were placed in front of them.

"Thanks, Betty," Madison said. She looked at Nell, who was already stuffing her mouth with mac and cheese. "About the hotel—the nice ones are in Asheville or Johnson City. There are a couple in Erwin. They were built a few years ago for the Apple Festival crowd."

Nell hesitated. "I'd hoped to find something right here in Cold Creek."

"Are you kidding?" Madison said. "But wait, maybe you could stay in Shirley's old guest house. We affectionately call it 'the shack,' but Jess keeps it in decent repair, and it shouldn't take too long to make it habitable."

"I'd hate to impose on you." Nell took another bite from her lunch.

"It doesn't have central heat and air, but the commode flushes and the shower has lots of pressure. If you don't mind roughing it, you're welcome to stay."

"Is it that quaint little house across the street? I noticed it when I came into town. That's the original architecture of the old homes, from settlers way back—I don't remember exactly, but the 1800s, if I recall correctly."

"How'd... Well, you are a reporter. Guess you've done stories on the local housing?"

"I took any assignment I could get. But those early stories gave me an appreciation for Appalachian heritage. You can be proud to have one of the oldest homes right here in your midst. I feel fortunate to have this experience, just like in the old days," Nell said. "Does the shack have heat?"

"Yes, Jess had natural gas piped into the original fireplace. I love it. And I am proud to own that property now. I've been considering renovating it for my own home, but don't want to mess up the historical value. You know?" Madison pushed her plate away. "I'll call my friend, Holly. With two of us working together, you'll have a comfortable room in no time. Besides, what else do I have to do? I guess I'm unemployed, after the argument with my boss."

"I thought you worked for your aunt, the dentist?" Nell looked inquisitively at Madison.

Madison flipped open her cell phone. "Yeah, long story—another chapter."

Holly agreed to meet them at the shack in an hour. Madison excused herself and went to the back to gather supplies for the cleaning job. While in the kitchen, she advised Jess of her intent.

"I can help you as soon as the lunch crowd is gone. You'll be surprised how little work you'll have to do. I've been keeping it up all winter. You know how folks tend to get stranded up here when a sudden snow comes."

"Yes, and we didn't have our usual snow this winter, mostly rain. That reminds me, did you manage to stop the leaky roof?" Madison asked.

"Sure did. But those old shingles aren't holding up well after nearly two centuries. We might need to replace it with a tin roof," Jess said.

"I've been looking into renovating, and a metal roof is acceptable on that type of home. I'm happy you agree with me. We're going to have fun with that job."

"We can get Henry to give us a hand. He loves the older houses too, and is all for keeping them true to history," Jess said.

"Thanks, come on over if you want; Holly is meeting us there shortly. See you later." Madison took the cleaning supplies out front and said to Nell, "I've got what we need. Let's go and take a gander to make sure you want to stay in the shack." Madison started for the door.

"The first time I heard that expression, *take a gander*, I thought we were looking for a goose. I've learned so many colloquialisms I decided to put them into a book." Nell walked out the door and held it so Madison didn't have to set down the bucket of cleaners or the handful of rags and mop.

"You should get some ammunition for a book from listening to Shirley's patrons; they have some doozies!"

"I've heard some already!" Nell's laugh didn't sound like a mockery, but excitement.

Holly's pickup pulled into the yard as soon as Madison and Nell stepped onto the porch at the shack.

"Hey, Madison." Holly turned to the other woman. "I'm Holly, and you must be Nell."

"It's nice to meet you, Holly." Nell accepted a brisk handshake.

Soon the three women were laughing and talking like schoolgirls, and the shack began to sparkle.

"What do you think?" Madison said.

"This is no shack. It's a lovely cottage," Nell answered.

"You're right. We'll call it The Cottage from now on. Holly, Shirley deeded the shack and acreage to me for my birthday."

"Really? Are you going to move in here now?" she asked.

"I'm thinking about it." Madison tugged at her ponytail. "Did you bring your kit?"

"It's in the truck. Does Nell want a touch-up?" Holly asked.

"No, it's for me," said Madison. "I want a haircut."

"You're kidding me! What will Jess say?" Holly stared at Madison as if she had just uttered a string of expletives.

"He'll quote the Bible verse *a woman's hair is her crowning glory*. He'll be disappointed, but it's my crowning glory, not his." Madison sounded defiant, even to her own ears.

"You've been doing a lot of thinking, I can tell." Holly paused at the door. "How much damage do you want me to do? Remember, once it's cut, there's no going back. We can't glue it back on."

Nell spoke up. "I did a story last year about a church where women were instructed not to cut their hair. It's interesting how religions limit women's choices. Long hair and a dress code are not that different from the restrictions of a habit or burka."

"I've never looked at it that way," Madison said. "It just makes me feel different from other women." Madison clapped her hands together. "Let's do it."

"The dawning of a new woman," Nell laughed.

"Seriously, Madison, how long have you considered the change?" Holly was not convinced.

Madison took in a breath. She blew it out slowly, thinking back over the last weeks. *The time it takes to dry my hair limits when I can wash it. There are only two ways to wear it, up or down. Some days my head hurts from the weight of the braid or ponytail. Other times pulling it up in a clip makes my head sore for hours. Letting it hang loose with nothing constricting it is only possible when at home.* Finally, she said, "It's always in the way at work; once my braid fell into the patient's mouth while I cleaned cement off a temporary crown." Madison closed her eyes and cringed as that memory bounced back. "I will just have to face the consequences, but my heart is set on shortening my hair."

Holly walked out to her truck and returned with a purple nylon bag. "Wet it in the bathroom. I'll cut the length first, and then I'll style it." She took combs and a pair of scissors from the bag and put them on the small kitchen table.

"If you ladies will excuse me, I need to check in with my boss." Nell went outside.

"Come back for the unveiling. You'll be the first judge," Holly said.

Nell waved over her shoulder as she went down the steps. "Can't wait!"

Madison sat in a chair next to the kitchen table. She pulled the cape around her shoulders and shut her eyes.

"Honey, you'll have to stand for the first cut." Holly reminded Madison that when she sat, her hair hung almost to the floor.

Solemnly, as if out of respect for the growth God had given her, Madison stood and stepped away from the chair. Holly drew a thick-toothed comb through the length, gathered it into one clump, and fastened it neatly with a strong rubber band. Soon, twenty-seven inches of ponytail lay on the floor.

"We can't throw this beautiful hair away," Holly said. "Would you mind if I send it to Locks of Love?"

"That's excellent! It makes me feel better about the whole idea." Madison tilted her neck and straightened her shoulders. Truly, a huge weight had dropped away; not only from her head but from her mind.

"You're not having second thoughts, are you?" Holly squeaked, her laugh nervous.

"Not at all. I'm glad to donate to such a worthy cause. It's good, the way they make the wigs out of discarded hair for patients with cancer and whatever else causes them to lose their own hair." Madison's smile felt relaxed. She had no regrets.

Holly straightened the bottom edges and measured the front to make sure both sides were equal. "Let's stop here and see what you think."

Madison's face lit up when she looked in the mirror. The length rested against the pocket of her shirt. She felt the movement as she tossed her head. She took the hand mirror from Holly to look at the back. The hair hung in a straight line across her shoulder blades.

"I love it." Her laugh sounded like a child's giggle over a colorful balloon. "Guess that's silly of me to react this way. But Holly, I've never even *liked* my hair before. And now I do."

By the time Holly finished drying and styling, Madison's hair draped her shoulders like a silk curtain. As she looked in the mirror, Madison felt like a different woman—an *attractive* woman. The hair she viewed was a shiny, dark chocolate, all the same color from ends to her scalp. No more lightened, frayed ends to tangle and pull. She felt pleased with how beautifully each strand swept her back with the slightest movement.

Holly drew close to her best friend. "Are you sure you're okay?"

Madison tipped her head to the side. A tear trickled down her cheek. "I never knew my hair could look so..." she wiped the tear away. "Anyway, I like it, and Jess will too, eventually. All he has to do is see me for who I am. I'm a woman now, not his little girl. He'll come around."

CHAPTER 10

H olly and Madison waited in the cottage until Nell returned.

"You really did it, girl! Any regrets?" Nell asked.

Madison shook her head, but didn't say anything.

"It's so shiny and healthy looking! Holly, did you put something on it?" Nell ran her fingers through Madison's dark strands.

Holly shook her head, answering, "No, it's that healthy."

"Well, that's a huge change. What do you think, Madison?" Nell's eyes grew wide with anticipation.

"I don't know why I've waited all this time. In school I got ribbed about my horse's tail. The only thing I dread is facing Jess."

"Then let's do that together," Holly suggested.

Madison nodded. The trio walked as if they were the three musketeers straight to Shirley's Restaurant. Nell opened the door, let Holly lead, followed by Madison, and then she stepped in.

Madison felt her heart pounding heavily in her chest. Her feet could not move beyond the swinging doors of the kitchen. Shirley peeked over to see who had come in; she gasped, but said nothing.

Jess came to her side, his eyes widened. He pushed open the swinging door and stepped toward Madison. "Child, what have you done?" Jess heaved a sigh. "Guess this was bound to happen, since you haven't been moved to join the church. You're an adult, responsible for your own actions." He turned and went back to the grill.

Shirley stepped closer, her voice barely above a whisper, "You know our beliefs. We love you, but loving and condoning what you do are two distinctly different matters." Shirley made her way to a stool and sat down. "I know there have been times when you had a rough road following the old ways. You made it through, and I knew you'd be stronger for it. You've never hinted that you disliked your long hair enough to cut it."

Madison knelt in front of Shirley, "It isn't that I disliked my hair; it was just *too* long. At work, my hair was always in the way, and if I expect to get a job in Johnson City, I have to learn a better way of managing it. Yours isn't as long or heavy as mine, yet you say it causes your neck to hurt."

She moved to the stool next to Shirley. "This is not an impulse! It was time. I'm not Jess' little girl, and I'm certainly not the old Madison. I'm going in a new direction, under my own power and for my own reasons. I love you Momma, and I love Jess, but no one is telling me what to do and not to do anymore. Not Denny, the sheriff, and most definitely not Weird Willy."

"You haven't called me Momma since you were six. I guess you have considered your situation. I don't know where you're headed, but you *are* a good girl. You know right from wrong, and you'll make the right decisions. I have faith that you will."

They hugged, and Holly joined them. "Shirley, doesn't she look lovely? We saved the ponytail, and I'm sending it to Locks of Love."

"That's nice, Holly. I'm glad to know it won't be in the trash can." Shirley wiped her tears on her apron. "Nell, you must think we are odd folks here in Cold Creek."

"No, Ma'am, I don't. I did a story on religions last year. I understand this was not an easy decision for Madison. But you're right. You have raised her in the best way you knew. Too bad more young girls haven't had that influence. This world could use more old-fashioned morality." Nell slid her arm around Shirley and embraced her in a warm hug. "You remind me so much of my grandmother—God rest her soul, I miss her."

Madison heard the back door of the kitchen close. "Will Jess hate me?"

Shirley shook her head. "He'll be all right. Doesn't accept change easily, and in spite of growing into a woman, you'll be his little girl even when you're my age."

"Does that mean the cook is gone, and we can't get supper?" Nell looked worried.

Shirley laughed. "No, it means you have to eat what I cook."

After dinner, the three young women walked back to the porch of the cottage. Holly told them goodbye, placed a to-go container with supper for Henry in the front seat, and then drove away in her truck.

Madison pulled two chairs from inside onto the porch so she and Nell could enjoy the evening air for a while.

"Are you afraid of staying here in the cottage alone, Nell?"

"No, I'll be fine. This is a unique opportunity."

"I can bring my sleeping bag and sleep on the floor. I've been thinking of doing that anyway, for a while. Maybe it would be a good test for me."

"What kind of a test?" Nell asked.

"This is just between you and me; I've considered moving into the cottage for a long time, but don't want to hurt Shirley and Jess's feelings. They've been good to me. Now that I own the cottage, I feel it might be best, you know, with things awkward between Jess and me."

Nell looked toward the door as if considering the interior. "I'd make some upgrades, at least in the kitchen. Maybe add a laundry room and a fresh coat of paint over the old wallpaper—I see possibilities."

"I have a plan for that back room off the kitchen; it's the perfect size for a laundry room."

"If you move in here, where else will occasional guests stay?" Nell asked.

"There's an apartment over the restaurant," Madison answered.

"Why doesn't someone live in it?"

"It is noisy during the day, and hot in the summer. Shirley keeps it as it was in the eighteen hundreds, when her great-grandparents built it. You should see the antiques. Jess has considered putting a small air conditioner in the side window, but right now it only has a ceiling fan."

"How charming." Nell appeared to be deep in thought. Then she said, "If you want to stay here tonight, it would be more fun than being alone."

Madison jumped to her feet, nearly overturning her chair. "Oh I forgot about Bud! He's been in the house all afternoon. What was I thinking?"

The two walked to Shirley and Jess's house. Bud met them on the porch, with excitement wiggling all through his body.

"Jess must have let you out. I guess he figured I have my head in the clouds and forgot about you. I could never forget you Bud."

When they returned to the cottage, Madison ran across the street to tell Shirley her plan.

"You do look refreshed, Madison. The hair style is growing on me," Shirley said.

"Did Jess say anything else?"

"No. He'll come around. You know, I didn't join the church until after Jess and I had been married a couple of years. He had such high hopes..."

Madison listened for the rest of Shirley's sentence. When nothing came, she asked, "What do you mean, high hopes?"

"Oh, I just meant that he wanted you to be saved while you're young. It is easier if you haven't been out in the world all that long."

Madison wasn't convinced that's what Shirley started to say. "And what else?"

"That's all." Shirley turned away. "Did I give you that extra key to the shack?"

"Not a shack anymore. We're calling it a cottage."

Shirley fumbled through the drawer of the small desk in the kitchen. "Oh, here it is."

"Thanks, I'll see you in the morning."

"Good night, Madison. You girls be careful."

"Not much gets past Bud, don't forget."

Madison left by the back door and saw that Jess was standing at the edge of the creek, which flowed behind the restaurant. She approached quietly, "I'm sorry if I've disappointed you. You have no way of knowing how heavy that long hair was and what it did to my neck, my head, and my moods. I love you, Jess, and I hope that one day you'll accept me as the person I am and not who you *hoped* I'd be. Even though I look different, I'm still Madison inside."

He kept his back turned, looking into the creek and said nothing. Madison backed away, turned, and crossed the street to where Nell and Bud waited on the porch.

"What's the matter, Madison? You look sad."

"Jess still won't talk to me." She sat on the porch steps. "In just these few days my life has gone from carefree and happy to..." She shook her head. "I don't even know what to call this. My whole world is upside down, all because I found that skull. Why is this causing such turmoil in my life?" She rested her head on her knees.

"Madison, maybe you're looking at this all wrong." Nell settled onto the steps beside her. "If the bones prove to be Tina Denson, and if she *was* murdered, your life has to change because you've been lied to by somebody you love. Even if it was a stranger that buried her up there, just finding the truth *has* to change your life. As for the bones, whoever she ends up being, she deserves your help. Don't you think?"

Madison raised her head. "Shirley told me when I was learning to ride a bicycle that anything worth having is worth a little pain. I wrecked and skinned my knees and elbows, but I mastered riding my two-wheeled bike. Holly and I spent our summers riding back and forth from the restaurant to her mamaw's house. Otherwise, the two-mile walk took us all afternoon. My scrapes healed, and I gained a faster mode of transportation. Maybe the pain in my heart is the price for learning the truth about my mother."

"And maybe it's painful cutting ties to those who love you and brought you to this stage of life. Hmm? Do you think seeing his little girl mature into a woman isn't painful for Jess?" Nell stood up and extended her hand to Madison.

"That makes sense." Madison latched onto the friendly hand, helped herself up, and the women went into the cottage.

Madison's cell phone rang. "Oh, it's Lisa." And then she said into the phone, "Hey, mutual friend. How are you, Lisa?"

The conversation took a couple of minutes, so Nell carried her things to the bedroom and hung up a shirt so the wrinkles would fall out before she wore it.

Madison joined her. "Lisa warned me not to try going back up to Eagle Ridge. Cole says there are moonshiners in the area. He ran upon a still while hunting. If it's active, it could be dangerous. We can't tell anyone else."

Nell nodded. "She told me the same thing last weekend. I wanted to warn you, but promised I'd keep Cole's secret so no one will snoop around near their cabin."

"How do you know Lisa?" Madison asked.

"When Cole played football for UT, I did a story on the team. I liked him in particular. Then I met Lisa. She and I really hit it off. I even went to their wedding," Nell said.

"I missed it. I had to do something for Denny that weekend. I can't remember what, but it was important to her. I heard they had a redneck theme, and it was fun!"

"Oh, it was hilarious! I don't know when I've enjoyed myself more." Nell said. "You need to ask Lisa to show you their pictures. They used Mason jars to serve punch from an old-timey looking pump. You know, the kind on a well. The tables were bales of hay, with red-and-white-checkered tablecloths. The bride's cake was a white monster-truck and the groom's a chocolate one, and they were meeting in the middle of a mud puddle, made with chocolate pudding atop a chocolate sheet cake. It was delicious!"

"Oh, that really sounds fun. Well, never again will I miss anything like that, not for Denny at least," Madison said with conviction.

Late night shadows brought Bud to his feet repeatedly, disturbing Madison's rest. The couch was too short for her long legs, so she put the cushions on the floor and placed her sleeping bag on them. "That's much better." She patted the floor next to her and said, "Come on, Bud, lie down. If you don't sleep, I can't sleep."

Bud walked in a circle and then settled with his head resting next to Madison's on the sleeping bag. She patted him and left her hand on his neck as she drifted off once again.

A knock at the door woke Madison. She opened the door just a crack and recognized the sheriff standing on the porch.

"Wake up, sleepy heads. Why don't you and Nell join me for breakfast?"

From somewhere behind her, Madison heard Nell say, "That sounds good. Give us a couple minutes, and we'll meet you over there."

Madison shrugged her shoulders and Sheriff Perry stepped off the porch.

"Is that okay with you, Madison?" Nell asked.

"Yeah, sure. Bud kept me awake a lot last night, so I overslept. What time is it, anyway?"

"It's seven thirty. I woke up a half hour ago and didn't want to disturb you."

Madison started to close the door, but the wiggly dog stood at her feet. "Bud, do you need to go out?" She opened the screen, and he slithered past her.

"Stay in the yard," she called.

"Does he know where the yard is?" Nell laughed.

"Close enough, I guess." Madison walked into the bathroom and shut the door.

"I feel badly that you had to sleep on the floor. I slept great in this bed."

Madison answered over the sound of the shower. "Jess just put it in here last winter. The roof leaked onto the old one, so when he patched the roof, he extended the frame to queen size and put a brand new mattress and box springs in the old bed frame. You're the first to sleep on the new bed."

"So when are you going to move in here?"

There was a long pause. The bathroom door opened and Madison came out with her hair wrapped in a turban and another towel draped her body. "I made up my mind last night. Jess is uncomfortable because he realizes I am going through a change. So I'm going to live under my own roof." She pulled the towel off her head and began combing her shoulder-length hair. "This is such a relief!"

"Did the sheriff notice?" Nell asked.

"It was tucked behind my ears. He couldn't see the length." She pulled a sweatshirt over her head. "Did Bud come back in yet?"

"No." Nell walked to the screen door. "Bud?" she called out.

The dog came running and leaped onto the porch. He stood wiggling at the door, but would not come in.

"I think he wants to stay on the porch," Nell said.

Madison stepped into the only pair of jeans she owned and walked to the door. "Stay on the porch or the yard." She let him know his boundaries.

Bud walked in his usual circle and then dropped and curled into a ball on the porch.

"Good boy. He'll stay right there. He's a good dog." Madison slipped on a pair of leather penny loafers and the women crossed the street to the restaurant.

Sheriff Perry sat at a booth and waved to the women. He stood, "What's this?" He lifted a strand of hair from her shoulder. "Did Delilah pay you a visit?"

"Nope, it was Holly." Madison slid into the booth opposite Perry.

"Never thought I'd see the day that Madison McKenzie would cut her hair." He stared at her and smiled as though he liked what he saw.

"Doesn't it make a big difference? You should see it when it is dry. It swings freely and is so shiny. I wish *my* hair looked that healthy," Nell said.

"Your hair is beautiful, Nell. Envy of your look is what pushed me over the top to cut mine."

The sheriff whispered. "Madison, I think your hair is lovely this length."

"Thanks, Sheriff. It made me feel good knowing that women or children with no hair from cancer treatments will have a wig from my hair. Holly knew just what to do about that."

"Locks of Love; yes, I've heard of it. And I think that was a noble thing you did," Perry said. After a brief pause, he turned toward Nell. "Um, Nell, would you like to ride up to the site on the mountain with me? I need to check on the men, but I won't be long. I thought you might want to see the place for yourself."

Nell responded in favor of the outing. Madison didn't know if it was due to the investigation or the company.

Jess appeared at the swinging doors and then turned away. Madison dropped her fork, suddenly full. "I'm going for my run. You two can fill me in later about your trip to the mountain." She slid from the booth and out the front door before Nell or the sheriff could comment.

CHAPTER 11

Madison's mind was a jumble of thoughts as she ran the familiar trail. Things that had to be done and things she wanted to do were in conflict. If she moved into her own place, something she wanted to do, there would be hurt feelings. But if she stayed with her folks, the feelings would still be there, building with every passing day. She knew Jess loved her enough to get past her breaking his rule, but not without consequences. No, staying under his roof would be like rubbing salt in a wound. She hadn't considered how much cutting her hair would hurt him. But at the same time, she was an adult—she might even have to go away from home to find another job. The change was long overdue. She couldn't turn back; moving ahead was the only answer.

Denny packed dishes and linens last year when she'd cleaned out her house. Things she knew Madison would need one day, when she set up housekeeping. Who knew it would be this soon? First she'd get her clothes and personal stuff from her bedroom in Jess's house, and then she'd go out to Denny's for the boxes stored there.

Keep busy, look forward, stop worrying and do what you must; do what you want. That thought was unfamiliar to Madison. She'd never really done what *she* wanted. She felt dread and excitement at the same time. She wanted Holly's reassurance. Or was this more of a need? Yeah, she needed confirmation, backup. Holly was her support, always had been. After all, she could use help with moving the boxes. It wasn't likely Denny would be forgiving enough to help her today.

After her run Madison drove her Blazer to her folks' house to load her clothes and other personal items. "Bud, I need you to stay here while Holly and I get my things from Denny's house."

The dog whined and then lay on the braided rug next to Jess's chair. Madison set a bowl with fresh water on the floor, secured the doggy door in the kitchen, and checked to see that everything was locked down before leaving.

She noticed there were no cars at the dental office as she passed. Closer investigation revealed a note on the door that read, *Closed due to an emergency.* "I wonder what she considers an emergency."

"We're both adults; I just have to call her and talk this out." Madison said as she called her aunt's cell phone. When she answered Madison thought she heard fear in Denny's voice.

"What's wrong, Aunt Denny?" Madison asked.

"I'm taking two sick dogs to the vet in Johnson City."

"I'm sorry to hear that. What's happened?"

"How would I know? They're just sick." Denny said abruptly. "Emily canceled my schedule."

"Oh, Emily did it—well I hope the dogs will be okay," Madison said. "I'm moving into the cottage, now that I'm its owner."

"And so now you want your grandmother's dishes I've saved for you. They're packed into boxes cluttering up my storage room."

"You aren't surprised that I'm moving out on my own?" Madison said.

"Shirley said you'd cut your hair and you and Jess are at odds." Denny sounded as though there was a satisfaction in her tone.

"Yes, Holly cut my hair. But as far as Jess and I, well, I know he is disappointed, but we certainly aren't at odds."

"I heard you're looking for a job in Johnson City, now that I helped you get your certification. Does this mean you've quit your job at my practice?"

"After your harsh words, what would you have me believe?" Madison felt that her aunt was trying to lay the blame on her. "If you're expecting me to apologize, I won't. You owe me the apology.

"Why you little shit! Get *all* your stuff out today; tomorrow I might burn it!" Denny disconnected the call.

Madison parked her car in the yard next to the cottage and then ran across to the restaurant.

"Hey, have you talked to Denny today?" Madison asked Shirley.

"Not this morning, but last night she called saying she has to take her dogs to the vet."

"Did you say anything about me?"

"I mentioned that you'd cut your hair and the look is growing on me. She commented that you'll have to move when you get a job in the city. I ignored her; she was fishing," Shirley said.

"Yeah, she was fishing for an apology too." Madison picked up a carrot and walked to the door. "I'm going to get my stuff while she's gone. She told me she'd burn it, if I didn't get it today."

Shirley's mouth gaped open in shock. "Don't you go out there alone; get Holly to ride with you. There's no telling what that aunt of yours is capable of."

"That's true; she's been a strange bird lately." Madison punched in Holly's number.

Shirley waved. "Be careful."

Madison nodded as she left the restaurant and crossed the street.

"Hey, Madison. Too late, I've already sent your ponytail away," said Holly, laughing.

"Good, but that's not why I'm calling. I wondered if you'd ride to Denny's with me to pick up my things. I don't want to leave them there any longer."

"Sure, I'll head that way now." Holly sounded excited at the chance of getting away from their farm again. "Henry's plowing, and doesn't need me."

"Thanks, I'm at the cottage."

Madison unloaded her clothing, piling everything on the couch, and then walked into the small bedroom, which had no closet. Jess had explained once about these historical houses. Years ago, homes were taxed by the number of rooms. And a closet counted as a room, so to avoid paying more taxes, homeowners hung a curtain across one corner—crude, but efficient enough. They didn't have a lot of changes of clothing then.

Hmmm... If I take the wall out between these rooms. That'll make a spacious bedroom and place for a closet. Holly's truck rumbled into the yard, and Madison ran out to meet her.

Holly waved. "We can use my truck and get it all in one load."

"But look at those clouds. It might rain." Madison looked at the sky. "I've already put the back seat down to make room for the boxes."

"Ok, you have that look. You're on a mission," Holly said.

Madison glanced sideways. "How do you know that?"

"I'm observant, and I know *you*."

"I've dreamed of living on my own; it's time to breathe life into the cottage again."

Holly clapped her hands. "I love the idea; after all, you *do* own it. I can help you strip the old wallpaper and paint it. Henry can redo the hardwood floors to make them look brand new. He did ours, you know."

"That sounds like a lot of work to me. What will he charge?" Madison asked.

"Nothing, if he knows what's good for him!" Holly slapped her knee and laughed.

"Yeah, yeah. I hear you, Holly, but I know you'd never say a word to upset Henry."

"Guess you know *me* well, too," Holly sighed. "Henry likes you, and what's more, he respects you. If you need help, he'd be the first to offer his skills. I told him that Jess isn't comfortable with your haircut, and he knows Jess does the repairs to the shack, so Henry will understand that you can't ask Jess for help right now."

Madison stared out the windshield as she drove in silence for a few minutes. Then she turned and said, "I've put myself in this position. Both aunt Denny and Jess are upset with me—the people I love most. And they've done so much for me. Who will be next, Shirley or you?" A tear slipped from one eye and then the other.

"Don't beat yourself up! Jess will be okay in time; he just has to get used to his little girl growing into a woman who makes her own decisions. As for Denny, she brought this on herself with the way she has steered you toward *her* goals. It was bound to happen sooner or later. She'll come around too, as soon as she sees the good choices you make. And yours *will* be good choices. I know that, and so do you." Holly put her hand on Madison's shoulder.

Madison felt comforted by her best friend, and she knew that Holly spoke the truth.

The twenty-minute drive to Denny's property usually relaxed Madison; however, today she was tense. Would her aunt be there, waiting to fuss at her? She slowed the vehicle to a crawl as she turned onto the shady lane leading past the old woodworking shop, the barn with dog runs and kennels, and finally to the stately, two-story pale yellow farmhouse Danny and Tina Denson lived in when Madison was born. Usually, Madison felt like she was home. Today, a cold chill came over her as she and Holly walked up the steps to the white, recently painted wrap-around porch. Holly knocked on the golden oak door but there was no answer. Madison let out a sigh of relief and opened the door—a door that had never been locked, as long as she could remember.

A spare room off the den acted as storage. The double doors stood open and boxes were neatly stacked in one side of the room. Denny's Iditarod dog sled sat on the other side, covered with a brightly-colored blanket.

"She might be back anytime. We have to get this in one trip. I don't want to see her." Madison picked up a box marked dishes and carried it outside.

Holly carried a second box of dishes and set it on the porch. "Something puzzles me. If the Denson's original house burned, how'd these dishes survive?"

"Only the upstairs bedrooms burned. The kitchen had water and smoke damage, but the dishes were okay. When Danny rebuilt, he made the kitchen larger and turned the formal living room into the master bedroom. The two bedrooms upstairs now have their own bathrooms."

"So the basement must have only had water damage, right?" Holly walked inside for another box.

"This house doesn't *have* a basement." Madison sounded puzzled.

"Henry was in the old house, but never the new one. Maybe Danny had the builders seal off the basement. Your grandfather kept a gun collection down there. Henry's old man bought a shotgun from him; Henry still has it."

"Really!" Madison stood frozen in her tracks. "I've been all over this house, even in the attic. I've never seen steps to a basement."

After nearly an hour, the Blazer, loaded with all the designated boxes, drove away from Denny's property. Madison felt sad and a little guilty because she had snooped into Denny's past, but her aunt was not her usual self. What else was bugging Dr. Denson? Madison was sure the change began after she'd discovered the skull and thought, *why did I have to find that skull?*

The very next day, Holly got Henry to look at the wall between the two bedrooms at the cottage. He determined it was not a load-bearing wall, and in no time demolition of the wall was complete. After the dust settled, Madison and Holly worked on stripping the old wallpaper off and priming the hard-coat plaster.

The next morning the women went to Johnson City for window treatments, while Henry framed up the closet, hung the drywall, and installed the closet door. Madison stayed up all night painting to complete the room's makeover.

Henry refinished the bare wood floors that had never been sealed with shellac.

Days slipped by, and the cottage came to life. Madison plundered through the antique stores in Jonesborough and found a couple of tables, along with a dresser and chest of drawers. She chose a new couch for the living room, and then donated the old sofa to the Salvation Army. With all the components brought together, Madison felt a sense of gratification as she looked at the interior of her cozy home.

She heard a slight tap at the door. When she opened it, there stood Jess.

He smiled, looking past her at the newly painted walls, he said, "Can I come in?"

She opened the door wide and said, "Please. I'm glad to see you."

He looked at the remodeling. "This is nice."

"Thank you. I had a lot of help."

"May I?" he moved further into the room, then looked at the spacious new bedroom and said, "You eliminated the wasted hall space!"

"Yes, but that's not all—look at this." She showed him the new entrance to the bathroom. "That used to be the linen closet. Do you like it?"

Jess nodded in approval, saying, "Nice, very nice."

Madison met Jess's gaze. "I'm happy you approve. Henry did that for me, and the floors too. Don't they look great?" Then she added, "I'm glad you're here, Jess."

Jess nodded slowly, "You didn't have to move out of our house, you know, but I understand. This is perfect for you, and it's all yours."

Madison walked him back into the living room. "It was time. Besides, I've wanted to do this for a while." She surveyed the adjoining room. "I haven't decided what to do with the kitchen yet; that might be a while, because I don't want a modern look. But that little room off the back will be fine with a washer and dryer, not a couple of wash tubs and a scrub board."

She and Jess laughed together and on impulse, she hugged him. She was glad that they could laugh together again; she couldn't stand ill feelings between them.

In return, he held her in a warm embrace and said, "You're a smart young woman, Madison. I'm proud of you."

Surprised, Madison pulled back and looked straight into his brown sugar eyes.

"No, really; I *am* proud of you, even though I'm still not thrilled about your hair—but that's *your* business." He shrugged his shoulders. "You're all grown up now. There is nothing more I can do, you know?"

He walked to the door. "I just wanted you to know I'm not mad at you." He stared at the walls, and then asked, "Something is missing, what are your plans for the walls?"

Madison smiled, "I want flowers—oils, or maybe watercolors, I've even thought of the photos on canvas. You know me and flowers."

Jess said with a smile, "I do know!"

Madison stepped onto the porch. "Thank you for coming, Daddy."

He stopped at the bottom of the steps, turning to face her with a surprised look. "I heard you call Shirley, Mom, and now I'm Daddy again? It's been a long time, but we knew you loved us just the same. We are your folks, even if we're not blood kin."

"Yes, you're the best parents anyone ever had!" She felt proud of her words.

Jess walked slowly back toward the restaurant. Madison thought how he was the image of goodness, so handsome, tall and slim, but it seemed he carried the weight of the world on those broad shoulders. What about his early life—was there someone else before Shirley, someone he can't or won't talk about? She was sure there were secrets pushed down deep inside; the secrets she wanted to know, if she could only read his mind.

CHAPTER 12

Madison noticed the restaurant was extremely busy Saturday evening, so she went to Shirley and offered to help.

Shirley sounded elated. "Oh, if you'll just run the cash register it'll make my life easier. Betty and Rena can handle serving."

Madison took note of who was hanging around waiting for the sheriff's men to drop some hint about the investigation. There was Slim, the barber; Mr. Olsen from the hardware; Rex and Boyd, two members of the Volunteer Fire Department; Dan from the feed store; and of course, loudest of all was Deputy Will Franks, Jr. She'd heard that Sheriff Perry had assigned Franks to the office because he was familiar with running things there. But in actuality, Madison knew it was to keep Weird Willy out of the investigation.

Scattered throughout the room were a few faces Madison did not recognize. No one was in a hurry to leave, so Madison didn't have any tickets to cash out the first hour. She cleared tables of emptied plates and refilled coffee cups or other beverages.

Mr. Olsen was the first of the residents to pay his ticket.

"Thank you. Good night, Mr. Olsen." Madison handed him two dollars and change with his receipt. "Say hello to the missus."

He responded, "Keep it, you worked hard tonight. And if you are not work-ing—I know Shirley appreciated your help, and I figure you can use the money."

"Thank you, but I'm okay financially. I've worked since I was sixteen, and never had much to spend my wages on. My nest egg is plump; don't worry 'bout me."

One by one the locals gave up on hearing any secrets and went home before the law left.

Madison carried the last slice of carrot cake to the kitchen. "Take this to Jess before I nibble on it." Shirley laughed with such enthusiasm Madison realized she was exhausted. "Let me finish here and close up. You go on home to Jess."

"Thanks, Sweetie, I will." Shirley peeled off her apron and tossed it at the laundry hamper next to the back door, but missed.

"Good night." Madison locked the door behind Shirley, then picked up the apron and put it into the hamper along with her own. Nell, Sheriff Perry, and a cute guy she'd noticed sitting with the deputies earlier were the only patrons left in the dining room. Rena cleared their table while Betty worked at closing down things behind the counter.

Sheriff Perry joined Madison at the register. "I've been waiting for a chance to talk to you. Let's step into the kitchen. No reason to let anyone else hear this." After a short pause, he continued, "We found the lower portion of the skull." He watched Madison's reaction. "I want you to look at it when you're done here. Come to my office, okay?"

She nodded. "I'm just about finished."

They returned to the main dining room. Nell motioned from a table where she sat with the handsome guy. Madison had found her eye drawn to him all evening. Now she was hesitant about moving toward the table.

Perry placed his arm around her shoulders and nudged her closer saying, "Madison, have you met Rick?"

"Not formally," she extended her hand. "Madison McKenzie."

"I've heard that name. You and your four-legged friend discovered the bones." He took her hand and held it for a long shake.

"That's right." She looked away and pulled her hand back.

"I'll be at my office." Perry said. He tipped his hat to Nell and left the restaurant.

Madison stood as if her feet were glued to the floor. Her eyes made contact with Rick's and she felt a flip flop in her stomach. She drifted into an abyss of the deepest green, like emeralds. His eyes held her gaze. He loosened his tie and the top button of a white shirt fell open, showing a V-neck t-shirt. His neck was paler than his face, leading her to believe he spent a lot of time with the tie on.

Suddenly aware that her face was burning, Madison said, "Nice meeting you." She made her way to the register and busied herself with the cash left by the sheriff. She so hoped Rick had not seen the foolish way she'd stared. Had she been there for a minute, a second? Her thoughts halted as Nell and Rick approached with their tickets.

Madison quickly counted out their change and both declined. So she returned to the table and left it for Betty's tip. She saw them waiting outside.

"Betty, you and Rena can lock up can't you?" Madison asked.

"Sure!" Both girls answered.

"Good night." She flipped the closed sign on the door and joined them on the sidewalk. "I need to see what Perry wants to show me. You two make yourselves comfortable at the cottage."

Madison walked into Perry's office and he showed her to a chair. "This is under wraps, not to be mentioned to anyone. I'm sure you know my rules," Perry said. The skull Madison had found sat on the desk. He set a lower jawbone next to the upper. "Do they match?" he asked.

Madison leaned in close and raised her gaze to meet Perry's. As though he knew her question, he nodded. She picked up both portions and fit them together. They were a match. She set the top part down and closely examined the lower arch.

"She has a gold inlay. Not like we do now, where we send them out to a lab and they make it on a stone model. This one is like the older dentists made in their own labs. See the margins? It was artwork, and beautifully done. Each doctor had his own signature style. Nowadays we wouldn't make a three-unit inlay; the fillings would be individual, and most likely done in the tooth-colored resin. Dentists have stopped doing the old amalgam fillings now, too. So I'd guess this was made nearly thirty years ago."

Perry leaned in to look. "So certainly not one hundred years, huh?"

Madison shook her head. "How about DNA?"

"I sure hope so. And with that said, I need a DNA sample from you, if you feel the half heart pendant matches the one you have."

From a kit sitting on his desk, Perry got out a swab. He uncapped it and reached toward Madison. She opened her mouth. Perry swabbed the inside of her cheek, put the cotton swab back into the vial and recapped it.

"I'll get this to Knoxville immediately."

The sheriff and Madison stepped out into the night air and walked to her cottage, less than a block away. Rick and Nell waited on the porch.

Nell sat in a slim rocking chair. "When did this arrive?"

"Oh, Jess brought it this afternoon. I told him I'd need another one, but do you think it's too crowded?" Madison stepped as though measuring the front porch.

"Well, at least it's small. Another the same size will be fine," Nell said.

Madison leaned against the porch post. "I'd love to have the porch wrap around the side. It's nearly always shady on the side facing the creek. Wouldn't that be nice?"

"Oh, yeah that would be nice. By the way, where's Bud?" Nell asked. "I'm surprised he didn't come to the door when we walked up in the yard."

"He's probably asleep on my bed," Madison unlocked the door.

"I'd like to meet the famous Bud," Rick said.

She called his name, "Bud. Come here, Bud." And then she clapped her hands. Bud didn't come. She walked through each room, and then back to the doorway. "He's not here." Her voice was almost a whisper. A terrible feeling of dread crept from deep within her. "He doesn't go out of the yard without me."

Nell stood. "I'm sure he's out back somewhere. Come on guys, we'll look for him." The four of them walked around the house.

"Bud, come here boy!" Madison's voice felt shaky. She called again. "Bud!" Then she tightened her lips and made a shrill whistle. The sound echoed off the mountain. She listened for his bark. There was nothing but the wind in the trees and the sounds of night bugs.

Madison froze by the back gate. Her eyes combed the grassy field beyond, out of bounds for her beloved pup. Her heart pounded so loudly in her ears she didn't hear Rick approach. She jumped when he touched her shoulder. She wheeled around. Tears streamed down her face.

Rick pulled her close against his chest and held her there. "We'll find him, Madison. Dogs do this, especially males; he'll be back."

Madison shuddered. "He'd never leave on his own. Someone took him."

At that moment Sheriff Perry returned from his patrol car with a spot light. "Show me where you and Bud run. Maybe he was bored with being alone and just ventured out."

Madison stood zombie-like against Rick's chest. She'd forgotten how comforting a man's embrace felt. Yet even this wasn't enough to relieve her pain. Bud was gone. The thought cut her insides like shards of glass. She'd never felt pain from fear. But this was real.

CHAPTER 13

Sunday morning, Madison forced herself out of bed early and into the shower. Her eyes felt puffy from crying and no sleep. She ignored the ringing phone and Denny's voice on the answering machine. "Call me back. I've got to talk to you!"

After drying off, Madison stepped into a pair of faded jeans she'd picked up at a thrift shop and pulled a sweatshirt over her head. She didn't notice she wore house shoes until she walked into the restaurant. At that point, she didn't even care.

Normally Shirley's was not open on Sundays, but with so many people around town, Jess wanted to offer them lunch and dinner.

At a glance, Shirley recognized Madison's state and cried out, "What in the world is wrong?"

"Bud's missing. He wasn't home when I left the restaurant last night. The sheriff, Nell, Rick, and I looked for him until after midnight." She slumped onto a stool and rested her head on the counter. "Someone took him. He's *never* gone off by himself."

"Why? Everyone in Cold Creek knows he's your dog." Shirley patted Madison's arm.

Madison rocked her head back and forth. "That's what worries me; they *know* he's my dog."

"You must have had the door locked?"

Madison nodded.

"Why didn't you wake us?"

"Didn't need to. We walked through your yard. I knew if Bud was in there he'd have come out through his doggy door. He didn't. No point in waking you."

"Talk to Denny; maybe he went to her house." Shirley encouraged.

"Denny called and left a message on my machine. She sounded upset. I better call her back and see what's going on." Madison walked through the kitchen and onto the back porch to talk in private.

"Denny, it's me. What's happened?" She listened for a while and then said, "I'm so sorry. I hope Shep will be okay." She swallowed hard and tried to clear her voice.

"Bud disappeared last night. We looked everywhere for him." Again, she listened. "Call me later." She returned to the kitchen.

When she walked into the main dining room, Shirley was talking with Sheriff Perry at the register.

"Any sign of Bud this morning?" Perry asked.

"No, and Denny is at the veterinarian's office in Johnson City with two more of her dogs. They were poisoned. Rufus died, and Shep is critical. A few days ago, she had two others that got sick. Now it's happened again."

Sheriff Perry propped his fist on his hip and pinched his chin with the other hand. "There are some strange things going on right now. We don't normally have skeletons on the mountain and poisoned or missing dogs. I don't think this is at all coincidental."

Madison drew in a deep breath and slowly let it out. "I'm going to try to sleep for an hour or so, then back to hunting for Bud." She walked outside with the sheriff. "I guess Nell went back to Knoxville?"

"Yes, her editor had another assignment for her."

"Are you going back up on the mountain?" Madison asked.

Perry nodded. "I'll talk to you when I get back." He squeezed her shoulder gently. "Madison, he'll turn up. Bud's smart. Try to get some rest."

"I didn't sleep a wink." She waved at Shirley who stood in the doorway.

Madison barely made it to her bed. She fell into a deep sleep and dreamed of dogs: hanging from trees, in the woods, on the roof. By the time she awoke in a cold sweat, she realized she'd only slept an hour. She had to go look for Bud.

She put on running shoes and went to the back yard. Near the gate, where the meadow begins, the grass was flattened by wide tires, like the kind a four-wheeler has.

These weren't visible last night. She noticed the tracks turned in a circle, leading through the meadow where she and Bud played. The sandy soil showed paw prints on top of the tire tracks. *But why would Bud follow a four-wheeler?*

On the other side of the meadow, she lost the dog tracks, but the flattened grass was easy to follow. She ran fast, causing her eyes to burn and her throat to feel dry. At the entrance to the old cave, she stopped so suddenly that her feet nearly slid from under her.

The rocky ground gave up no tracks. Still, she slipped into the cave, crouched down, and waited as her eyes adjusted to the darkness. She remembered the small penlight in her pocket from the night before. She rotated the lens to a fine, sharp beam, then edged further into the cave. She called Bud's name, but heard no response.

The wall felt cool and smooth to her touch where large rocks protruded on both sides, forming a tunnel. *Is that light I see? I hear water.*

In the loose dirt, she followed small paw prints through a narrow passage into a room partially lighted by an opening overhead. A stream of water trickled to the floor. Then a hoarse whimper, low and strained, drew Madison's attention; there was Bud, anchored to a rock in the lowest part of the room. She moved closer and fell to her knees. He jumped into her arms yapping like a whisper. She removed the rope from his collar and lifted him as she stood. He felt small in her arms and didn't squirm to get down. Instead, he put his paws on each side of her neck and frantically licked her face. Finally, she set him on the floor. A small stream of water flowed near the wall. The rope holding Bud had allowed him to reach the stream.

Who did this? "Oh Bud, if only you could talk."

Madison heard a scraping sound and a huge bolder closed the opening to the tunnel. "Hey! Who's out there?!" Panic in her voice echoed around the room as she screamed, beating her fists against the stone till they bled. She and Bud were trapped underground. She moved under the trickle of water, yelling for help, but got no response.

So this was the motive for taking you—knowing I'd find you. And now they have me. Madison sunk to the floor with Bud in her lap. She felt her pockets. She'd left her phone at the cottage. "What now?" Her voice drifted from her mouth, nothing more than a whisper.

Madison and Bud sat for what seemed like hours waiting and listening for someone to come and rescue them. "No one knows we're here, and I don't intend to spend the night." She stood up and walked in circles.

Bud moved to where the water fell from the ceiling, looked up and yapped.

"That's too high, I can't reach the hole." She combed the room for inspiration. Most of the rocks were firmly attached to the wall. She finally found one that she could move, with a broken tree limb as leverage. The stone inched to the center of the room. She stood on it, reaching toward the hole.

Still too short. She stepped down, spotting another stone; it soon slid into place. She piled gravel and mud another six inches to fill in the gap between. Now Madison could reach the edge of the hole.

"I can't get out, but I can push you up to the surface." She stepped down and scooped Bud into her arms. "Go to the restaurant, get Jess."

Bud licked her face, and she heaved him over her head. His legs scratched at the opening, raining dirt and water down on her. His claws caught on a root, and he pulled himself out the opening.

He looked down and barked.

She repeated, "Get Jess." And the eager dog disappeared.

Madison leaned against the cave wall. After a while, she heard barking, not from the hole, but from the tunnel. The stone scraped, letting light into the room from Jess's flashlight.

"Madison?"

"I'm here. Bud brought you to the cave."

"Why are you here?"

"This is where I found Bud, tied with that rope over there." She pointed. "Someone closed off the tunnel and trapped us in here. I was able to move these rocks and build them up high enough to push Bud out that opening overhead." Her arms reached around her loving dog. "Oh, Bud, you're so smart!"

"That was pretty smart of you, too. I guess your gangly arms and legs aren't so bad now that they came in handy." Jess hugged Madison. "Let's get out of here."

When they were safely inside the cottage, she called Shirley. "Come over, as soon as you can."

"I'll be right there."

Seconds later Shirley burst through the front door.

"We're back here," Madison called.

Shirley appeared in the doorway of the bedroom. "Where'd you find him?"

"He was tied in the old cave on the other side of the meadow."

"Tied? But he came to the back of the restaurant." Shirley dropped onto the bed.

"She found Bud in the cave, and then someone closed them up in it." Jess said.

"The one I won't go into," Shirley added.

"Yes, but Madison did. Someone knows the secret, and put the stone in place."

"What do you mean, the secret?" Madison asked.

"It's perfectly balanced and pivots, sort of like the old pyramids. I can't figure it out, but I know when you lean on the top, it will move. It isn't strength, it's just that balanced." He scratched his head. "Anyway our girl was able to get Bud through the opening overhead, and he came for me."

"Dear me, who would do something like that, Jess?" Shirley cried.

"That's what I intend to find out. I'm going to see the sheriff." Madison said.

"No, let me. He and I have some things to discuss anyway." Jess left the room. "Madison, you stay at the restaurant with Shirley. Lock these doors, and bring Bud in the back way. Don't let anybody see that you found him."

An hour passed as Jess waited at the perimeter tape on Eagle Ridge before Perry approached from the trail. "I'm sorry I kept you waiting. We found more bones, and the forensic team is here from Knoxville. Every inch of the ground has to be photographed and marked, every bone, everything!" Perry ran his fingers through his hair.

Jess took a shallow breath. "More? What's going on?"

Perry shook his head, "Tell me why you drove up here, Jess."

"Madison followed a trail to the cave beyond the meadow and she found Bud tied up. When she went in, someone trapped her and Bud. She's smart enough that she figured her way out by putting Bud through the opening, and sent him for me."

Sheriff Perry looked confused. "What? I don't understand." Perry furrowed his brow. "You've got some explaining to do." Then he spoke into the microphone on the shoulder of his shirt.

Jess heard him telling someone that he'd be ten-nineteen.

"Let's go to Cold Creek; we can talk on the way," Perry said.

"Good idea, Sheriff. I have things I'd like to ask you, too."

The two men returned to Jess's truck and drove back to the restaurant together.

During the drive, Sheriff Perry confided in Jess. "When we found the second skull, I knew Madison was right. Something awful happened up there. Or somewhere else, and the bodies were dumped there. It's odd how they took the time to dig so many graves." Perry stared out the window.

"Maybe it took place over a period of years. Not a mass shooting or anything, but one killing every now and again," Jess suggested.

"Well, it does make more sense that way, but it's basically out of my hands. Knoxville's team will do all the forensics. What bothers me is it has to be a local. You know? Maybe someone we see every day. Doesn't that bother you, Jess?"

"Absolutely! And to think, my Madison was there alone and discovered the first one. It keeps me awake nights, worrying about her. She's hardheaded, and will go back up there if we don't keep her under guard."

"She won't now. The site and surrounding area is off limits and guarded." Perry shifted in his seat. "Just the same, I want to keep an eye on her. If the killer is still in our area, she might be in more danger than we know. I'll need your help, Jess."

"I know, and I'll do anything I can to help."

Sheriff Perry questioned Madison in the security of the kitchen at the restaurant. She told him about the tracks. "They might be from a four-wheeler."

"Tracks? We didn't see any last night." He propped his thumb on his forehead and massaged with his fingers. "Did you hear anything during the night?"

Madison shook her head, "No, nothing."

Sheriff Perry placed both feet firmly on the floor. He rocked on his heels and back down several times. "I'll get up there before dark and have a look around. You," he punched his index finger into her shoulder. "Stay with your folks tonight. No argument, you hear?"

Madison nodded but said nothing.

"Madison, you were right. This is something bigger than even you realized. We're still uncovering new bones. Last count was six, and there could be more. You've got to promise you'll stay away from the mountain—and don't go anywhere alone! I mean it, and Jess agrees."

Madison swallowed hard. She felt sick and dropped into a chair. "I wish I hadn't been right."

After Perry left the restaurant, Madison went upstairs and watched over the town from a window facing Main Street. Bud followed; his toenails tapped a rhythm on the steps.

She pulled the swivel chair to the window and stayed behind the sheer lace curtains. A cool breeze blew into her face, making her sleepy. She lay across the bed and Bud curled up below her on the floor.

Hours passed and darkness brought a thunderstorm, waking Madison. She jumped up, pulled the window down, and spotted a person walking beside her cottage. She remained motionless waiting for them to show again. She knew all her windows and doors were locked and eventually they reappeared at the front of the house. It was Weird Willy.

What is he up to? She watched him try to raise the bedroom window. No luck, so he slipped back into the shadows and disappeared.

Downstairs Jess turned off the lights. "I was coming to wake you. We're ready to go to the house."

"I saw Weird Willy trying to open a window of my cottage. He slipped all the way around, and then vanished in the shadows. What do you suppose he was up to?"

"I don't know. Maybe I should call and ask him," Jess said.

"Or tell Sheriff Perry," Madison said.

"He'll probably use the excuse that the deputy was checking to be sure your house was secured." Jess put his arm around Madison leading her to the back door. "Shirley's in my truck waiting for us."

They ran together under an umbrella. Bud jumped in the floorboard ahead of them. Shirley dropped a towel on his wet back. "Sit, Bud," she said.

"I'm taking you home and then going to find the sheriff. Madison, you and Bud don't even *think* of leaving our house," Jess warned.

"We won't. One scare is enough for me in a day," Madison said.

Bud was first out of the truck and up on the porch shaking vigorously. Madison held the umbrella over Shirley, supporting her on the wet steps and into the house.

"First thing I'm going to do is call Denny. My cell phone was at my house; if she tried to reach me, she couldn't."

"Are you sure that's a good idea?" Shirley asked.

Madison stared at her and then put the phone down. "You don't think she had something to do with this?"

Shirley shrugged her shoulders and walked into her bedroom. "Madison, I don't know what to think these days. I never would have thought she'd turn on you, but she did." Shirley flopped down on her bed and closed her eyes.

"Does she know about the cave?" Madison looked at Shirley.

"Anyone raised around here knows," Shirley answered.

Madison went to the living room and picked up the phone again. "Hey, it's Madison."

"Madison, what's wrong? I've called you all afternoon." Denny spoke sharply.

"I'm sorry. I was upset about Bud and forgot to take my cell off the charger. How's Shep?"

"He's going to make it, thank God. I can't believe I lost Rufus." Denny sniffled and her voice cracked. "I, I... can't imagine who would do this to our dogs!"

Madison felt Denny's pain. "Me either. Did the vet have an idea how the poison was administered?"

"It wasn't in their stomachs." Denny's tone changed. "Killing women and dumping their bodies, and now someone hurting animals. That really disturbs me."

"We're the ones meant to suffer, and it's working," Madison blurted out. "Maybe it's because I found the bone yard."

"I'd say you're right. That was nothing to be messed with." Denny sniffled and then blew her nose. "You're not still messing around up there, are you?"

"The forensic team is here from Knoxville," Madison remarked.

"The TBI is in on it?" Denny was barely audible.

"Knowing Weird Willy, word will be out tomorrow anyway. Sheriff Perry's team found additional skeletons." Madison hesitated. "We're not supposed to know about them yet."

"This is way over Drew Perry's head," Denny said.

"Rick Malone, the TBI investigator, called them in," Madison added. "He's young, and nice looking."

"Careful, girl; you'll get your heart broken by a cop from the big city."

Denny's voice sounded like chalk on a blackboard to Madison. "I can look, can't I?" Madison didn't mean to sound indignant. Stress and fatigue tugged at her normal sweet nature. No matter who she looked at, Denny always said, *watch out, he'll break your heart.*

"Careful, you're sounding a bit rude, Madison. That isn't like you. I just don't want you hurt," Denny said.

"Is that what happened to you? Is that why you hate men?" Madison heard a click. She looked at the phone in her hand and slammed the receiver down. "Heaven forbid I get rude with Aunt Denny!" She yelled. "Just because Denny lost interest in men. I don't intend to be an old maid."

Bud stood up and put his feet on her leg.

"I'm okay, boy. She just knows how to get under my skin, and that isn't easy to do."

Shirley called from her bed. "What's wrong now?"

Madison stood in Shirley's doorway. "Denny's being her usual self. She told me not to let that cute Rick break my heart."

"He is cute. Will he be around for a while?" Shirley propped a pillow behind her head.

"He's staying at the Mountain Inn in Erwin. So was Nell, and anyone else that comes from Knoxville, since we have no hotel." Madison walked to Shirley's side and kissed her forehead. "Good night, I'm going to bed."

"Good night, Sweetie," Shirley said.

CHAPTER 14

Just past midnight, Madison was awakened by the sounds of voices and the smell of smoke. The room lit up with a yellowish glow. She pulled on her jeans and shirt and hopped toward the front door, putting on her shoes. Bud ran past as she went out onto the porch. Jess and Shirley were already there.

"Where is it?" she asked.

"I don't know; stay with Mom." Jess jumped off the steps followed by Bud.

"No, Bud, you stay." Madison put him in the house and ran after Jess. In a minute, she could see Denny's office was blazing.

"Oh no!" She slid to a stop and looked at the crowd that had gathered nearby.

Moments later, a Unicoi County fire truck arrived and the fire was knocked down. Madison stared as Rick pushed the crowd back, out of range of falling embers.

He caught Madison by the hand. "Sheriff Perry kicked the back door in, but the lab was engulfed, and then something exploded."

"Was he hurt?" she cried.

"No. He got out before the explosion."

"Denny was working in the lab when we passed last night," Madison said.

"On a Sunday?" Rick frowned.

"She does lab work all hours of the night on weekends. She must have forgotten to turn something off." Madison looked at Rick through teary eyes. "Has

Sheriff Perry called her?"

"Yeah, she's on her way." Rick led Madison to Sheriff Perry, who was talking to a fireman.

"I'm sorry, Madison. I hope your aunt was insured," Perry said.

She nodded, turning away to dry her face.

Denny's Suburban slid to a stop a few feet from the fire truck. She ran toward them screaming, "What happened?! Was anybody hurt?" She looked past her niece to the sheriff.

Madison asked, "Did you turn everything off before you left?"

"Well, of course! There must have been a short in a wire or something."

"I'm really sorry, Dr. Denson. There was nothing I could do. Something exploded." Sheriff Perry stepped closer to the burly woman.

"There was a propane tank, and what about the oxygen and nitrous tanks?" She moved toward the back of the building.

Perry caught her arm. "No, I managed to drag them out of the way. Stay back until the firemen get their job finished. There are hot spots."

"Yes, yes of course." Denny yanked her arm away. She returned to her Suburban and sat in the driver's seat, leaving the door open.

Madison joined her. "I hope the clock wasn't burned. It's wet, but maybe not ruined."

"Clock, what clock?" Denny kept her eye on the scene.

"The grandmother clock that Danny built?" Madison reminded her.

"Oh!" Denny's hand covered her mouth. She started to get out of the vehicle.

"You can't go in there." Madison held to Denny's arm. "Are you okay, Aunt Denny?"

"No, I'm not okay. Someone killed one of my dogs and burned down my office! How could I be okay?" She shouted.

The crowd stared. Madison felt uneasy with people watching their private life exposed.

"Why don't we go to my house? The sheriff will let us know when the firemen are done. Besides, the electricity is off. You'll have to wait 'til morning to go inside. Let's get out of the night air."

"No, I'm going back home to my team. Someone may have done this to draw me away. I can't risk losing another dog." Denny started her vehicle and sped away.

Rick stepped up and whispered, "Let's go in and let the crowd disperse."

Madison turned and walked with Rick's lead. He leaned in close to Sheriff Perry. "You know where we'll be."

Perry nodded, and then he caught Madison's arm. Surprised, she jerked and then relaxed as he said, "Things will get better, Madison. I'm on to something..."

"What is it?"

"I'm not sure what it means, but your aunt told me a different story about the gold inlay. She says it could be over a hundred years old," Perry said.

"Why, that is absolutely not true! The first gold used to fill cavities was in 1884. It wasn't until the early 1900's that it became common practice for wealthy people. They didn't have the refined methods until the mid... Anyway, this is different. This is kiln fired, and they just look different. She's lying to you."

"I'm not taking her word for anything. Just wondered what she'd say. Don't let it upset—"

A sharp crack sounded from somewhere in the darkness. Madison screamed. Her hands went to her face. She felt the spatter of warmth, and on her hands there was blood, but she felt no pain. Then she watched a dark stain spread across Sheriff Perry's shirt. He grasped his shoulder and fell to one knee.

Madison and Rick caught him, keeping his face off the street as he collapsed. A fireman ran to help. Perry's eyes closed. His body went limp.

An EMT, there because of the fire, rushed over with his kit. He packed bandages into the wound to stop the bleeding. Perry tried to get up, so they fastened him onto a stretcher and loaded him into the ambulance.

Madison felt as though the scene was in slow motion. The ringing in her ears muffled the sounds around her. She heard Rick's voice from far away. Then she felt his arms embrace her. His lips moved but she couldn't make out what he said.

Rick escorted her back to Shirley's house. When they were inside in the light of the living room, Madison looked at the blood on her hands.

"Am I shot? I don't feel anything."

"No, that's the sheriff's blood. Shirley, can you help me clean her up?" Rick guided Madison to a chair.

"Perry was shot?" Shirley grabbed onto Madison's hands and looked her over. "What was the fire? What happened?"

"Denny's office burned, and someone shot Perry in the shoulder. Madison and I were right next to him. An ambulance is taking him to the hospital in Johnson City." Rick explained as best he could in the confusion.

Shirley rushed out of the room and returned with a wash pan and cloth. "Let's see what we have here." She took her time wiping away the red, making sure it wasn't coming from Madison's skin. "You're okay, Madison. It's not your blood." Shirley disappeared again.

Bud took this opportunity to check Madison for himself. He jumped into her lap and licked her cheek. She wrapped her arms around her pup and held onto him. Then she stood and walked to the bed where she'd been sleeping earlier. She held Bud and pulled the sheet up to her neck. Bud didn't try to escape.

Madison heard voices but couldn't make out the conversation. It didn't matter, at that point; she just wanted to close her eyes, and hoped when she opened them again this would all have been a nightmare.

On Monday morning, Madison squinted toward the window; light seeped in, but no sun. Her head felt like a jackhammer pounded inside it. She made her way to the kitchen, following the smell of fresh coffee. She filled a mug and went to the front door. Rick sat on the steps.

"You still here?" She said.

"I'm back." He stood and stretched his arms over his head. "Perry wants to talk to you. I told him we'd come over soon as you woke up." He looked down at her mug. "Got any more of that coffee?"

Madison nodded. "Yeah, come in. Is Sheriff Perry in the hospital?"

"No, he wouldn't stay. He's in his office."

At that moment Bud charged onto the porch, barking excitedly.

"You guys awake in there?" a familiar voice called out.

"Yeah, come on in," Madison met him at the door. "You should have stayed in the hospital. What were you thinking? You look exhausted."

Perry stepped around her and went to the kitchen, dropped a note pad on the table and sat down. "You're right, *Mommy*, but I have work to do." He laughed, poking fun at the way she hovered. "You got any of that to spare?" He gestured toward the coffee mug.

"Go ahead and laugh at me. Someone needs to take care of you. You aren't doing it yourself." Madison poured two mugs and slid one to Rick. And then the sugar bowl and the other in front of the sheriff.

"I guess I've got the right to look exhausted. How 'bout you, Madison?" Perry's left arm was in a sling. His shirtsleeve hung empty at his side, still stained with blood. A large bandage encompassed his entire shoulder and left side.

"Why would you ask how *I* am? You're the one who got shot."

"Yeah, the bullet did hit me. But was it aimed at you."

Madison gasped, "What are you saying?"

"I leaned over to tell you not to worry. In the dark, was the shooter that good a shot—or was he already lined up on you?" He stirred sugar into his coffee.

"Now wait a minute, Sheriff. Do you really think she was the intended target?" Rick leaned on the table.

"Shucks, I don't know anymore. I wouldn't have thought I'd be in someone's sights, either. They could have been aiming at *you* for all I know, Malone." Perry lowered his head. "I've got to get some sleep."

"Until we know who did this, and who the target was, we should all stay together." Rick straightened up and looked out the window.

"Hmmm," Madison said. "Shirley has a room upstairs above the restaurant. No one has stayed in it for years. It's the safest place in town. You can sleep up there." She smiled.

"We're probably all three targets. And that tells me we're getting close to something that's making the right person very nervous," Perry said. "She's got a good idea, Rick."

Madison stared into nothingness. "I'm so tired. I want my life back. No!" she stood slamming her fist on the table. "It was never *my* life, and everything I ever did was someone else's choices. Now I'm an adult, and I'm making my own choices."

Rick said, "And you will, soon. Perry is right; someone's nervous, and that's when mistakes are made. We're going to figure this out.

Madison glanced at Perry.

He winked. "Soon, Madison, you'll get your chance. And I must say, I'm surprised and happy to hear you're ready.

"Okay, then, let's go to Shirley's." She heaved a sigh.

Fog hung close to the ground from the evening's rain. The morning air smelled of cold ashes when they neared the remains of the dental office.

"Gee, it's completely gone. Somehow it didn't look so bad in the dark." Madison paused to survey the shell of what used to be her place of employment. "I thought Denny would be here."

"She was, but I told her to wait until the fire marshal finished his investigation. She got mad and tore out of here." Perry pointed to tracks left by spinning tires.

Surprisingly, there were no patrons in the restaurant. Shirley met them at the front counter.

"Sheriff, what are you doing out of the hospital?" She stood with her fists propped on her hips.

"Can't keep a good man down." He smacked a kiss on the woman's cheek. Madison looked upward.

"Until Rick figures out who tried to kill him, the sheriff needs a safe place to rest. The safest place we can think of is right here in the room upstairs. Jess can guard him while he sleeps."

"That's a great idea." Shirley pushed through the swinging doors of the kitchen, the three of them following.

Jess sat at the desk, scribbling on papers. "What's the excitement now?"

"We're going to use the upstairs as a hideaway, so Sheriff Perry can get some sleep with you guarding him," Shirley said.

"Good idea. I've considered offering the room to Rick. Beats that Holiday Hotel down the mountain," Jess said.

"Let's let him see it first," Shirley started up the stairs, but then leaned against the wall. "You show them, Madison. Jess and I cleaned it just the other day. I had a feeling."

Madison noticed Shirley's breathing was shallow and her face looked pale; she didn't have her usual apple-cheeked glow.

She led the way up exposed stairs along the back wall of the kitchen and located the key on a ledge. As she opened the door, she said, "This is the only key."

The view opened onto another century.

Madison walked to the bolstered bed and began folding back the cotton chenille bedspread. Perry used his good arm to assist her.

She placed the coverlet on a quilt stand at the foot of the bed. "Make yourself comfortable, Sheriff."

He sat in the straight chair next to a round table, removed his boots and gun belt. "Thank you; this will be fine."

"Okay. You get some rest now. We'll be close by."

Madison joined Rick on the far side of the room. "That gas lamp is a relic of the eighteenth century."

Rick ran his hand across a roll-top desk. "Let me guess, these old spectacles, the ink-well, and quill were left here by Ben Franklin." He laughed. Then he sat in the dark mahogany swivel chair. Its wheels creaked when he leaned against a tired leather cushion back. He ran his fingers across years of nicks and scratches that hinted of historical treasure.

"Don't make fun of these antiques. They're real, and Shirley is proud of them." She pointed to the low table in front of a settee. "That's a Richmond newspaper dated October 1865."

Rick rolled the chair closer and read the headlines aloud. "'War Ended Five Months Ago...'" He squinted at the smaller print. "'Battles between North and South still fought.' I'm sorry. This is a museum!" Rick wheeled around carefully and placed the chair back at the desk. "I want this room."

"I thought so." Jess commented, leaning against the doorjamb.

Rick walked to the corner. Behind a folding Oriental screen hid a bathroom with a large, footed cast iron tub. Beyond, in a small closet-like stall, was an old-time commode, with a long pipe leading to a water tank nearly at the ceiling and a cord to pull for a flush.

"I've never even *seen* one of these, except on TV. Does it really work?"

"Yep," Jess said.

The floor creaked as Rick walked across the clean but scuffed hardwood and looked out onto the street below. "I can imagine horses and wagons; I love this."

"Shirley's grandparents lived here for over thirty years. Her mom was born in this room." Jess surveyed the room with a satisfied smile. "You can have the room, and you're welcome to stay here as long as you need." He turned to go back down the steps. "Oh, Sheriff, if you want, I'll bring you something to eat."

There was no response from the sheriff.

"He's already asleep," Madison whispered.

Rick followed Jess out the door. "You have to let me pay something."

"As long as you're watching over my baby girl, that's payment enough."

Madison liked the idea of Rick sleeping just across the street. She wasn't sure why, but it made her feel warm inside.

Shirley sat at a small table near the swinging doors. Jess bent to kiss her forehead, "We have a guest sleeping up there now and one planning to move in."

"That's good news," Shirley said.

Madison smiled, feeling her earlier concern was unwarranted. Shirley's color had returned, and her breathing was no longer labored. "I can sleep in the cottage again, with Rick or Sheriff Perry sleeping up there. So, I'm going home."

"Absolutely *not*! You don't stay alone until this mess is over. And that comes from the law, Perry himself. You are to be accompanied by a bodyguard at all times." Shirley sounded like a drill sergeant.

Madison laughed. "Okay, I give up. Who's my bodyguard today?"

"Me. I have to make a trip to Johnson City and you can be my guide," Rick said.

"I'll be your prisoner, you mean."

"And what's wrong with that?" Shirley raised her eyebrows. "Why, if I were twenty years younger and not married..." She laughed and walked to the kitchen. "What do you two want? Breakfast or lunch?"

"How about brunch?" Rick looked toward Madison.

She nodded.

"So, leave the hound dog with me to help keep watch," Jess said.

"Sure! Bud, stay with Jess." She pointed to the swinging doors.

"Maybe we should hang a badge around his neck, you know, Deputy Dawg?" Rick laughed.

Madison and Rick finished brunch as Nell came in. "Where's Sheriff Perry? I have something to show him, and you. My cameraman was with the fire department last night, filming the excitement. You'll never guess what showed up on the tape." Nell made her way to a booth and opened her laptop. "I want you to see this one special part."

Rick and Madison crowded into the booth, watching the small screen intently. Nell pressed skip until the flames were down and Denny's Suburban drove away. She tapped skip again to the point where the lens focused on Perry, Madison, and Rick as a shot rang out. The camera panned toward the sound. In the darkness, the camera zoomed in on the outline of a truck with no lights, speeding away from beside the hardware store. Denny's headlights illuminated the area just enough to silhouette an older model truck.

"Rick, there's the shooter. Not a clear picture, by any means, but maybe enough for Sheriff Perry to recognize it. I went to the hospital, and they said he hadn't been admitted. Do you have any idea where he is?" Nell had tears welling up in her eyes.

"He's upstairs, sleeping," Rick whispered. "We aren't sure he was the target last night, so until we catch the perpetrator, we're keeping him under guard. Jess is in the kitchen, with Bud stationed on the stairs."

Nell let out a sigh. "Thank goodness. I couldn't imagine where he was, and why he wouldn't answer his phone." She pulled a flash drive from the computer and gave it to Rick. "I guess you should hang onto this."

"No, Madison is going to show me around in Johnson City. You wait here and give it to Sheriff Perry."

Nell nodded.

Madison and Rick slipped from the booth and went out the door.

Madison felt strangely excited. She'd never been anywhere alone with a man she didn't know well. Oh, she'd ridden with the sheriff, and Franks, and even Mr. Olsen. But never a handsome young stranger that caused a stir inside her; not like this. She hoped it didn't show on her face.

In her scattered state of mind, it dawned on her that Rick had been at the fire quicker than she and Jess. She turned toward him. "How did you happen to be on the scene last night before me?"

Rick glanced at her and smiled. "What, now I'm a suspect?"

"No, of course not! But why were you still in town so late?"

"Perry and I were going over some ideas. He was going to stay at the jail, and told me I could crash at his place. I was just about to head over there when

I saw the flames. Perry and I were first on the scene."

Madison nodded, "Okay, I was just wondering. Well, now you can be here at night and not have to return to the hotel."

"I'm looking forward to staying here in town. You can believe *that*. I like your part of the country, but these roads are dark once the sun is gone. I'm always afraid I'll hit a deer; they're all over, on the sides of the road."

"Yeah, they're dangerous, that's for sure." Madison grinned at the thought of him being in town and just across the street from her.

Rick scanned the horizon as he drove onto the westbound lane of I-26. "This is a beautiful drive. You're lucky to live in the prettiest part of the state."

"So I've been told." Madison's smile warmed the atmosphere.

"Well, I've seen Tennessee all the way to Nashville and Memphis; there's just no comparison. It's the Blue Ridge, I think." Rick stole a glance toward Madison. "What will you do now? I mean, with the dental office burned? Do you think she'll rebuild?" He asked.

Madison turned toward him as she answered. "That's so hard to predict; she's not herself lately. I'm not sure I can work for my aunt anymore."

Rick felt surprised that he didn't detect disappointment in Madison's tone. "That doesn't bother you?"

"No. I've been doing a lot of soul searching. I realize I don't want to spend the rest of my life looking into peoples' mouths all day. Trying to convince them to care about their teeth is a futile effort when they don't want to be educated. They say dumb things like 'my folks had plates when they were in their thirties, so I will too.' Like its hereditary; it's not! A dirty mouth leads to disease and loss of teeth. I used to say back to them, is your dirty face hereditary?"

Rick laughed. "Dirty faces? What did they say to that?"

Madison rolled her eyes. "Do you know how hard it is to educate people who don't want to learn?"

"I've seen a few in my time." Rick looked in the rear view mirror. "What did they mean by 'plates?'"

"Older people used to call dentures plates. Around here, they still do." She looked over her shoulder. "That's the third time you've looked in the mirror. Do we have company?"

"Possibly. Where does that exit lead?" He nodded as they passed the Clear

Creek Exit sign.

"To the old road, and eventually down the mountain into Erwin. We'll find out if they're following us; nobody takes the old road anymore."

Rick veered off at the exit ramp. He watched as the car sped past, staying on the interstate. The stop sign gave him time to pause. "We can get back on, or..." He looked to Madison.

"Let's take the old road." She pointed left.

Was Rick being overprotective, or did he really sense danger? Either way, the feeling of someone watching out for her warmed Madison, and she liked the feeling. She stared out the windshield at familiar territory as she experienced unfamiliar emotions.

CHAPTER 15

Holly was anxious to talk to Madison, after Henry told her about the fire at the dental office and Perry getting shot. But her call went straight to voicemail as soon as the phone rang. "Madison, why aren't you answering? Uh, call me back, please."

"Maybe she don't wanna talk to nobody. That's why I don't keep my phone turned on all the time." Henry slipped his arm around Holly's shoulder. "She's all right, I just talked to Jess—stop worrying yourself. I told him to get 'er to call you. He said she rode to town with that TBI feller, Rick Malone."

"Oh, the one Madison thinks is so cute!" Holly giggled.

"Madison thinks he's cute?" Henry scratched his ear lobe and looked at his wife awkwardly. "Has, um, she ever even dated?"

"Not much; mostly in a group. She doesn't trust men. Denny influenced that. I think she's rethinking that whole philosophy now, though."

"Well, that's good, I guess." Henry leaned on the kitchen sink and pulled his wife against him. "Know how you said you wanted to learn to quilt?"

Holly nodded.

"Mr. Olsen says the missus wants to revive the quilting club. You know, since old Ms. Simpson passed and her son sold the farm, the quilting club's got no place to meet. I told him about Momma's room upstairs, and he thinks Mrs. Olsen might be interested in getting a group of women together."

"But Henry, it's so hot upstairs. Your momma quilted at night when the exhaust fan pulled the night air in through the windows."

"I know, but Mr. Olsen figured since he's puttin' a central unit in at the store, if I'd help him install it, we can have his big window unit from the store building. It's a good 'un, kept that whole store cool. But now that he's adding an upstairs, he reckons a central unit will be more efficient."

"Are you saying that you don't mind if I have something to do besides housework and cookin'?"

"Well, you don't need to be out in the heat working the garden now that I have that new plow. Plus, I stay at the lumberyard a day or two a week. You're apt to go stir crazy without somethin' to keep you occupied. Besides, Madison needs a distraction. Jess said she's thought about taking up quilting. Shirley says there's not many folks quilting these days, and it's a dying art."

Holly threw her arms around his neck. "I can't *wait* to tell Madison!" She pushed redial on her phone.

"Maybe you ought to talk to Mrs. Olsen about all this first; at least she'll answer her phone." Henry went out the back door, looked back, and winked.

Holly ran up the stairs to the room with the dormer windows. She hadn't been in there in months, and then it was only to look for thread to patch Henry's britches. The door creaked as she pushed it open, not a scary sound but one of loneliness, bidding her to come inside. She crossed the room, dust rising like fog from the scuffed boards, and slid the windows up. A crisp breeze blew in, whished out the door, and whooshed down the stairs. *Maybe that's why Momma Jacobs chose this room for her sewing; it's got a good draft pull.*

The curtains appeared dingy in bright sunlight, so Holly took them down, piling them in a heap in the doorway. The quilting loom was covered by a plain white sheet, which she carefully removed and added to the pile of curtains. Mrs. Jacobs's Singer Sewing Machine waited under a flowered pillowcase atop its mahogany wood cabinet, nestled in a dark corner. "I'll get Henry to help me move you in front of one of the windows."

Behind the door stood a distressed oak chifferobe. Holly had never even noticed this lovely tall cabinet. She opened the door on the left side to discover three drawers filled with different patterns and colors of fabrics folded neatly, stored out of the dust of the room. Inside the doors hung lengths of ribbon, yarn, and binding. The right side door hid three open shelves filled with embroidery hoops, small flat boxes of multi-sized needles, yarn and scissors. Across the bottom was one long deep drawer, now empty, but there was evidence left behind: quilt batting fragments and an envelope, yellowed from age.

What I need now is the vacuum cleaner to remove years of dust and allergens. This is going to be fun!

She stooped to pick up the dusty curtains for removal to the laundry room and then set out to get the vacuum, a mop, and some cleaning rags. Holly was right at home with cleaning. She'd learned it from her Granny, and loved making things shine.

While the washer filled, she gathered the cleaning items and took them back upstairs. All the while she kept thinking about that lone envelope. It felt out of place with all that was in the room. So Holly opened the drawer again and picked up the dingy paper. A black and white photo fell to the floor. She stared at the figure of a young girl as she stooped to pick it up, turned it over and read, *Mariah Davidson Jacobs, age 9.*

Chapter 16

N ell stayed with her at the cottage Sunday evening, sleeping on the new
sofa bed while Madison and Bud slept in the bedroom. Having Rick on
guard across the street gave the women a pleasantly secure feeling. The two law-
men lingered until midnight, telling stories after eating the tortillas, chips, and
salsa Nell fixed.

Madison couldn't remember when she'd laughed and enjoyed herself so
much. Maybe never, at least not with a girlfriend and two handsome men, all
friends. The four of them really liked each other, even under the strained circumstances. This was a world she'd never experienced, and she loved it.

Nell was fun to be with, and Madison had never realized what a sense of
humor the sheriff had. He even insisted she call him Drew, but she thought
that would only work in private. She'd show more respect in public. And as for
Special Agent Rick Malone—he truly was special. He was easy to look at, fun
to laugh with, and had such a great personality. She'd have to keep tabs on her
heart, because it tended to flutter whenever he looked her way.

Having her own place was so different from being under her folk's roof.
She could never have had friends over that late. Not girls *or* guys, simply because
Shirley and Jess got up at 4:30 each morning to open the restaurant. They
served homemade biscuits and gravy with all the trimmings for the working
people: regulars, who either didn't have a cook at home, or had wives who
didn't get up before the chickens and give them a proper send-off. Shirley's

mother, and her grandmother before that, had always set a hearty breakfast table for anyone who wanted to eat early.

The sun rose before Madison felt like tipping her toe to the cold floor. Bud needed to go out, so she tiptoed past her bunkmate asleep on the sofa. She wanted to run on the trail, but had been warned not to go alone. Still, she felt keeping her under guard was completely unnecessary.

As she wrote a note at the little kitchen table, Nell peeked over her shoulder saying, "You're not really thinking of going against the sheriff's wishes, are you?"

Madison crumpled up the paper. She let out a sigh, "Busted, huh? I *need* to run. I have all this energy piling up and want to let it out. Come with me, why don't you?"

Nell studied the situation for a moment. "I'm not much of a runner. If you promise not to get into trouble, I'll shower while you're gone. When you get back, you shower and I'll meet Drew at the restaurant. When he asks about you, I won't be lying when I say you're in the shower."

"Works for me!" Madison headed to the door. "After breakfast, I want to go to Johnson City to the News Press. Bud will be with me, and that's not really the same as alone."

"I'll make you a deal. We'll go together; I'll drop you and Bud at the Press Building and I'll stop in at WJHL News to talk to Sara Desmond, the evening news anchor." Nell made her best offer.

"Do I have any choice?"

"Nope!" Nell grabbed her clothes and went toward the bathroom. "How long 'til you'll be back?"

"No more than thirty minutes. Promise." Madison pulled the door closed behind her and slipped off the porch, weaving her way through the wooded lot of her property. She had a new way to get to her running trail now, without going through town. Even better this way—no one saw her and Bud head up the mountain.

The contrived story held up to scrutiny, making Madison feel empowered. She and Bud stopped by the restaurant after her shower to let Nell know she was ready.

Bud always enjoyed riding and didn't seem to mind going in with Madison when they arrived at the JC Press. He accepted his role as watchdog when she snapped on his leash.

Inside the 1920's revamped building between Market and Maine, Madison found a strictly business atmosphere. In the corner, nearly hidden by a large palm-like plant, she spotted a neatly-dressed young woman sitting at a desk, smiling as they approached.

"Good morning," she said. "Can I help you?"

Madison returned a friendly smile, "I'd like to research your archived issues."

"Sure, come with me, please." Six-inch heels clicked on the ceramic tile as the receptionist led the way through a thick-glassed door. "I'm Roberta."

"Madison McKenzie, and this is my guard dog, Bud. Is it okay that I keep him with me?"

"Sure. This way to the dungeon, Madison. Are you familiar with the microfiche method? No one has ever bothered to put the old files on CD, the way recent years are stored."

"Yes. I did research in school that way. When did they switch to CD?" Madison asked.

"Five years ago. So if you need to see something in those backups, we keep them upstairs in our library." The woman pushed open a heavy door at the bottom of dark stairs.

"You see why we call it the dungeon." Roberta switched on overhead lights.

Before Madison stretched a narrow room filled with shelves. At the entrance to the room stood a couple of wooden tables holding the microfiche machines.

"Don't you think it's creepy down here?" Roberta hugged herself.

"No, not really. It's quiet and well lighted, perfect for research." Madison set a notebook and pen down at one of the tables. "I'd like to start about the mid-seventies."

"They'd be right here." The young woman pointed to the second row of shelves. "1950 starts the row, and it goes higher toward that end."

"Thank you; I'll be here for a while." Madison took the first canister under the date 1975 and began to feed it into the machine. "It's working fine." She nodded to Roberta.

"Very well, then I'll leave you. Here's an intercom to my desk, and there's a bathroom through that door." She pointed and bent to pet Bud. "You're a cute fellow."

"Thanks, Roberta. Looks as if he likes you."

"Okay, you know where to find me."

She sat and scanned the film. Bud walked the perimeter of the room and then settled himself against Madison's feet. By the end of the seventies' records, she found no missing persons or anyone unaccounted for. She replaced that canister and took down the next ten years.

The scanning went smoothly until she reached January of 1993. Then she read the small print on the Sunday paper's front page: *Cold Creek businessman dies in own workshop. (Story on page A-3)* She held her breath as she paged down to the column identified as *Cold Creek businessman.* There was a small photo of Danny Denson. It was the first she'd seen, other than the one of him as a teenager on Denny's desk at home. He was a handsome man with a warm smile. Madison swallowed hard as she read the story.

Denise Denson reported that her brother, Danny was involved in a tragic accident. Sheriff Willard Franks arrived on the scene minutes later, to learn Danny had fallen into the stripping vat in the workshop basement. He was too late to do anything to save Mr. Denson. The chemicals are immediately fatal. Young Denise was hysterical and required sedation by the local doctor, who was called for the coroner's jury. Doc Wilson ruled the death accidental, as Danny was working to fish out a heavy door by himself. Denise said she had arrived just in time to see her brother fall head first into the tank. No charges were filed, but the sheriff ordered the tank to be sealed off as to prevent further accidents.

She continued reading, her mind spinning with questions.

Danny took over the woodworking business after his parents' tragic deaths in a fire that destroyed the family home in 1982. The Densons were one of Cold Creek's founding families. Nearly every household in the area owns a piece of fine Denson Furniture.

Denson's death ends a long-standing tradition in the business community. All who knew him will miss his smile and his talent. Danny's specialty was making grandfather clocks.

Funeral arrangements have not been completed. Burial will be in Cold Creek Family Cemetery, alongside the late Mr. and Mrs. Daniel Denson Senior.

Madison felt the loss of a good man. But at the same time, it felt strange; not like he was her father—instead, like someone she'd only heard of briefly. Jess was the loving dad she knew and she shared his name, not Danny Denson's. She wondered if that might be the source of ill feelings between Jess and Denny. After all, Jess had adopted her; so his name was certainly appropriate, wasn't it?

Madison glanced at her watch. She'd been in the dungeon for nearly an hour, and from the looks of it, she figured it would still be a long while.

As Madison reviewed the ninety's headlines, Bud stood up and stretched his legs. Madison looked to see a large man standing on the stairs.

"Hey, how would you like to sell me this mutt? Why, he ain't big enough to be a real dog; can't be worth much." The man approached her table. "I'm Ed. I've been publishing this paper for over forty years. What exactly are you looking for?"

"Certainly not to sell my guard dog." She laughed. "I'm Madison. It's nice to meet you, Ed. I've enjoyed your paper all my life."

"Where are you from?" He asked.

"Cold Creek." Madison shook a strong grip. She took in his look, a tall stout frame topped with unruly gray curls and kind blue eyes.

"Lovely town. I'm surprised I've never seen you at Shirley's. I eat there every chance I get." Ed pulled a chair from another table and sat down.

"I worked behind the counter at Shirley's all through high school, until four years ago. Don't see how we missed each other."

"Hmmm," Ed pinched his chin and gazed at the table. "Maybe I have seen you. I always sat at the little table in the corner near the window." He looked up and pointed his finger as if they were in the main dining room. "Usually it was Thursday mornings, for breakfast. I love Shirley's biscuits and gravy. Reminds me of the way my own mom made them. That Shirley is a wonderful cook."

"Oh, yes, she is. I had long hair and wore it in a braid. I never wore make-up until recently. Hardly ever made it up on a Saturday, you know, trying to ready the Sunday paper. If I'm going to compete with Knoxville, I've gotta' put out all the news."

"Yes, and you do a great job. I'm interested in missing persons, specifically women who went missing and were never accounted for, over a period of twenty or so years. Any come to mind?" Madison shuffled through her notes.

He nodded his head. "The women they found on the trail. That's horrible. Don't you think I haven't already wracked my brain?" He leaned forward resting his hands on the table.

"Those women might not be from Cold Creek, or even the surrounding area, for that matter."

"That thought occurred to me. Somewhere in the nineties, I made a note." Madison scanned her papers.

Ed spoke as though on cue. "Fall of 1995, I'll never forget the mangled mess the cars were in. A year and a half later, the driver was released from prison and disappeared. Her name was De-De Fontaine." Ed recited as if it was yesterday.

"Yeah, Fontaine. Phillip Fontaine's family?" Madison's eyes widened.

"Yes, Mayor Fontaine's baby sister. She was a real embarrassment to his family. He didn't run for reelection. Just kind of dropped out of the limelight, if you know what I mean."

"The woman and baby that were killed were Jacobs. Was that Ross Jacobs' wife and baby?" Madison referred to her notes.

"Yeah, shame too. Ross was the best one of those Jacob boys. He and his surviving boy, Russell, moved to Arizona, somewhere. Took his mom with him, I hear."

"So, De-De never turned up." Madison studied Ed's face.

"Not to my knowledge. Not that anyone would care."

"That's a start. Thanks, Ed. Are there others?"

Ed studied Madison for a moment and asked, "What do you do, Madison?"

"I was Dr. Denson's dental assistant," she smiled. "Guess I'll be looking for a job here in Johnson City now."

"Yes, I heard about the fire. Just glad no one was hurt. You have any suspicions as what happened?"

"We think an electrical short might have ignited the gas. It's usually turned off, but was left on that night. Just an accident, I guess."

"What else did you find?" Ed asked. He craned his neck to see her notes.

"That's about it. Thanks for coming down to talk with me," Madison stood.

Ed screwed his mouth into all sorts of strange shapes as he pecked his finger on the table. "Come back anytime. If I can help you, just give me a yell." He got up and walked to the steps.

"Thank you. I'll remember to call on you."

Ed walked up the stairs with Madison watching. *He acted as if he wanted to tell me something. Wonder what it was, and why he chose not to?*

Madison worked carefully to put the canisters back in their proper order. She gathered her things, clicked the light switch, and climbed the stairs. It was nearly noon. She might as well call it a day. As she reached Roberta's desk, Ed appeared from a door on the opposite side of the room.

"Madison, I've been thinking. There is another name. Tina Denson, Dr. Denny's sister-in-law. I'm sure you've heard of her."

Madison nodded, but didn't say a word.

"Denny said she left no forwarding address and just skipped out after her husband died. I always felt suspicious about that, you know." He scratched his head and stared out a window. "Well, I met a lawyer in Knoxville who looked for her, too. He said she owed him money. Anyway, he's checked all over the US and wasn't able to locate her. Either she's left the country or"— he looked back to her. "She might be one of your skeletons."

Madison felt her heart stop. "I'll check it out." The words finally made their way past her lips. She so hoped that Ed couldn't see the turmoil she felt inside.

Ed knelt in front of Bud. "You watch after her, oy. I'll be looking for you real soon."

Nell drove up as Madison and Bud walked onto the sidewalk.

All the way back to Cold Creek, Madison thought of Ed's words. "She might be one of your skeletons."

"If he only knew." She said aloud.

"Who?" Nell asked.

"Oh, did I say that out loud? Just thinking of something Ed said." *Unbeknownst to Ed, Tina Denson is a skeleton in my own family closet. Good move, not revealing my connection. He might be a good source, as long as he doesn't realize I'm Tina's daughter.*

"So what were you doing all that time, anyway?"

"Research on women missing in the area for the last twenty or so years. I talked to Ed, the editor, a really nice guy. He has a feeling that Tina Denson could be one of the skeletons. I didn't tell him she's my mother." Madison felt her time was productive.

"Madison, you are too stubborn for your own good."

"I know."

Nell smiled approvingly. "I can see you'll be successful on your own."

"Thanks, Nell. That means a lot to me."

"You're welcome."

"Oh, I need to call Rene Kiplinger about the shooting classes in Erwin. I want to get my license to carry a weapon. But don't tell anyone! You've gotta' promise."

"That's one more thing we agree on. I have my carry permit and a revolver. It's like my American Express: don't leave home without it." Nell said.

"You're kidding me. Well, that's great!" She fist-bumped with Nell. "Are you packing now?"

"Yes, and I have since the day I first showed up in Cold Creek. So you see, I am a worthy bodyguard."

"So you are. I'm impressed." Now, more than ever, she wanted to have her own gun and learn to shoot. *Nell is a good role model.*

CHAPTER 17

Later in the afternoon, Nell suggested they ride out to see Holly and Henry. Madison jumped at the chance so she and Bud could get out of the house. Maybe they could get a run in while at the Jacobs' property.

As they passed by the mill, she commented, "Henry's the third generation operator at Jacobs' Mill. His family has been around Cold Creek from the beginning. They worked hard logging, and then cut lumber from the logs. Now they can only mill logs from out of the county, unless you own your own wooded acreage. Unicoi County is largely government land: you know, national forests."

"Good information to know," Nell said.

The Jacobs' two-story farmhouse came into view as they rounded a curve and crossed the cattle guard at the creek. Smooth slopes of green pasture land were terraced above a backdrop of outbuildings and a large barn behind the house. Once painted white, now the house appeared somewhere between gray and natural wood. Madison wondered how many years it had been since a fresh coat was applied.

Two dormer windows protruded from a rust-colored metal roof above the wraparound porch. A worn wooden door stood ajar behind an old screen door with new mesh, allowing a breeze to enter.

Holly stood with her broom at the steps. She waved, greeting them with her enthusiastic smile. "Hi! Get out and come in."

"Hey, you! I hope we're not interfering with your chores. Is Henry home?" As soon as Madison asked, Henry answered from the passenger side of her vehicle.

"Who's asking?"

His gruff voice startled Nell. She turned to look at Henry's smiling face just inches from hers. He stuck his hand in the window. "You must be Nell."

"It's nice to meet you, Henry. Even if you did just give me a heart attack." Nell grasped his hand in a gesture of friendship. "I've heard a lot about you from Holly."

"Yeah, I've heard you might come snoopin' out this way. But there ain't no story here." He sounded like he'd prefer to see them drive right on back out the way they came.

"I wanted to see what you can tell me about four-wheelers," Madison leaned forward looking around Nell.

"Why?"

"Been thinking of getting one to ride."

"Where?"

"On my property, or out on Denny's farm."

"Four-wheelers will get you hurt. They ain't meant to be toys."

"So many kids ride them—I don't see how they're dangerous."

"Can be."

"So there are different sizes? Maybe Madison wants a small one," Nell added, sounding a little timid.

"I've never driven one. Maybe if they are dangerous, I'd better have lessons. Holly said you're a good teacher."

"She did?" His voice softened. He straightened, looking over the Blazer at his wife. "Come 'round back, I'll show you what I ride."

Madison winked at Holly and motioned her to follow.

She put down her broom and hurried down the steps. "What are you up to?"

"Shush, I'll tell you later. Go along with me on this," Madison whispered.

"You coming?" Henry yelled. "I ain't got all day to fool with you women."

"Be right there, Henry." Madison called out.

"I've tried calling you all day. Henry's gonna let me use our upstairs for the quilting club. Isn't that nice? He and Mr. Olsen worked out the idea; he even offered an air conditioner unit from his store. I'm so excited! Couldn't wait to tell you. I talked to Mrs. Olsen; she's all for teaching us." Holly jumped up and down as they rounded the side of the house.

"Henry? The man you live with?" Madison laughed.

"Yes, my *only* Henry!" Her look said she was proud of him.

Bud raced around the house behind Henry. They stood next to a green and brown camouflage ATV.

"That's a big four-wheeler!" Madison stiffened when she saw the machine.

"Sold my old one last year. This is a stronger model. It can pull my tractor out; sometimes I get stuck in the tater patch." He kicked a clod of dirt off one tire. "These are called ATVs, all-terrain vehicles. Yep, it's a 4-wheeler with an attitude."

"Wow, don't think I'll need one of *those*. Thank you, Henry."

Henry shook his head and then looked at his wife. "You told her about the plan for the quilting club?" He picked up an old rag in the yard, turning toward the barn. "Why don't you show the ladies your room?"

"I will, thanks for reminding me. Supper's on; I'll let you know when it's ready," Holly said. "Come on in. I just made some lemonade."

"Oh, Henry?" Madison called, stopping him in his tracks. "Jess loves the remodeling job you did in the cottage."

Henry turned around. "Glad he approved. Tell him to call when he needs me. I got some ideas that might be good in that kitchen. You wanna keep it simple, I know, kind of like the old days—but it ought to be functional too."

"Yeah, that'll be good. We'll call you." She started to walk away, but spun around and followed him. "Oh, one more thing."

"What?" His eyes narrowed.

"I found some old articles of the Press, and wondered if you knew anything about that Fontanne woman who caused your sister-in-law and nephew to die."

"Why would I know about her? She's trash; the law should never have let her out of prison." Henry didn't make eye contact as he spoke.

"Do you think she could be one of the skeletons? I heard she vanished."

"All I know is, Russell and Mom was gone by then, and I didn't ever hear of her again. I wouldn't be surprised if she's dead. She ought to be!"

Holly and Nell were almost to the house.

"Thank you again, Henry. I'll let you get on with your work." Madison turned to go.

"I'm glad you gals want to carry on with the quilting. Mom made quilts up in that room. It's a worthwhile art, and should keep going with the younger generation."

"Yes, it surely is," she said, watching Henry disappear into the shadows of the barn.

Holly led the way upstairs with Nell and Madison following.

Nell was the first to comment. "This room is large." She gazed at the shelves lining the walls on two sides, piled high with folded fabrics. Below the shelves stretched long worktables with Formica tops. In front of one window sat an old Singer sewing machine. "I guess that was your mother-in-law's?"

Holly nodded as she opened the cabinet doors, revealing spools of thread—every color imaginable, along with cutting tools and scissors of all shapes and sizes. "Isn't this great! Mrs. Olsen brought some of the quilting club's supplies. She said she'd forgotten this room had so much working space."

"So Mrs. Olsen and Mrs. Jacobs must have been friends." Nell watched Holly.

"Yeah, they made a few quilts together. I think Mrs. Jacobs stopped doing much of anything after that wreck. She kind of withdrew from the world." She took her time closing up the cabinet doors and then stood there, her hands caressing the woodwork. "It wasn't long afterward that she left. That's when me and Henry moved in here."

"Thanks for the tour. It looks like you all will have fun." Nell turned to Madison, "Don't you think we should go now, and let Holly finish supper?"

"Yeah. This is generous of Henry; we don't want to wear out our welcome!" Madison smiled, "Quilting *will* be fun!"

Just then the kitchen timer sounded and the women walked down stairs.

"Thanks for the lemonade," Nell said. She and Madison stepped onto the porch.

Henry knelt next to Bud in the shade of a dogwood tree. He stood up, looking at the women. "Madison, Sheriff Franks told my old man that he'd put De-De in jail if he caught her in Cold Creek. The next week he bragged that she'd

115

never hurt anyone else with her behavior. I always wondered what he knew, but Dad told me to stay out of the law's business." He stepped closer to the porch. "You might be right about that skeleton."

"You ever tell anyone this?" Madison asked.

"Not my business; my old man taught me to stay out of people's affairs."

"I appreciate you telling me, Henry. It was sad for your family. I remember the news. I didn't know your brother's wife or your nephew well. I'm sorry it happened—and then to lose the rest of your family, too. Do you ever hear from them?" Madison touched Henry's arm as she walked past.

Henry dropped his head and whispered, "Not often enough."

On the way back toward the mill, Madison and Nell saw the sheriff's vehicle coming toward them, with Rick in the passenger seat. Knowing they were headed to the Jacob's place, because it was the only house on that road, Madison jokingly said, "Hey guys, where you going?"

"As if you don't know." Sheriff Perry glanced at Rick and laughed. "It's business, and I can't discuss it. Henry home?"

"Yep, and they were just about to have supper. You might not want to disturb him before he eats. He's like an old dog when he's hungry."

"I'll take that into consideration." The car continued in the direction of the Jacobs' farm.

Madison grinned as they drove away. "He's a looker!"

"Which one? I could learn to like your sheriff," Nell said.

"Both of them. But I meant Rick. I bet he has a lot of girlfriends."

"I wouldn't know about *that*, but he's a nice guy. I've run into him a time or two before. He's always appeared shy, but not with you. I think he *really* likes you."

"Aw," she shrugged off the comment. "I'm too young for him."

"No, you aren't."

"A man like that could never care for a country girl like me." Madison let out a sad sigh. "I'm sure he'll be happy to leave the sticks when the case is solved."

"Listen to you! I've seen the way he looks at you. Don't let your aunt's feelings cloud your mind. Girls like you are hard to find these days."

Madison's jaw dropped. Nell's words echoed in her head. *I trust Nell's opin-*

ion. *Maybe I have let Denny's negativity influence my self-esteem.* "Thank you. I'll keep that in mind."

Had cutting her hair and moving into her own place made enough of a difference already? Or was Nell being kind? It was encouraging, and that was enough for her; she felt different, so it made sense that maybe she looked different, too.

Back at the cottage, Nell typed notes on her laptop. "Madison, Sheriff Perry told me they've unearthed eight skeletons."

Madison stared straight ahead. She felt a ringing in her ears. Finally, the words came. "Eight; yeah, Ed told me... I thought he was exaggerating."

"Yes, and all women. Not one has any hair, soft tissue, or muscle. It's like they were dipped in some kind of acid," Nell said.

Madison couldn't concentrate on Nell's words. She leaned forward and supported her head in her hands on the counter. Her stomach churned. She reached for a glass. It slipped from her hand and splintered into the sink.

Nell grabbed her at the elbows. Madison felt her body sinking toward the floor. The next thing she knew, Nell was bent over her laying a cold cloth on her forehead.

"Just lie still. Breathe, and let the color come back into your face."

Nell sounded far away. After a while, Madison sat up. Nell helped her to the sofa. She shut her eyes, and eight skulls looked back at her.

"What happened up there?"

"I don't know. But Perry and Rick said keep this to ourselves. The whole town doesn't need to know the details. In fact, Rick told me not to tell you. But just in case you heard it, I wanted to be the one you heard it from." Nell leaned against the sofa back. "I wonder how Ed knew."

"I don't know. He acted like he was holding back some information. Then, as I was about to leave the building, he caught up with me and told me about Tina."

Madison's arms felt heavy and her stomach turned cartwheels. "I feel sick."

"When did you eat last?" Nell asked.

"Last night." She closed her eyes and leaned her head back. "I need to eat, I know."

"Stay right there while I fix you something." Nell looked in the pantry.

"Just bring me some crackers. That'll help until we get to the restaurant." Madison tried to stand. She fell back to the couch.

"Here, drink this orange juice." Nell handed Madison a plastic cup, then opened a new sleeve of saltine crackers and gave her one.

Madison ate it and reached for the stack. She sipped the juice and ate several more crackers. "That's what I needed. I hadn't realized I was so hungry."

"Why don't you take better care of yourself?"

"I do take care of myself—this is not normally a problem."

"So you say. I've seen how you eat. You're afraid you'll gain an ounce."

Madison stared at Nell. She didn't like what she heard. *You have no right to judge me.*

"I'm fine." She finished off the juice and set the crackers down on the table next to the couch. "I'm okay; we should go to the restaurant."

Nell had been sure that low blood sugar was the reason she'd fainted. Madison let her believe that, so she didn't have to explain what really turned her stomach. Maybe the dead women had not been exposed to acid, but she knew where a pretty mean furniture stripper could be found. She had some snooping to do, and a trip to Asheville was the place to start.

But how could she get away from her so-called bodyguards? Old man Franks held a wealth of information, if she could just get it out of him. She couldn't slip away from Nell, so she did the next best thing.

"Nell, let's you and I go see old sheriff Franks."

"In Asheville? When?"

"In the morning. We can slip out of town and see what he'll tell us." Madison crossed her fingers. "And hope that Weird Willy hasn't convinced him to keep quiet."

"Okay, we'll do it," Nell agreed.

CHAPTER 18

The drive across the mountain, south on I-26, was a new experience for Nell. Whenever her assignments landed her in Asheville, she'd taken I-40 out of Knoxville; she hadn't seen the new highway, running the full length of Unicoi County.

"I thought I-40 was a beautiful drive; this is amazing, too. These mountains are breathtaking." Nell asked Madison to pull into the welcome station on the North Carolina side so she could take a photo with her phone.

Madison had a mental list of keywords to use with Sheriff Franks, but she needed to pull this off without tipping Nell to what she suspected. Nell was sharp, and becoming closer to Sheriff Perry. This wasn't the stage of *her* investigation to bring the law into the mix; no, that would *not* do at this point. There are too many loose ends to tie up before she shared her suspicions.

About forty minutes later, Madison exited onto Tunnel Road. Soon she drove into the parking lot, bordered by weeping willows sweeping the mirror surface of the duck pond. There wasn't a single duck in the tranquil picture.

"Oh, where are the ducks? They kept Bud entertained when I was here last." Madison slipped from behind the wheel. She cupped her hand over her eyes, looking across the water for the decorative fowl.

"Maybe they're nesting." Nell pointed toward the tall grassy area on the opposite bank.

"I bet you're right. That's where the trail leads away from the water's edge, and meanders through those rocks. Bud and I walked all the way around the pond the other day." She lowered the windows a couple of inches and locked the doors. "He'll be fine here until we get back. Then we can walk the trail again."

The women entered the Veterans' Nursing Home by the main door. Madison spotted the old man sitting at the same game table, staring at the checkers on the board.

"He loves playing checkers. I'll introduce you and see how he reacts." She knelt to look into the stooped old man's face. "How are you today, Sheriff Franks?"

"I'm just fine. Who are you?" He hadn't moved his eyes off the checkers.

"I'm Madison, remember? You and I played checkers my last visit."

"Oh, yeah... Madison, all grown up. Do you play?" He looked up and squinted toward Nell. "Who's with you?"

"This is Nell, a friend from Knoxville. Nell, this is the famous Sheriff Franks." She winked at Nell.

"I'm pleased to meet you, Sir. I love to play checkers. May I?" She seated herself before he had a chance to answer.

He slid the black side of the board toward her. "I like the red ones. They're lucky for me." He made his first move and then looked up at her.

The conversation was only about checkers during the first game. Nell chose poor moves so that she'd loose.

"I haven't played in a long time. Can we do that again?" She asked.

"You'll still loose." A confidence oozed from the old man's smile.

"You think so?" Nell laughed.

"What have you been doing since I saw you the other day, Sheriff?" Madison pulled a chair from across the room, sitting close by his side.

"Never do nothing but play and eat, and sleep and play." His voice had a sing-song tone. "I want to get out and go back to work. I have business to tend to."

"Yes, you mentioned business before. Oh, and I took your advice. I talked to Victoria Vance about Denny. You were right; they did have a fight." Madison kept her eyes on the old man. And then she whispered, "You've got a jump."

He grinned and jumped Nell's black checker. "Denny won't like that Victoria told on her. No, she won't like it one bit." He pushed one of his red checkers into Nell's back line. "King me."

"Oh! How'd you slip *that* one in on me?" Nell put a second man on top. "Tell us some of your best arrest stories, and some bad guys you've put behind bars."

"Mostly moonshiners, a few drunks, and even a couple prostitutes. Can't have that riff-raff loose in Cold Creek." He pushed his shoulders back, sitting up straight for a moment.

"Oh no, you certainly can't. We're glad you cleaned up our town," Madison said.

In the next half hour, the proud old man told the ladies everything he could remember about the bad guys of Cold Creek. Madison played a game after he became bored with beating Nell. This time, she hadn't let him win.

"Nobody beats the law in Cold Creek. Not Hiram Jacobs, Denny Denson, or that blood-sucking Melungeon, what was her name? Aw... Mariah: she was Hiram's girl."

"I remember Mariah," Madison said. "But what does that have to do with beating the law? What did she do wrong?"

"She loved Hiram, which was enough to make your aunt mad. They had a real battle going. Well, until I stepped in. He-he," the old man chuckled to himself. "Denny always went for older men. Couldn't figure that out. Guess she missed her dad."

"Were you and Denny friends?" Nell asked.

"Oh, yeah. Denny would do anything for me. Humph," he muddled under his breath, "to a point." He laughed once again. Then he looked up and said, "You need a drink? I sure would like me a root beer."

"I'll go and find us one." Nell stood, "I love root beer too."

She walked away, and Madison questioned the old sheriff again. "Do you remember a woman named De-De Fontaine? I heard she got out of prison and came back to Cold Creek."

The old man's eyes narrowed as he studied her face. "Who told you that?"

"Hiram Jacobs," she lied.

"Hiram, huh? He hated that woman. Told me he'd kill her if he could ever get the chance." Then the old man did something very surprising; he signaled with his index finger for Madison to lean in closer. "He never had a chance, but I did."

"So, you put her back in jail?" Madison played along.

"I did more than that. I locked her below the ground where no one would hear her screams. She dried out real fast down there. Wasn't no good to nobody anyhow. I'll let her out one of these days." Sheriff Franks scratched his head and looked at the root beer Nell handed him. "I don't like root beer; got any cream soda?"

Nell's face went blank. "I'll check." She walked away and looked back at Madison.

After a minute or so Madison had a thought. "Here you are Sheriff Franks, this one is cream soda, and I'll drink that root beer." Madison handed him the root beer.

He turned it up and gulped a mouth full and then said, "Aw, nothing better than root beer." He lowered his bottle and asked, "Do you play checkers?"

Nell returned empty-handed and looked at the old man. Her disappointment was obvious. Their time was up with old sheriff Franks. He was back to the present, when his mind didn't know what happened five minutes ago.

They thanked him for his time and promised to come back again soon. This time, when Madison looked back and waved, she saw that he raised his head and smiled. He attempted to raise his left hand in a wave. But all he could manage was to lift it off his knee. She realized she'd never seen him move his left hand. That gave her reason to wonder, because she recalled the stories about how fast he could draw his pistol from the holster, and he was a leftie.

No sooner had Nell and Madison gotten on the interstate heading back to Tennessee than the wheels of thoughts turned. Nell keyed notes on her iPad. Then she looked straight out the windshield, saying, "You've got to be thinking the same thing I am."

Madison threw a sideways glance and nodded. "I have an idea." She spilled her thoughts to Nell as they drove over the mountain.

Did Aunt Denny lead a double life? Why had she become so fixated on older men? Could old Sheriff Franks have been the father of her baby? And what happened after Denny left school?

Nell hadn't heard the old sheriff's confession, if it was one, but Madison felt he had indeed told her what happened to De-De Fontaine.

122

CHAPTER 19

Madison planned to turn the bodyguard idea into an advantage, affording her the opportunity to snoop wherever and whenever necessary. Bud's playful nature instigated the runaway dog trick. When she and Nell came out of the cottage Bud ran away, hiding until one of them followed. They figured he'd enjoyed escaping from the cave and getting Jess to "find" Madison. Who would realize the little dog was a decoy for the investigating team?

Nell's fascination with Henry's family background of milling lumber and farming prompted her to set up an interview with the couple as a means of learning about the history of Cold Creek.

The women drove to the Jacobs' farm for a second visit in just a week.

"You don't think Henry will be suspicious, do you?" Nell paged through her notes of questions outlining the interview.

"I have that covered. Henry knows I've been forbidden to run alone lately, and Bud needs exercise after being cooped up. I'll just ask if Bud can run around the farm without his leash," Madison said.

A clever plan; Bud and Madison could get some running exercise safely, and Nell would gather information for a human interest story. At least, that was the idea.

While Nell sat on the front porch with Holly and Henry for an informal interview, Madison and Bud set out across the garden perimeter and up a steep hill behind the barns. Their first pass was a challenge, since Madison hadn't run in over a week. She stopped to stretch her calves by one of the smaller buildings. She noticed through the crack in the door that there was a dark-colored pickup truck inside, and fresh tire tracks in the soft soil.

Her first thought was to take a photo with her cell phone, to compare the image with the one Nell's cameraman had discovered on film from the night the sheriff was shot. Curiosity drew her inside the shed to peek into the cab. A shell casing on the passenger side floorboard beckoned her. Not wanting to smudge any fingerprints, she wisely chose to shoot another photo and not touch the evidence that could be incriminating for Henry.

Even though she wanted to learn the truth about the mystery of the skeletons, the last thing Madison wanted was her best friend to suffer. She reasoned that if he was the perpetrator of the evil deeds, he was no good for Holly anyway. But in her heart, she prayed he was not involved.

The downhill run crossed a small creek at the back of the Jacob's house. When she rounded the front of the house, Holly was serving tea and lemonade. "Okay, even the furry runner needs a drink." Holly set a bowl of water down on the steps for Bud.

"One more pass; I cramped up on the climb. I need to run it out now. I'll be right back. Save me some lemonade, will you?" She ran by the porch and out of sight again.

"That girl loves to run more than anyone I know," Nell said. "And she really missed it when we kept her corralled."

"Why would you keep her from running?" Henry asked.

Nell studied his face and then said, "With all that's happened–the sheriff getting shot and someone trapping Madison in the cave–Perry feels she's in danger. Surely you can understand why he can't let her take her usual freedoms."

Henry appeared to weigh Nell's words. Then he said, "Madison's not in danger. Maybe the cave incident was a freak happening. That stone moves easily when the conditions are right. We had an aftershock that day from the earthquake up in Virginia. I'd bet that's what put it into play. Why would anyone harm Madison? She's just the unfortunate victim who discovered the bones."

"And I guess Bud just happened to tie himself up with a rope, to lure her in there in the first place," Holly said.

Henry looked at his wife and made a very surprising comment. "Willard

Franks likes to think he's a taxidermist. When he was a young boy, he tortured and killed small animals so he could stuff them. He doesn't like dogs—especially one that's smarter than him."

Nell felt her jaw drop. "Henry, are you suggesting Willy put Bud in the cave to die?"

Henry cut his eyes to meet her gaze. "You'd be surprised at what that man's done. He's just not right."

Madison and Bud rejoined them on the porch.

Henry declared that the interview was over, because he had a field to plow. "You gals can talk all you want. I gotta get busy."

"I want to photograph you in action, Henry." Nell followed him off the porch. "I promise to stay out of the way."

The two walked around the side of the house and out of sight.

"Well, Nell sure has an interest in Henry." Madison accepted an iced glass of lemonade from Holly.

"Yeah, they talked the whole time you were running. I'm surprised at how Henry's mellowing," Holly said.

"Holly, do you remember your father-in-law and Denny being friends?"

Holly pursed her lips. "Not that I recall. But I overheard an argument he and Mariah had. She told him something that upset him, and I heard Denny's name mentioned. I couldn't make out what all they said. Henry came in, so I couldn't listen. He blamed Mariah for his mom and brother leaving. We walked up to the barn while they argued. She was gone when we got back."

"So you didn't know Mariah well?" Madison asked.

Holly shook her head. "I felt sorry for her. She was sad all the time. Don't think she had any family. I could relate to her, in that way. If she was shunned by the man she loved, she was on her own. If I didn't have Henry, I'd be in the same fix."

"What happened to her?"

"After that day, we didn't see her anymore. Hiram didn't mention her to me. He told Henry she was gone, that he didn't know where or even care—but I think he did care. She was a pretty woman, and a hard worker. You know, she was the only Melungeon I ever met." Holly looked out over the field, where Henry's tractor soon drove into view. "Since his daddy passed, Henry has changed."

Madison wished she didn't know about the truck and the spent shell she discovered. "Could you see the fire from here the night Denny's office burned?"

Holly's forehead furrowed and she said, "We weren't here. That's the night we spent in Knoxville. I told you Henry had an appointment with a doctor, remember?"

"Oh, was it that same night? I guess it was."

Madison suddenly felt confused. *If Henry was in Knoxville, then who drove his truck?*

Nell returned smiling like the photo shoot had been pleasant. "Thanks for your time, Holly. I really appreciate you and Henry being so cooperative. I think the real story of Cold Creek will be successful. Especially since Henry's ancestors are an important part of the foundation of this community."

"Well, I didn't realize I was married to a celebrity. I'm glad he warmed up to you. He doesn't take to strangers easily." Holly gathered the glasses and refreshments. "Either of you want any more to drink?"

"No thanks. We need to get going," Madison said. She clapped her hands to call Bud and loaded him into the vehicle. "Come to town and see us soon, will you?"

"When that field's ready, we'll plant our vegetable garden. We do live on a farm, you know." Holly laughed from the door.

Nell and Madison waved as they drove away.

"You couldn't get away fast enough. What happened?" Nell leaned toward Madison.

"I found something, but I don't know what to do." She stared out the windshield.

"Listen, we're in this together; we'll make the decision together."

Madison handed over her phone. "Look at the last few photos."

Nell pulled up the picture gallery, looking down at the small screen. Her eyes grew wide and her expression asked the question.

"In an outbuilding above the barn. I noticed the tracks, and saw the truck through a crack between the doors. The shape is right, and those tracks mean it's been out recently. I looked inside the cab, and my heart nearly stopped when I saw the shell casing," Madison explained.

"I can't tell from this photo what caliber it is." Nell flipped through the photos again.

Madison said, "This could be the proverbial smoking gun. And just when I was beginning to like Henry." Then she added, "But Holly said they were in Knoxville the night the dental office burned. Are we looking at a mere coincidence?"

"I don't believe in coincidences, Madison. Everything is another clue. We just have to fit them all together. We're going to have to print out the photos. If we mishandle the evidence, it will be thrown out."

"The law isn't going to use it. I am." Madison turned into her driveway. "You are either with me or against me, Nell. Which is it?"

"You know I'm with you!" She opened the door and stepped out of the vehicle. "But you have to show this to Perry. He'll get a search warrant and take it from there."

"No, I don't want him to know yet. I'll check this out on my own." She unlocked the door and went inside her cottage.

"You're not Sherlock Holmes. You *have* to tell the sheriff!" Nell stood at the door, glaring at Madison. "You saw it—so you tell him, or I will."

"Alright! I'll tell him. Best you stay out of this." Madison hung her head. "This will break Holly's heart."

"Henry told me that Willy has a history of cruelty to animals. He hinted that might be who tied Bud in the cave."

"Bud would never go with Willy. He hates that man," Madison said.

"What if Bud was chasing him?" Nell tightened her lips.

"Now that's a possibility," Madison said.

Nell stepped onto the porch. "I'm going to leave so you can download your photos and make notes. If I'm not here, I don't have anything to hide. You know?"

Madison nodded. "I'll call Sheriff Perry. It'll be easier if I'm not looking at him."

"I think you know more than you're telling me, but that's okay." Nell held her hands up. "I'm supporting you all the way."

Madison watched Nell cross the street to the restaurant. She felt a bond with her and wanted to share her thoughts—but at the same time, she needed to go it alone. Nell and Sheriff Perry were close. As much as she wanted to solve this mystery herself, she knew Nell was right. Sheriff Perry and Rick could handle an anonymous tip. She couldn't have Holly knowing her best friend turned Henry in. Madison picked up the phone, her heart heavy.

CHAPTER 20

Early the next morning, Madison heard a tap on her door. She was already dressed and ready to go. She peeked out the window and saw Jess standing there.

"Hey! Are you my bodyguard today?" She swung the door open wide. He carried a long object wrapped in a towel. "What's this?"

"Maybe a start at decorating your walls, if you like it." Jess uncovered an 11x14-inch framed canvas.

She recognized the painting was one of her favorites, the Gray's lily: a beautiful, bright orange wildflower found in the southern Appalachian Mountains, specifically on Roan Mountain.

"That's awesome; where did you find it?" She took the frame in her hands. "Jess, that's your signature! You painted this?"

He nodded. "I'm pleased with the way it turned out. Is it good enough to hang up in here?"

"Good enough? Are you kidding? It's beautiful! I never knew you painted." Madison felt awkward but she said what she was thinking. "One more secret you've hidden?"

"I used to paint when I was young. My oils are in the storeroom over the restaurant. I hadn't touched a brush in a long time. Then you inspired me, and it felt good. Flowers are easy for me. What I always wanted was to do portraits. Never had much luck making them resemble the person they're supposed to be, though, so I lost interest."

"Jess, this is wonderful! Will you do more? This looks exactly like the blooms we saw on Roan Mountain. I remember you said they're rare. And orange, of course; being a UT fan, you know I love orange." Madison held the painting up to the wall behind the couch.

"Probably need a larger one there. Try it here." He put his hand against the short wall separating the kitchen and living room.

"Yes, that's perfect." Madison set the frame on the floor, leaning it against the wall.

"I brought a hanger; get your hammer." He raised a small nail with a hook attached. "About here, don't you think?"

Madison retrieved a small hammer from a kitchen drawer. "That looks good."

They both stepped back to admire the art.

"Thank you, so much!" Then she hugged him.

"You're welcome. What do you think about a lady slipper, with some ferns?"

"I think I'm going to be spoiled." She hooked her arm in his and they headed for the restaurant.

Madison poured herself a cup of coffee as she gazed around the restaurant. "I hoped to find the sheriff here this morning."

"He was in earlier." Shirley reached into her apron pocket. "He asked me to give you this." She handed over a folded piece of paper.

Madison sipped her coffee, read the note, and stuffed it into her pocket.

"Why don't you have something to eat?" Shirley suggested.

"I've had breakfast. Bud is waiting for our run."

Shirley shook her finger at Madison. "You're not supposed to go anywhere alone."

"I know; Nell is going with us."

"What can she do to protect you?"

"Maybe I don't need protecting."

"You're so thin. Must you run every day?" Shirley said.

"Look at Denny; she's built like a bull, and she stays active with her dog team. She's my nearest blood relative. I don't want to be obese, so I stay in shape by running. It's great for stress relief. Maybe you should try it. At least

I'm healthy!"

"Are you saying I'm fat because I don't exercise enough? I put in twelve or more hours a day in this restaurant. I don't have time to run." Shirley turned and shoved the swinging doors as she burst into the kitchen.

"That's not what I meant..." she called after Shirley from across the kitchen. Shirley ignored her.

Madison slammed the front door as she left the restaurant. She recognized that she found a satisfaction in running she couldn't explain. It meant free time to do and go wherever she pleased, just Bud and her; that was more incentive than any. *Why can't others understand? I'm not anorexic. Why does everyone want to tell me how to live my life?*

Nell sat in the rocker at the cottage. "Ready to run?"

"Did you go inside?"

Nell shook her head.

Madison pushed the door open, and pointing at the painting, asked "What do you think of my first art?"

"That's beautiful. What's it called?" Nell looked closely at the canvas. "Jess McKenzie?" She turned to Madison, her mouth wide open.

"It was a surprise to me, too. Jess and I hiked up Roan Mountain one summer. They're Gray's lilies, and are somewhat rare this far south. Roan Mountain is one of the few places along the Appalachians they're found." She took in a deep breath. "I'm really proud of my dad."

"Wow, this is unbelievable! What else has he done?" Nell asked.

"Nothing lately, but he'll do another one soon." She pulled Nell toward the door. "We better go, or Bud will run without us."

Later that afternoon, Madison pulled her running pants off and the note fell out of her pocket. The more she thought about the Sheriff's message, the more curious she became. He'd asked that she come by his office after sundown so they could talk.

On the door of his office, she found another note.

I'm on the mountain at Eagle Ridge. If you have urgent business, drive on up.

She ran back to the cottage. "Nell, we're going up on the mountain."

"We are?"

"Sheriff Perry left a message on the door, and he sent me that note this morning."

"I don't think he had in mind for you to come up there." Nell stood firmly with both hands on her hips.

"Oh, stop pretending you don't want to go. I'm leaving in two minutes."

"Okay. Why argue? I'm already guilty of concealing evidence. Why let a little thing like trespassing stop me?"

In record time the two women stopped at the turnaround on Eagle Ridge. There were so many vehicles, Madison could barely turn and park.

There was a deputy from Erwin standing at the trail. "I'm sorry ladies, Sheriff's orders; no one beyond this point," he said.

"Sheriff Perry asked us to come up here. Can you contact him?" Madison asked.

"Perry, this is Buck. You've got a couple of visitors at the trailhead."

She heard the sheriff's voice ask, "Who is it?"

"Nell and Madison," she said into the little radio.

"What are they—oh, never mind. I'll be right there." Perry's voice sounded irritated.

After a few minutes, Perry appeared. He walked between Nell and Madison, put an arm around each, and escorted them back to her Blazer. Bud followed close behind.

"Okay, now what's this about?" He patted his leg and Bud jumped up to get a petting.

Nell cut her eyes to Madison, who pressed her lips tightly together and frowned at Nell.

"What is it? Come on. I know you discovered something." Perry looked sternly into Madison's face. "Don't mess with me; I'm tired and frustrated, not to mention hungry."

"You said you were going to call him. You didn't, did you?" Nell stared, letting Madison know she was disappointed.

"I tried. Willy answered, and I didn't want to talk to him about it. Just tell me what caliber of rifle shot you." She held her ground.

"It was an ordinary twenty-two: the type any hunter might use for small game. Every kid from twelve years old to one hundred has them. Why? What's so important about that?"

"Twenty-two caliber? Is that why it didn't put a big hole in you?" She asked.

Perry nodded. "And I am grateful it wasn't an elephant gun. Now, can I get back to work?"

Nell moved closer to Perry. "Sheriff Perry, you look exhausted. Why don't you come back with us? You could use a hot meal and a good night's sleep."

Perry took a deep breath. His smile widened as he relaxed into a slump, his forehead touching hers. "And a hot bath?"

"Especially a hot bath—*and* a massage." Nell's lips were millimeters from his.

"Twist my arm. I can be persuaded," he whispered.

"Oh, puh-*lease*! You two! Why don't you just kiss, and get over the drama?"

Perry backed away. "What? We're just having a conversation here."

"Yeah. You should try having a conversation like this with Rick!" Nell said.

Madison dropped her head and turned away. She had a sinking feeling—she didn't think *any* man would ever look at her the way Sheriff Perry looked at Nell. She moved to the driver's side of her Blazer and opened the door. Bud jumped in and immediately climbed into the back seat.

"I'm going to Cold Creek. Anyone who wants to ride along, jump in."

Nell reached for the passenger side door handle.

"Hold up, I'll ride back with you," Perry said. He spoke into the small radio on his shoulder and told someone on the other end that he'd be back in the morning, and for now they were in charge.

Madison felt as though someone was watching them. She snapped her head toward her open window at the sound of a branch cracking in the woods.

Bud growled from the back seat.

"No, Bud." She listened, but heard nothing else.

Nell climbed into the front seat, and Perry shut her door and climbed into the back.

"Did you hear that?" Madison looked at Perry. "It sounded like someone moving around, right there in the woods."

"I heard Bud growl. And I was followed out the trail. Act normal and drive away."

"Is it Franks?" She whispered.

"It better not be! I left him in charge." Perry leaned close to the front seat.

"When we get around the first curve, slow down so I can jump out. Don't stop; don't hit your brakes. It's a slight incline, so just let the vehicle slow on its own."

"Jump out? You could get hurt!" Nell cried.

"Not if we're going slowly. Wait for me around that next curve, and lock your doors. I'll catch up." Perry put his hand on the door latch.

"I don't like this," Madison said.

"If car lights come up behind you, let them pass. I'll be right behind it."

"What if they don't go on around?"

"I'll shoot out the windshield." Perry laughed.

"Oh, shit!" Madison cried.

"Why, Madison! I'm surprised at you." The car slowed and Perrys stepped out and hit the ground running. The door swung shut, and he disappeared into the woods.

Madison continued on to the next curve and followed the sheriff's instructions. After what seemed like an eternity, they heard a tap at Nell's window. Both women screamed.

Perry shone his penlight under his chin. "It's me, silly. Unlock the door."

"What did you see?" both women asked at the same time.

"No one left the parking lot, but I heard a four-wheeler driving through the woods," he answered.

"That darn four-wheeler again!" Madison pounded on the steering wheel. "Who is it? And why can't we catch them?"

"We will, if I have to patrol the woods myself." Perry rested his head against the rear seat.

Nell spoke softly, "I'm shaking; it's a good thing I'm not driving."

Madison started the vehicle and drove in silence for a while. She handed Nell her cell phone, nodding her head toward the back seat. "Don't tell anyone how you found out about this. I took those photos yesterday at the Jacobs farm."

Nell located the pictures and handed the phone across the seat to Perry.

"That's Henry's dad's old truck. And that's a .22 long shell casing. What's this about?" He handed the phone back to Nell.

"Could that be the truck in the video?" Nell asked.

"Could be, but why would Henry do something like that?" Perry looked at

Madison, who was watching him in her rearview mirror.

"Henry and Holly were in Knoxville that night. Henry couldn't have done it," she said. "But *someone* took the truck out; there're fresh tracks in the soil. Don't you think you should check it out?"

"I will, tomorrow. I won't say who told me. I've wanted to search his out-buildings, and this is a good excuse. I need you to download the photos to my computer. There are files on the desk in the basement. Look through them while you're there."

"Thanks, Sheriff. I don't want Holly hurt. Henry wouldn't do something that bad." Madison drove a few miles in silence before looking in the rear view mirror again.

She whispered, "He's asleep."

"He's worn out. But a promise is a promise; I'll give him a soothing massage." Nell fluttered her eyelashes.

"I wouldn't expect any less. The poor man deserves it," Madison said.

As they approached Cold Creek, Madison turned on a side street behind Jess and Shirley's house. Perry lived in a garage apartment over an empty machine shop.

Nell got out and opened the back door. She shook Perry to wake him.

"Good night, Madison. You lock your doors and stay there until I come in the morning. We'll go for breakfast together."

"She doesn't need to be alone, Nell." Perry stepped out from the back seat.

"Bud is a better bodyguard than you tonight. Go, and don't argue with the lady," she protested, and watched as Nell and Sheriff Perry ascended the steps along the outside of the concrete block structure. Once the light came on inside, she drove toward her cottage. As soon as she opened the car door, Bud jumped out, making a dash for the nearest tree.

"Come on, we have to barricade ourselves inside." Madison put out fresh water and some dry food for Bud, then took out a carton of yogurt for herself and sat on the couch. Thoughts twirled like a whirlwind in her mind.

Denny was definitely guilty of something. Madison knew that Denny was lying about her brother's accident, and Sheriff Franks covering it up meant they might be in cahoots. Was Franks following orders from his dad? What happened to the prostitutes Sheriff Franks arrested? Could *they* be the skeletons? It made sense. And what about the argument between Denny and Mariah? Was that why she'd disappeared? And if so, did Denny kill her? The timing was all off; if Mariah was here when Madison remembered her, she couldn't be one of the skeletons.

Maybe I'm looking at this all wrong. What do I know about investigating, anyway?

Madison started to undress. No. *I'm on the right track; just not looking in the right place.* She put her clothes back on.

While the sheriff is occupied, and Franks is up on the mountain, I can investigate those files in the basement at the jail.

CHAPTER 21

Madison pulled her cottage door shut and left the porch light on. She locked the deadbolt and the door handle. *There, no one will get through that.*

She found the lights on in the office, and the basement door was open.

"Anyone there?" There was no answer. She and Bud walked down the steps. *I wonder why he left the light on.*

She found the files Perry left for her and sifted through them, her hands shaking. *Are there answers here, right under my nose? Or just more questions?*

Bud sniffed every inch of the basement floor, the files, and a closed door. Madison heard him growl. She watched as he stared up the stairs. Then she returned her attention to the file in her hand.

Her heart felt as though it was in her throat as she sat down and began reading Tina Denson's case file. Bud growled again and the light went out. Madison heard the door at the top of the stairs slam shut.

"Hey, I'm down here! Sheriff, is that you?"

No one answered. She made her way to the top of the stairs and beat on the door. It was locked. She called out again. And still, no one came. Her hand found the switch and she went back to the bottom of the stairs.

"Let's see if there's a phone down here."

But there was no time; the light went out again. Bud growled and ran up the stairs. She groped her way to the top and flipped the switch. It didn't work that time. She dropped onto the top step.

I don't even have my cell phone! Surely whoever that was heard me. I shouldn't have come here. What am I trying to do, get myself killed? Not just me; poor Bud, too. She pulled him close and hugged her dog.

After a while, she remembered she'd seen a flashlight on one of the file cabinets. She felt her way in the blackness and located the light. "Thank goodness." She turned the small beam on.

Bud scratched at a door behind the stairs. She'd noticed him sniffing there earlier, so she opened it, finding another set of stairs.

"Go ahead of me, let's see where this leads."

Bud eased down the steps to a landing, and yet another door. It creaked as Madison pushed it open. Musty air filled her nose and cobwebs hung across her path. She checked for spiders; not seeing any, she pushed aside the webs, stepping into an earthen-floored tunnel. To her right, she saw what appeared to be a jail cell. Dirt walls draped in cobwebs covered three sides. A door made of iron bars hung askew in the opening.

She shined the light to her left, illuminating a mineshaft barricaded by boards. She spotted an oil lantern hanging on a hook, took it down, and went back up to the basement room.

"That was creepy, Bud."

She fumbled through a desk drawer. *Maybe I can find some matches.* Bud stood close by her side. "Ah-ha," she said. She raised the globe of the old lantern. The wick accepted the flame, and she adjusted it to lessen the smoke. *We could be here a while, so I might as well read the rest of these files.*

An hour passed and she became sleepy. "This lamp might use up our oxygen." She walked to the door under the stairs and opened it. *It smells bad, but it's air. I'll put out the lamp and wait 'til morning; someone will rescue us.* She rested her head on the desk atop a pile of papers, with Bud curled up at her feet.

It wasn't take long until Bud began stirring. Madison felt stiff and needed to move, so she went to the steps again. *Maybe there's a way out down there.*

She let Bud lead the way. With the flashlight in her pocket, she crept along in the chill of darkness, guided only by the light of the flickering lamp. She kicked the boards loose and passed through. Careful of each step, she moved slowly toward a cool breeze blowing on her face.

Bud walked ahead like a sentry, constantly sniffing fallen rocks. None appeared to have fallen recently, so they pressed on.

The wick flickered, so she turned it higher until the flame was bright again. When they came to a fork in the tunnel, she removed the globe and watched the flame. It flickered and bent to the right, indicating the breeze came from the left fork. With the globe back in place, she continued.

In a few feet, Bud sidestepped a rock—but Madison tripped as she tried to go around the protrusion and clanged the lantern against the wall, splintering the globe. She cupped her hand in front of the flame and moved forward again. Each movement threatened to extinguish the tiny light.

They came to a hole, stretching almost the entire width of the tunnel. Madison pulled out the flashlight and shined it too, so she could keep sound footing as she edged around the wall. Her foot slipped on loose dirt, and she dropped the lantern into the pit. She listened as it hit at least twenty feet down, clattering among rocks.

I better not drop this flashlight. She slid her back to the wall. Bud stood between her and the hole. "Over there." She pointed.

Bud whined, but obeyed her commanding tone.

After a few minutes, she said, "Listen. That's water." *We might have found a way out!*

Bud rushed ahead, and soon she heard him lapping a drink.

She hurried toward him, hoping the water looked clear and safe. It did, and so she took a scoop and lifted it to her mouth. *It has a lot of minerals, but at least it's wet and cold.*

The water flowed into a large room. Now they were out of the tunnel, and in a cave. The flashlight beam bounced off the wall. Overhead she saw boulders protruding. Reflections of layers of earth and rock gave her the feeling of a cavern, but there were no columns or stalactites. The smell of earthy dampness was like caves she'd been in on school trips.

"Oh, boy. Have we gotten ourselves into a bigger mess, or are we closer to getting out?"

Bud waded into the water. At first it came only to his belly and then Madison realized he was swimming. "Come back, Bud." She snapped her fingers. *That looks deep.*

Bud circled back, returning to the side. He climbed out of the cold water and immediately shook himself. Madison stepped backward to escape the shower and lost her footing. She slid down a slippery slope and into another room. Bud barked from high above her.

"Stay," she yelled to him.

Bud sat watching as she put the flashlight in her mouth and tried to find handholds up the side of the wall. But it was too wet, and she slipped right back down. She turned around, shining the flashlight along the walls. *There.* She spotted a narrow passage.

"Stay, Bud; *stay!" I'll see if this way goes out.*

The passage led upward to yet another cavernous room. She realized the water ran under the wall, and possibly out. Should she try to go with the water, or back to where Bud waited?

Bud's bark answered the question for her. He'd disobeyed her and followed down the slippery slope, right to where she stood.

Well, we're in this jam together; I suppose we'll have to swim under that wall. I know you don't understand. How do I make you stay while I check it out?

Madison sat down and pulled Bud onto her lap. She felt scared for him. Had she rescued him from the little cave on her property only to bring him in here to meet his death in a deeper cave?

She rested her head against Bud's neck, praying and crying at the same time. She wondered how long they had been in the tunnel and how far they'd walked. She tried to fight back the fear and retrace their steps in her mind.

Surely they weren't far enough to be near the river. She remembered when she and Jess had been fishing one time, he'd told her of a stream that flowed from deep within the mountain and formed a waterfall where the creek cascaded into the river. The terrain was steep, so he wouldn't take her up to see it, but he told her that he'd been foolish enough to do it when he was young. It wasn't a fable; the stream surfaced in the middle of the creek, and after a hard rain it gushed out like a geyser.

Madison sat for a long while, pondering what she could do. She rested her head against the wall. Soon she saw that the flashlight was dimming. She turned it off to reserve what battery power was left. The room was plunged into complete and total darkness. She closed her eyes and fell asleep, praying for a way to resolve their confinement.

Bud nudged her hand, waking Madison from a dream. No, not a dream; she was really trapped again, this time in a much larger scene. *How do I get myself into these fixes?*

Her eyes were accustomed to the dark, but that wasn't darkness Bud was staring into. She was surprised to see light under the water. Could it be daylight? Was it her imagination? Were her eyes playing tricks on her? There *was* light under the wall, where it had been dark before; not much, but at least it meant she'd slept long enough for the sun to come up. The longer she sat looking at the water, the lighter the water became. Images on the bottom began to take shape. There were rocks of all sizes. That was *not* her imagination! She believed she had an answer to her prayers.

The cold water took her breath. Bud came in behind her as though he knew what she was thinking. She stepped carefully and edged her way to the wall. The water was deep, to her waist now, and Bud paddled to stay afloat. She wondered if he would dive, so she ducked under water to see if he'd follow. At first he didn't, so she resurfaced and pulled him into her arms.

"We have to go under to get out, Bud. Trust me, I'll hold onto you. We'll do this together, or die trying." Madison hugged her best friend and kissed his nose. And then she took a deep breath and ducked under the water, taking Bud with her under the wall.

After a few seconds, Bud pushed off with his back legs against her stomach and swam ahead towards the light. She swam hard behind him. Her lungs burned; she wanted to breathe, but had to push harder. The light grew brighter. The distance between her and Bud grew. The light still looked far away. Could Bud make it? Could she hold her breath long enough?

She concentrated on forcing small amounts of air from her lungs. She felt like she'd burst if she couldn't breathe, but she forced more and more air out, trying to stretch her time. Her focus became fuzzy. The hole the light came through was narrow. She could see the edges closing in. She swallowed to keep from opening her mouth. Her shoulders felt the walls, very close. Could she fit through the opening? One last lunge was all she could manage. All of a sudden she bobbed up to the surface, and her lungs filled with clean air. The water bubbled around her, keeping her afloat. She saw Bud crawling out on the bank a few feet away.

When she crawled up the bank beside him, he licked her face with pure excitement. She had found a way out. *Just like Jess said, years ago. Who else was trapped in that cell?* They were safe, and Bud understood. She knew he did—even though he couldn't say the words. His behavior relayed the message as clearly as the daylight overhead.

Thick rhododendron made descending the steep hill treacherous. Madison fell, and slid the final thirty feet on her backside. Bud stayed right next to her.

Her body felt cold in the early morning air when they reached the bridge, where the gravel road crossed South Indian Creek. She'd never understood why a body of water this wide and full was only a creek. When she saw a truck parked on the other side of the bridge, she didn't care what it was called. She was glad to see the man walking toward the water with his fishing pole.

"Hello," she called out to him, and waved.

"Howdy." The man stopped at the path and watched her and Bud cross the bridge. "You fall in the river, or what?"

"You might say that. I'm freezing. Could I talk you into giving us a ride into Cold Creek? I'll be glad to pay you."

The man took off his hat and scratched thinning gray hair. "I'll give ya a ride, but no need to pay me. Aren't you Jess's girl?" He slapped the dirty cap back on his head. He met her at the truck and put his fishing pole in the back.

"Here, I got an old jacket you can put on, if you can stand the smell. It's my fishing jacket and might be a bit ripe, but it'll keep you warm."

"Oh, thank you. You know my Dad?" She accepted the lined flannel jacket and put it on over her wet clothes.

"Yeah, me and Jess are ol' fishing buddies. I seen you at the restaurant a time or two."

He lowered the tailgate to allow Bud to jump into the back. When Madison started to climb in the back too, he said, "No ma'am, you can't hurt these old seats. Climb right up in the passenger side here." He opened the door for her.

"Thank you. My name is Madison. I really appreciate this."

"I'm Jack Kelly." He offered his hand.

"Pleased to meet you, Mr. Kelly," Madison said.

The ride into Cold Creek took about fifteen minutes, because the road went around the mountain and away from the river. But as the crow flies, the cave and waterway had been closer.

Mr. Kelly stopped in front of the cottage, and Madison again offered to go inside and get him some gas money. But he declined, and drove off waving to her.

Madison went quickly to the house, checking her pockets as she climbed the steps. Luckily the keys had stayed in her pocket. She opened the door and she and Bud went inside without anyone seeing them. She looked at the clock on her dresser, and let out a sigh of relief. It was only 6:45—hopefully no one had even missed her yet.

CHAPTER 22

Madison was showering when she heard Nell's voice. "In here."

"Good, you're up." Nell stood at the door. "Rick and Sheriff Perry want us to meet them at Shirley's. I'm going to change clothes."

Wrapped in a towel, Madison slipped into her bedroom. "You have a glow about you. No need for blush *this* morning."

Nell stepped into the bathroom and checked her face in the mirror. "I have no such thing!"

"Oh, yeah, you do. Say, you can use your talents to make me up. What do you say?"

"Sure. I'll be happy to. You don't need much; you're naturally beautiful. Now go and dry your hair while I change."

Madison's impulse was to tell Nell about her horrible experience, but she held back. *Maybe I should keep a few details to myself.*

When Madison and Nell strolled into the restaurant, both Sheriff Perry and Rick stood up. The women joined them at a booth.

"What?" Madison said. "Did we do something wrong?"

"Absolutely not!" Rick slid into the seat next to her. "Looks like you did everything right!"

Madison felt her face burn. She smiled at his reaction. "Nell is some artist, isn't she?"

Shirley joined them. "You ladies look especially lovely this morning."

"Thanks," Nell and Madison said.

"Besides coffee, what can I get you?" Shirley took their orders, surprised that Madison ordered eggs, wheat toast, and a side of grits.

"Now *that's* what I'm talking about," Shirley said as she turned away. She put the ticket up in the pass-through window, and returned with mugs and a pot of coffee.

Rick and Sheriff Perry stared at Madison, causing her to feel self-conscious. She looked out the window, thinking of some way to distract them. "Are you feeling rested this morning, Sheriff?"

That was the wrong thing to say. Nell giggled, and this time, Sheriff Perry blushed.

"Oh yes, he got a great night's sleep. He fell asleep in the bathtub. So I left him in there until the water got so cold he had to come to bed to get warm."

"Lucky him. I can't recall the last time I had a warm body in bed next to me." Rick said.

"Maybe you should get a dog," Madison added quickly.

They all laughed. The subject changed when Shirley brought their food to the table.

She asked, "What's the special occasion?"

"Nell and I have things to do in town. Do you need anything from Asheville?"

Nell turned to Madison. "Asheville? I thought we were going to Jonesborough."

"After Jonesborough, I mean," Madison nodded.

"What are you up to?" Perry's look was stern.

"Nell hasn't checked out the antique shops in Jonesborough."

"Can I join you? I haven't visited Jonesborough yet either," Rick said.

Madison swallowed hard and cut her eyes to Nell. "It's girl stuff. You'd be bored."

"Not to mention I don't have sightseeing time." Rick glanced at the sheriff.

"Neither one of us do. But when this is over, we want a rain check. Okay?" Perry smiled.

Nell nodded and Madison shrugged her shoulders.

After breakfast, the foursome walked outside. Madison whispered to Perry.

"We need to talk in private." She nodded toward Rick and Nell.

Perry said, "We can trust them, but what's this business in Asheville?"

"I realized I haven't picked up my glasses. And there's this great art display downtown. You want me staying out of trouble, don't you? Then there's that awesome shoe store. Now that I don't have to live in Softspot clinic shoes, I can buy fashion." Madison batted her eyes.

"Give me a break! Now, what was it you wanted?" Perry shook his head, lips tight.

"You know you agreed to let me read some of the case files?"

"Yeah," Perry nodded.

"After I dropped you and Nell off, I went to your office. Lights were on and the door was open, so I went to the basement—"

"You went down there *alone?*" Sheriff Perry grabbed her shoulder.

"No, Bud was with me. Anyway, someone turned the lights out, not realizing I was down there. The first time it happened, I turned the lights back on. But the next time, they wouldn't come on and the door was locked. I found a flashlight and checked for a way out, through the closet and stairs—what was the cell used for?" She searched his face for some recognition.

"What? That's a storage closet. There aren't any files in there." His eyes narrowed, his hand holding firmly to her shoulder. "Are you ever going to listen to orders?"

"Probably not!" She jerked away from his hold. "You tell me what you're hiding! Closet? Not by any stretch of the imagination! It leads to a staircase, a mine shaft, a jail cell, and eventually into a cave!" Madison folded her arms, glaring at the sheriff. Was he lying to her? Or did he really not know what was under his own jail?

"Show me." Perry stomped across the street followed by the other three. The door was locked, so he retrieved a key from his pocket. The door to the basement was locked, also. Perry's neck veins bulged. "This door is never locked. I don't even know where the key is." He kicked the door in, snapped the light switch, and snapped it again. "Well, the circuit has blown." He went to the circuit breaker. The main breaker was thrown. "What the h—"

"Take it easy, Sheriff." Nell put her hand on Perry's arm. "Maybe Franks locked the door, not knowing she was down there. Then the breaker flipped somehow."

He picked up the phone on his desk. "How do you explain the cut phone line?" Perry's voice returned to his normal tone. He huffed out a breath, gritting his teeth. "In the first place," he turned to Madison. "I could arrest you and lock you up. That way I'd know where you'll be at all times! But whether you realize it or not, someone might just want you dead! And until I know who that person is, I want you to *stay put*! Do I make myself clear?" His face reddened. His jaw set, he glared at Madison.

She and Rick looked at each other. Neither said a word.

"So tell me, how did you get out?" Perry asked.

"One thing at a time." Madison led the way to the closet. She kept her distance from Perry.

Rick moved close beside her, as though he felt her tension. He placed his hand on her back, gently informing her he was at her side.

"There—that's a door, not a storage closet." Her voice was shaky and her hand shook when she pointed. She quickly withdrew it.

"That door had an old, rusty padlock." Perry ducked his head and walked in. He switched on a flashlight and led the way down the creaky stairs.

Rick suggested Madison and Nell wait, but they ignored him and followed. At the bottom of the stairs, they found exactly what she had described: the barricaded tunnel and primitive jail cell. Perry's flashlight was brighter than the one Madison had and the beam highlighted curious dark stains on the floor.

Rick put samples into clear plastic bags he pulled from his jacket pocket. "These could be oil spills, but I'll get them tested just to be sure."

Sheriff Perry used his knife to scrape a sample of residue from the bars. He placed it in a baggie as well. "I'll test this upstairs in my office. I'm betting it's blood."

Madison pointed out a pair of handcuffs secured to the back wall with a thick chain. "This looks like something from a torture chamber." She watched Rick and Perry's faces. "What?"

"How many torture chambers have you been in?" Rick smiled.

"Okay, I used to watch old Vincent Price movies when I couldn't sleep," she admitted.

The two men laughed, and walked in the direction of the tunnel. Perry's light shined the way to where Madison had knocked the boards down.

"Don't tell me you got out that way," Rick looked intently at Madison.

"Yeah, I did! What would *you* have done?!" She snapped at Malone, but her anger was intended for the sheriff.

Perry stepped across the boards.

"I don't recommend it." Madison grabbed Perry's arm. "Not unless you plan to take a swim."

"I don't understand," Nell said.

Madison took a deep breath. "First, you have to promise not to yell at me."

"Okay, back upstairs with you, all of you," Perry ordered.

They sat in Perry's office, eyes wide and mouths open as Madison explained every detail.

"I just don't believe this. I mean, I believe you, Madison, but the cave and the stream; why that's like a horror movie! Are you sure you weren't dreaming?" Perry paced back and forth across the room. "First, Rick, you and I are going to process that cell as if it were a crime scene, which it very well could be. Nell, I think you should take Madison to Knoxville with you. She can't stay out of trouble, so take her away so she won't be tempted."

"No. You can't make me. I haven't done anything wrong."

"You could have died, Madison, twice at least. Who knows what else you've done that I don't know about? I told you to stay put, and you run all over the county like you know what you're doing. You don't! You don't know who you're dealing with, and how dangerous a serial killer can be!" The sheriff slammed his fist down on his desk.

"Maybe something was hidden here. Maybe that's why the light was on." Rick suggested.

"All the more reason I don't want her to stay alone," Perry said. "If something was hidden and she interrupted whoever knew it was there, they expect her to be dead, or at least scared half to death from getting locked in all night. This could work for us."

"We can spread the word that you and Bud are missing. But you'll be in Knoxville with Nell," Rick said.

Madison went out the door and Rick followed. "Madison, wait, please. Come on, Madison." He caught her by the elbow and wheeled her around in the middle of the street. "Talk to me?"

"Old sheriff Franks is the first person I'd interrogate," she said. Madison was evolving, and she made sure everyone around her noticed the change. She jerked her arm away from the TBI hunk and barely made it to her cottage before her weak knees brought her to a halt.

Bud rushed to lick her face as she buckled and fell to the floor.

"Thanks, ol' friend. We've been through a lot together, haven't we?" She held his warmth close and wished she could hold a man that way; Rick, maybe. "No, out of the question. He's just a cop; here because it's his job—job! Oh no! I forgot." She ran into the bedroom and changed her clothes. She had an interview with a dentist in Johnson City, and if she didn't get out in a hurry, she'd be late.

"Stay here, Bud. I have to go alone." She petted her pal and got into her Blazer.

"Where are you going?" Rick joined her at the car.

"I have an interview in Johnson City. I suppose you want to ride along."

"Why not?" He went to the passenger side door and got in.

"Oh, come on. Seriously?"

"You don't need to be alone. We'll get lunch. I'd like some seafood."

"Okay, seafood sounds good to me too—after my interview."

Madison drove toward Johnson City, wondering if she even wanted a job. She had entertained the idea of going to college, but wasn't sure what she wanted to study. Would her family and friends laugh, if they knew what interested her? *I'll see how it feels when I get there.*

CHAPTER 23

The drive was quiet; Rick made small talk and sometimes Madison answered. When they reached the first Johnson City exit off I-26, she turned west on University Parkway and then onto West Walnut Street. She pulled up in front of a new brick building, looking out of place between an older machine shop and an unoccupied, possibly condemned, structure.

"Here we are, 712 West Walnut." As she exited the vehicle, she tossed Rick the keys. "If you get too warm, you can move to the shade. Just don't leave me!"

"I'll be right here." Rick settled his head against the doorpost.

Rick no more than relaxed when Madison returned. Her face looked as long as his tie.

"What's with the short interview? You weren't late."

"He said he doesn't need anyone; the receptionist forgot to call me." She slid into the driver's seat and shut the door.

Rick stuck the key in the switch and turned it. "Shall we go to lunch early? We might get a bottle of wine and make it happy hour."

"I don't feel happy. He was so nice on the phone, and sounded like he really wanted to meet me." A tear slipped down Madison's face.

"Want me to drive?" Rick offered.

"You don't know your way around. I'll be okay." She put the vehicle in gear and backed up.

Rick was watching Madison's attempt to swallow her disappointment, so he hadn't noticed the car whip in behind them. His head snapped, and he heard a loud crashing sound.

"What the hell?" He jumped out of the Blazer.

A man ran from the old car that rammed them, sprinted into the street, and was nearly hit by a transit bus. Rick gave chase.

He returned after a few minutes to see that Madison was out of the vehicle. "I lost him behind that warehouse. It was like a maze; boxes stacked everywhere."

Madison looked at the damage to her six-year-old SUV. Rick slipped his arm along her shoulders. "It's not so bad, Madison. The car got the worst of it."

Rick noticed a couple of men standing out front of the machine shop next door. He walked over and talked to them.

The dentist who had declined to interview Madison came outside. "Are you hurt?" he asked.

Madison shook her head. She stared at the crunched Blazer. "It's never been wrecked." She glared at the dentist. "Did you know him?"

"No, I've never seen him before. I have no idea why he'd turn in here so fast," Dr. Johns said. "My receptionist called the police. Are you sure you weren't hurt?"

She shook her head. "Did you see it happen?"

Dr. Johns nodded. "I'll be inside. The police will want to talk to me."

By this time a siren had sounded; soon a city police car pulled onto the scene.

A brunette woman wearing scrubs stood close behind Madison. "Your former employer told Dr. Johns not to hire you. Please don't say that I told you. I have to get back to work." She disappeared into the crowd of onlookers.

Madison felt confused and stunned. She watched Rick explain how the crash happened, then the policeman walked up to her.

"Did you hear me?" The short man in a dark blue uniform removed his hat. "Ma'am, did you hear me?" He stepped closer. "Have you had anything to drink?"

"Excuse me, Officer; she's in shock." Rick stepped between the persistent policeman and Madison. "Hey… are you sure you're okay, Madison?" He took hold of her arm. "Is your purse in the car? Where's your insurance card?"

Madison pointed at the Blazer. "The console." She moved in an attempt to get what Rick asked for.

The officer said, "Hold on." He turned to Rick, "You get it for her." He raised his hand in a signal to the EMT unit that pulled onto the scene. "Check her out."

An EMT approached and led Madison by the arm back to the ambulance.

Rick kept one eye in her direction as he handed over her license and insurance papers.

"Madison McKenzie? Isn't she the one who found the bones up on the Trail?" said the short officer. "What business did she have here?"

"A job interview. Why would you ask? This was no accident; that car crashed into us! You should be checking to see who was driving it, not harassing Madison."

Rick's voice sounded on edge as Madison returned. "I'm all right, Rick. Just a little overwhelmed, I think. I've never been involved in a wreck." She turned to the rude cop. "I'm sorry," she read his badge, "Officer Borski. No, I have not had anything to drink, I'm not under the influence of any drugs, I'm simply not used to being threatened, stalked, and crashed into. What else do you need to ask me?"

Officer Borski stepped back as he said, "I have what I need. Excuse me, Ms. McKenzie." He turned and walked briskly to his patrol car.

Madison watched as he talked into the radio in his car. She turned to Rick and said, "Denny told Dr. Johns not to hire me. Maybe she sent that guy to run me down."

"Aw, come on Madison. Your aunt is a bit odd, but she's not a killer. She didn't cause this."

Madison stared at the crunched rear bumper of her vehicle. "I'm not as sure as you, Agent Malone."

The JCPD confirmed the car that hit them was stolen from a garage down the street. They interviewed the witnesses, who all agreed the man appeared to have deliberately crashed into the Blazer. There was no question that the collision was no accident.

Nearly an hour later, Rick drove Madison's Blazer off the site and to the Chevrolet Garage. Her insurance company wanted an estimate. Rick drove to

Red Lobster. Madison repeated for a third time that she was not hungry.

"Well, I am." Rick opened the door for her and they went inside.

Madison sat quietly rubbing her neck. After they were seated, Rick placed an order for drinks, a beer for him and unsweet tea for her.

"You should probably see a doctor. You might have a whiplash injury." Rick reached across the table and touched her hand. "I wish you would go to Knoxville with Nell."

Madison pulled her hand away when the waitress brought their drinks. She hadn't looked at the menu.

Rick said. "I want the seafood platter, Cesar salad, and steamed carrots, please." He looked at Madison. "Shall we make that two? I'll take your leftovers for a midnight snack."

Madison smiled as she said to the waitress, "Fried shrimp, baked potato, butter only, and Cesar salad, please."

The waitress gathered the menus and walked away.

Madison's hand returned to her neck. "I'm sure I have whiplash. I felt it. Maybe Nell can recommend a good doctor in Knoxville."

"Thank you for that. At least now you're beginning to understand that Perry could be right." Rick smiled at Madison. "I'm working with him, Madison, not against you. The sooner you realize that, the better for us all. Give Knoxville a chance, and let us do our job here. And don't tell anyone where you're going. Especially not Holly."

Madison glared at Rick but said nothing. *You're keeping secrets too; I know you are.*

CHAPTER 24

Sheriff Perry picked Rick up in front of Shirley's restaurant at daybreak. They drove to the Jacobs' farm with a warrant. As they pulled in front of the old house, Henry sat on the porch tying his boots.

"Morning, fellows. What brings you out so early? I know you're not here to help me plow."

"No, Henry, we're here on business again." Sheriff Perry handed him a piece of paper. "I have a warrant to search your property. Everything is legal and self-explanatory. Show me where you keep your dad's old pickup truck."

Henry looked at the paper for a few minutes. "Do I need to call my lawyer now or later?"

"You aren't under arrest," Perry answered.

"This way," Henry said. The three walked around the house and climbed the hill to the truck, parked in a shabby outbuilding. "Help yourself."

Agent Malone pulled the doors open and stepped inside next to a faded blue 1955 Chevy pickup. He walked around to the passenger side, and Perry opened the driver's door with a gloved hand. He sprayed to check for gunshot residue, or GSR.

"How long has it been since you drove this?" Perry asked.

"Been a while, back in the fall," Henry said.

"Do you own a twenty-two rifle?" Rick asked.

Henry nodded.

"When was it last fired?" Rick continued.

Henry cupped his chin and said, "I guess that was last fall, during hunting season." He leaned against the side of the barn. "Sheriff, if you'll tell me what you're looking for, I'll help."

"Those are fresh tire prints." Perry pointed to tracks. "We had a hard rain the night Dr. Denson's office burned. If the truck hadn't been out, the tracks would be washed away."

Henry said, "I don't know if it'll even start. I usually have to jump it off."

"Where's the key?" Perry asked.

Henry walked to a peg on the wall and found the one to the truck. "Give it a try, if you like."

Perry sat on the front seat, put the key in the switch, mashed the clutch, and then turned the starter. The old six-cylinder fired up on the first hit. Perry drove it out of the barn.

Rick leaned in the passenger window. "Got a flat on the rear."

The sheriff turned the truck off and walked to the opposite side. "It's got a nail in it. Henry, I'd change it if you've got a spare."

"No spare. Tires were too thin; that's why I stopped driving it," Henry said.

"I'll send a guy out with a tire. I want that nail."

"Okay," Henry walked closer to the truck. "Did you pull the seat up?"

"No, I didn't touch it," Perry said.

"Too close to the steering wheel for either of us to drive. Holly can't drive a stick shift. Whoever drove it was short," Henry said calmly.

"True. I'll check the lever for prints. Good observation, Henry."

The law officers followed Henry back to the house. Henry went inside for his rifle.

Perry said, "He doesn't act like he's worried about the truck. Steering wheel was wiped clean as a baby's bottom, but they left the GSR on the door. If you were going to wipe down a crime scene, wouldn't you also include the GSR?"

Rick took in a breath. "Someone's trying to frame him. Let's check the rifle."

Henry returned with the gun. Holly joined the men on the porch.

"You all want something to drink?" she asked with a sweet smile.

"Thanks Holly, but we need to get going." Perry looked across the fields.

"Do you work in the gardens with your husband?"

"Yes, I do. I love getting my bare feet in the fresh plowed dirt." She laughed.

"You're a strong woman. Henry's lucky to have you." Perry walked off the porch.

"No, Sheriff. I'm lucky. He's a good man." Holly linked her arm with her husband's.

Henry kissed the top of her head. "I always clean firearms after I've used them. If it's been fired, it wasn't by me."

"I'll get this back to you soon, Henry." Perry put the rifle on the back seat. "Ready, Rick?"

"Don't work too hard, Holly." Rick got in the sheriff's car.

As they drove, Rick made a couple scribbles in his notebook. "You know, maybe we should keep an eye on Franks. Madison says his old man has a good memory at times."

"I've thought about that," Perry said. "But I was taught to follow the evidence. And as of now, I have no evidence against my deputy. Do I suspect he's sneaky? Yes. But so far, he's not made any mistakes. If this print is readable, his luck might change."

Madison and Bud were playing on the braided rug in her living room when the dog's attention diverted to the door.

She reached up to unlock it. "Come in, Rick."

He dropped to his knees to greet Bud. "You heard me coming, didn't you?" He rolled the dog onto his back for a quick tummy rub. Rick moved to the rocker. "Want to hear the latest news that I'm not going to share?"

"Sure." She sat on the sofa.

"One thing Dr. Geri Baker is sure of, the women were not killed on the mountain—at least not where they were buried." Rick studied Madison's face. "You don't seem surprised."

"I'm not. Nell told me there was no trace of hair, and I know hair doesn't disintegrate, so even I knew they died somewhere else. That's pretty easy to figure out, Rick. Tell me something I don't know."

Rick glared into her face. "I don't know any more."

"I promise I won't say anything. What's the harm?" Madison protested.

"That's all I know. Geri didn't share any other details." He turned away,

"Except that the last skeleton they found was put there as recently as five years ago."

"Five years? So it could be someone I know," she said.

"Did anyone leave suddenly? That should be easy to find out, in a town this size." Rick stood up.

"Presuming she was from here. I mean, what kept them from bringing the bones from somewhere else?" Madison held on to the hope they were not local residents.

"Think about it. The road wasn't there three years ago. It was built to access the new fire tower on Eagle Ridge. Before that road, there wasn't much chance of just happening upon the area on foot unless they lived here, and knew the mountain." Rick had a convincing argument.

"Yeah, you're right; that road is new." She rolled her shoulders. "There's that creepy feeling again."

"See why I don't tell you anything?" Rick moved to a position behind Madison. "I'm across the street. If you're scared, call me. I'll be here in two minutes."

She felt his strong touch on her shoulders and her muscles tensed. Rick squeezed slightly and then massaged with his thumbs. "The feeling I get isn't worry, so much as it is awareness."

He was silent for a minute, then said, "Isn't that better? You've been under a lot of stress these past few weeks." His hands stopped their motion. "You still need to see a doctor."

"I will. I mentioned it to Nell."

"Good. Oh, one other thing; the most recent victim would have walked with a limp. She had a steel plate mending a compound fracture in her right leg."

"A limp, five years... Mariah walked with a limp." Madison spun around. "She worked for Denny." Her eyes focused on his smile.

"And where is she now?" He asked.

Madison shook her head. "She took care of things while Denny ran the Iditarod. When she got back from Alaska, Mariah was gone. The dogs had been well cared for, and everything was in order at the house. Denny figured she'd just moved on. She was Melungeon; some called her a gypsy."

"Uh huh, I'll check into that. Do you know her last name?"

"No. She lived near Gatlinburg before Old Man Jacobs brought her here."

"Jacobs? Henry's dad?" Rick frowned. "That name keeps popping up. I've got to speak to Sheriff Perry about this." Rick said, "As usual, whatever I say to you is between us. Do I have your word on that?"

"Of course!" She said.

"We checked out the truck at the Jacobs' and Perry took his rifle. It required testing to determine if the shell came from his twenty-two."

Madison nodded. "I don't want it to be Henry because of Holly. Someone is sure trying to make him look guilty."

"I agree." Rick stared at her for a moment. "Geri wants to be at the scene at sunup. Knowing her, she'll stay up there as long as there's daylight." He walked onto the porch with Madison and Bud following.

"I'm going to run in the morning. Nell promised she'll go with me."

"Don't take any chances. This is not a game."

"Goodnight, Rick. Thanks for sharing with me. I'll help all I can."

She watched him disappear around the back of the restaurant before closing the door.

Almost immediately, she heard a tap at the door. Nell called out, "It's me, don't shoot."

Bud tilted his head and yapped.

Madison opened the door again. "Come in."

"Want to hear my rough draft? You can help me if anything is wrong."

"Sure, read it to me." Madison sat in the rocker.

Nell went to the table and sat down. She straightened her posture as though the camera was on her. She smiled and began reading from her laptop, "Cold Creek, Tennessee is a lovely town with all the right amenities—good people, beautiful mountain scenery, and wonderful home-cooked food at Shirley's Restaurant. However, the past weeks brought unimaginable terror to the community. A lifelong resident and her dog discovered a scene from a horror film: eight skeletons, all of them women, buried on the slopes of Eagle Ridge. Details are sketchy at this time. From this reporter's view, it's straight out of a Stephen King novel."

She tilted her head as if needing a signal from Madison.

"Keep going." Madison sat forward.

"Renowned Forensic Anthropologist Dr. Geri Baker, from Knoxville, is in Cold Creek to analyze the site herself. The bones appear to have been placed carefully over nearly thirty years, and as recently as five years ago. Stay tuned to this channel for the exclusive story as it unfolds. This is Nell Nielsen for News Three, reporting from Cold Creek." Nell looked at Madison. "What do you think?"

"Thanks for not using my name. Considering what you're reporting, sounds like that's about it in a nut shell."

Madison stared out the window into darkness. It seemed like only hours ago she and Bud were carefree and happy, just the two of them living out a fantasy in a small corner of the world. Now the world was looking in at their day-to-day lives, waiting to see what other secrets would arise. She wished her hometown could return to its peaceful existence. Somehow, she knew it would never be normal again—nor would she.

What exactly is normal, anyway? Compared to others, her life had never been normal. That was changing, and she held the key to her own success. Rick was getting close, but was that just for his own purposes? To get the information Madison knew? She had her guard up, and was not letting him into her heart.

Denny knew more than anyone, and Madison had to find a way to gain her confidence. She'd have to resort to an apology and beg forgiveness if Denny was ever going to open up to her. Madison felt that if she was right about her suspicions, the knowledge she might learn from Denny could be her undoing. If Denny was capable of killing, she might not hesitate to kill her own blood kin.

CHAPTER 25

First thing the next morning, Madison placed a call to her aunt. Getting no answer at the house, she tried her cell number. Still no answer, so she left a message this time.

I bet she's out early, messing with her dogs. Maybe she'll call back.

She bent to tie her shoes and then walked out the front door with Bud alongside. "Nell's late. We'll go without her." She stopped to lock the door and Bud ran into the yard, barking excitedly.

She spun around to see a lean form in sweats and a t-shirt. Her eyes moved down to find running shoes, and then back to Rick's face. Her heart leaped into her throat. *My, he's handsome in the early morning light.*

"I thought you ran early." He looked at his watch, "It's nearly seven."

"Yeah, I overslept and Nell didn't show up." She stepped off the porch. "I thought you were going with Dr. Baker."

"Change of plans. Mind if I join you? I *know* you weren't planning on running alone." Rick's eyes narrowed.

"Can you keep up?" Madison stretched her legs at the steps and then walked across the yard to the gate. "Let's go."

Madison and Bud set the pace, a moderately brisk walk to the park, around the obstacle course, and then they sprinted up the steep hillside. Rick stayed in step.

When they reached the tall grass, Bud went on his usual bird hunt. He didn't scare up any game, so he returned to the path ahead of Madison just as she reached the tree line.

Rick walked alongside when she slowed at the top of the ridge. "When you found the skull, did anyone in particular come to your mind?"

"No," Madison quickly answered.

"What about when you heard they were women?"

"Yes. Henry Jacobs."

"Really? Why is that?"

"The day before I found the skull, Holly came in the office with a broken bicuspid. Denny patched it with a root canal and medicated filling. Holly said it was an accident, but Henry hit her in years past."

"Hmmm," Rick stopped to admire the town overlook. "Did Henry ever hit any other women?"

"Only Holly, far as I know. But he didn't need an excuse to fight." Madison looked over her hometown below. "To look at Cold Creek from here, you'd never guess her residents are all in an uproar. I feel their caution when I pass them on the street. They don't look me in the eye anymore—people I've known all my life."

"Looks like a peaceful town from here. But I've noticed cold shoulders from some. They're frightened, and don't know how to deal with this." He propped his foot on a stump and retied his shoe. "So, you were born here?"

"No one was, except for older folks born at home, like Shirley and Mr. Olsen. Doc Whitaker delivered a few emergencies at his clinic, but most of us were born in Johnson City."

The downhill run ended their talking.

Madison caught up with Bud at the creek, but continued running. Bud followed them to the porch. Rick stopped at the gate to catch his breath.

"Maybe Geri is ready now. We'll meet up later." He struck out for the back of the restaurant.

Madison called Holly's number, and not getting an answer, she drove to their farm. *I bet they're planting the garden.*

As soon as Madison pulled into the drive, Holly came out onto the porch.

"I thought you two might be in the garden, since you didn't answer your phone." Madison stepped out, followed by Bud.

"Henry's waiting for me to bring another bag of seeds. Come on, you and Bud can help." Holly bent to pat Bud's head. "I want a dog so bad."

"Henry has dogs, doesn't he?"

"Yeah, but I mean one for me, to stay in the house and be my companion when Henry's gone, like Bud is with you."

Madison nodded, "He is great company. Why don't you get one?"

"Henry doesn't like a dog in the house. We've argued over it for a long time."

"You hear that, Bud? You'll just have to win Henry over and change his mind."

The two women laughed as they walked into the freshly plowed dirt. Madison stopped and took her shoes off, like Holly. She liked how the cool dirt soothed her feet.

Henry explained to Madison to drop one bean in the holes where Holly put the corn. He went behind them, covering the holes with his hoe.

"I never realized you did this by hand," Madison said.

"Some folks use a corn planter. That works fine, if you only plant one type of seed. But we're planting three. I'm dropping the squash seeds between the hills of corn and beans," Henry said.

"Squash, yes, I've heard of that." Madison stood straight and watched Henry. "It's an old Native American tradition, called Three Sisters planting. The corn grows tall for the beans to climb. The bean vines reinforce the corn stalks, making them less vulnerable to wind. And the squash runs along the ground to shade it, keeping moisture in and weeds out."

"That's exactly right, Madison. I learned it from my dad, he learned from his, and I'd say back along the line, my ancestors learned it from the Native Americans."

Henry walked toward one of the barns, leaving the two women alone for a short time.

Madison and Holly sat in the shade of the willow tree.

"Holly, was Henry's dad mean? I've heard stories about him."

"You mean do I think he put those bones up there on the mountain? I've thought a lot about that. And I think Henry's worried, too."

I hope that's all he's worried about. "Was Henry scared of his dad?"

"He called it respect. I saw the old man backhand Henry and knock him off his feet once."

"Are you serious?"

Holly nodded.

"How did Henry react?"

"He had a hard time holding his temper, but he never back-talked his dad," Holly said.

"Henry does have a temper, and he is controlling. I see how he is with you."

Holly sat quietly for a moment and then said, "Denny has always ruled you; outta love, you said. Well, Henry says he knows what's best for me. What's the difference?"

"Denny never hurt me physically. Henry hurt you more than once."

"Mentally, or physically, what's the difference? Denny controlled you since you were a toddler, and she's moody. At least Henry loves me." Then she gasped, "Oh, I don't mean that your aunt doesn't love you—and she's always been good to me. I shouldn't have said that. I'm sorry."

"No, don't apologize. You're right. She guided me toward her goals. I never had a choice in the matter." Madison took a deep breath, and blew it out slowly. "In the last few weeks, I've seen a side of Henry that I like. He's nice to me. I'm the one that should apologize." She patted Holly's hand. "I'm sorry. You're right, and I'm glad I don't work with Denny anymore. I don't want to be the mousy person you've always known. Henry *has* mellowed. I am changing too."

"Is that why you told the sheriff about Henry's truck?" Holly's tone sounded harsh.

"I told Perry that I thought Henry was framed." Madison breathed a sigh and hung her head. "Please forgive me, Holly. I never meant to hurt you. I believed Henry was innocent."

Neither woman spoke for a long time. Then Holly made a surprising statement.

"I love Henry, and he's the only person in the whole world who has ever loved me, besides you. Remember, we said we'd always love each other, like sisters?"

"Yeah," Madison smiled.

"From now on, if you want to know something, ask me, don't go behind my back and snoop around. That shows you don't trust my husband."

Madison nodded. "We have to stick together; you're the one person I *do* trust."

As the afternoon sun heated the soil, Henry finished with the last row of vegetables. He found Holly and Madison wading in the creek behind their house.

"You two are like children." Henry sat on the back steps. "When Russ and I were kids, we played in that creek; we dammed it up so we'd have a swimming hole. Weren't any deeper than our knees, but we'd lay in it and act like we were swimming."

Madison walked to the porch and leaned against the stair rail. "Do you ever hear from Russell?" she asked.

"Last time he called was after we'd buried the old man." Henry watched Holly splashing water at Bud. "Mom was sad when I spoke to her. She wants to come home. I hoped Russ would bring her back for a visit."

"Maybe they will, someday." Madison patted Henry's shoulder.

"You worked hard today, Madison. I didn't know you liked to get dirty." Henry laughed.

"I find farming intriguing. There are some things I'll get dirty for."

Henry removed his boots and rolled his pant legs up. He walked to the creek and began stacking rocks in a semi-circle where the creek was widest. Holly watched for a minute, then helped gather rocks. Madison carried some from farther up the creek. Soon the three had built a dam, making a pond.

Henry walked up the hill where the creek tumbled over large boulders. He shoved his hands into the pockets of his overalls and looked toward the pooled creek.

"Holly, would you like a waterfall here? With our bedroom window on the back of the house there, it would sound like the machines that city folks buy," Henry said.

Holly ran up the hill and hugged him. Madison watched, a bit envious. When they returned to the porch Holly explained, full of excitement, about Henry's plan.

"That sounds lovely. And let me throw in one little idea."

Henry stepped closer to listen to Madison's suggestion.

She told them that a little arched bridge would look nice crossing the creek under the willow tree, and leading to a garden of flowers.

"That sounds nice, and I know just the person to help me create the look," Henry said.

"Jess?" Madison smiled.

"Yeah, Jess is good with landscapes," Henry said.

"Just this week, I learned he's an artist. He painted a beautiful lily for my cottage."

"Jess is full of surprises, Madison. He's a fine man." Henry smiled.

Madison accepted dinner with the Jacobs and then drove back into Cold Creek at dusk. Rick waited for her on her porch.

"Good thing you checked in with Shirley. I was upset, with you going off on your own. But since you were with Holly and Henry, I won't give you any grief." Rick rubbed Bud's coat. "You've been in the creek, haven't you?"

"It's okay for me to be with your suspect, Agent Malone?" Madison folded her arms.

"It's obvious Henry was framed." Rick mimicked her, folding his arms.

"Good, you're on my side." *Maybe I'll confide in Rick after I talk to Denny.*

Madison went into the house. Once again, there was no message; her attempts to reach her aunt were wasted effort.

Denny is definitely avoiding me. That speaks volumes about her guilt. Is this the time to share with Rick? Maybe—or maybe not quite yet.

CHAPTER 26

The next morning, Madison was awakened more by a feeling than by a sound. And Bud was also disturbed. He stood at the bedroom door as though he was ready to go out.

"Okay, Bud, let's go." *No one is here to run with us or to stop us from running; let's be mischievous.*

The eastern sky glowed with a hint of pink, but more of an orange hue. Madison stretched at the kids' neighborhood park like always. Then she and Bud ran up the steep incline into shadows of the trees.

The air felt cold on her face, causing her eyes to water. Bud led the way, which suited Madison. She wasn't quite focused on the path.

When they reached the meadow, she kept running, knowing it was too early to scare up birds. Bud stayed right with her. She checked her heart rate as they took a cooling walk along the top of the ridge.

I'm burning some calories; today might beat my record time.

At the overlook, a bright orange sky glowed in the background of Cold Creek. "That's an odd color, not exactly red, but I bet it means the same thing." Bud looked up and then back at Madison, as though he agreed.

The downhill path took on a strange hue. Madison imagined running in an animated setting with orange grass and golden sky. The evergreens even appeared more brown than green.

How unnatural her surroundings felt, in this early light! As they approached the last leg of the run, Madison smelled smoke. It was then that she realized the orange glow was not a natural color. It meant there was a forest fire, and it was close.

Her speed increased as she raced closer to town. Ashes fell on the street and her front yard. She put Bud inside the cottage and ran to the restaurant.

"What's burning?" She asked as she burst through the door.

"What do you mean?" Shirley looked up from the register.

"There's smoke, and ash falling."

Shirley rushed to the front window. "Jess, come here!"

"What is it?" Jess strolled from the kitchen.

"Look!" Madison pointed out the window.

Now larger pieces of debris fell. A cloud of brown smoke blocked the sun. Jess and Madison ran outside.

"Embers that big could catch the shingles on fire. I'm going to wet down your roof." Jess yelled, running across the street.

"I'll go to the sheriff's office," she yelled back to Jess.

She burst through the door, knocking Deputy Franks off his feet. He bounced off the wall and rolled into a chair.

"Where's the fire?" She yelled.

"Eagle Ridge Tower called, and the sheriff went toward Denny's farm. I haven't heard back yet."

Sheriff Perry called over the radio just then. "Franks, get the Johnson City Fire Department heading out here It's big. Unicoi County is on scene. We can't get through to Denny's place. Try to raise her on the phone."

"You call the fire department, I'll try Denny," Madison instructed.

In a few seconds, Franks turned to Madison. "Any luck?"

"No. She isn't answering."

"Don't you have a cell number?" Franks asked.

"I tried that already," she said.

Franks shook his head. "Someone already called the Johnson City fire department. They'll be able to get to her from that side, I'd say."

"See if you can get the sheriff back. Ask him where the fire's origin was."

"SO to Sheriff Perry, come in," Franks worked the radio.

"No time now, Franks," the sheriff said abruptly.

Madison jerked the mike from the deputy's hand. "Sheriff, it's Madison; can we get through the old logging road?"

"Don't think so. The Forestry Service helicopter is in route, Perry out."

Madison couldn't stand to wait. She ran back to the restaurant, meeting Rick on the steps.

"Come with me, Madison, we'll ride out there. Think you know the roads well enough so we won't get trapped?" Rick asked.

"You bet!" She started toward the dark blue Expedition. "Bud's in the cottage."

"I'll take him to the restaurant," Jess yelled. "The roof is wet. I'll keep an eye on it."

"Okay." She watched Jess turn off her garden hose and then let Bud out.

By this time, the street was filled with residents and merchants watching for falling embers. The last thing Cold Creek needed was to lose another old wooden building in their historic town.

During the ride toward Denny's house, Madison was quiet.

The wind shifted, blowing the smoke away from Cold Creek Road just as they arrived at the point where Sheriff Perry waited with the Unicoi FD.

"What are you two doing here?" He yelled and slammed his fist against his steering wheel.

Rick spoke up. "We couldn't just stand by. How can we help?"

"The wind shifted; that's better for Cold Creek. However, I'm not so sure it's better for Denny and the dogs." Perry stepped out of his vehicle.

Rick shut the engine off in the middle of the road. "Do you know where this started?"

"Near Denny's house, is all I could tell from the ranger's call." Perry rubbed his neck.

"What about the back road? Shouldn't we at least try it now?" Rick asked.

"Too dangerous. You never know when the wind could shift again. Wait until I hear from the helicopter." Sheriff Perry walked back to his radio. Rick followed.

Madison couldn't hear what Rick asked, but she had no problem hearing Perry's answer.

"I don't know anything, Rick. I really don't," Perry yelled.

Madison couldn't stay out of hearing range; she moved in closer.

"Patrol Helicopter to Sheriff Perry, come in?"

"Perry here. Go ahead, Patrol."

"Looks like it burned right up to the barn, and then turned south. The house is okay, too. Don't see anyone on the ground. The back road is clear. You can enter the property from that direction. The fire turned toward the river. Got two crews headed that way. Over?"

"10-4, Patrol. Perry out."

"Pull your vehicle off the road. We'll look for Denny." Perry said.

Heavy smoke hung in the air of the thick woods. He drove slowly over the rutted dirt road. When the vehicle emerged from the woods behind the barn, Madison gasped. She leaped from her seat and ran toward the dog pens.

"Wait, Madison. The ground is hot. I'm wearing boots; you get back here," Perry ordered.

Madison stopped in her tracks and spun around. "Then hurry. See if they're there."

Perry walked at a quick pace and disappeared into the barn. In a few moments, he came out. "Nobody's in there, not a dog one."

Madison looked toward the house. "Denny!" She called.

Rick reached inside the car and sounded the horn. There was no response.

"She probably led them into the woods, away from the flames. She won't let those dogs get hurt," Perry said.

"The Suburban is gone; she must have loaded them up and driven out." Madison looked to the Sheriff. "Can you contact the Johnson City fire department? Maybe she got out on that side."

"Sheriff Perry to Johnson City fire department, come in?" There was no response. Perry tried again. There was still no reply on the radio. "I say we head back the way we came. She's out, that's obvious."

"We should leave her a note," Rick said.

"There's a tablet in the glove box, I think," Perry said.

Madison yelled, "The workshop is gone! It's burned to the ground."

"Stay here, Madison." Perry walked toward the site where the workshop had been.

Rick moved up the steps of the house. Immediately after he opened the door, he yelled, "Wait a minute, Perry! The house is splashed with kerosene!

Perry said "Get in the car both of you. It left a crater where the workshop was!"

Perry grabbed for the radio mike. "SO this is Perry. Franks, come in."

"Right here, Sheriff." Franks replied immediately.

"Contact Johnson City fire department. I can't raise them on the radio. Get a cleanup crew in route to the Denson farm. Over?"

"If it's about that strange goop, Dr. Baker says stay away until her team arrives. Over?"

"What goop?" Perry slammed on the brakes.

"I forgot," Rick said. "It was something Madison found in the lower level of that workshop. I sent the sample to Baker's lab."

"It's my fault; I thought the dogs might have gotten into it through the coal chute, so I boarded it up. It stunk awful. Probably some kind of furniture stripper."

"Do you know how toxic that chemical can be?" Perry wheeled around looking at her in the back seat.

"Yes, that's why I thought it might be what made the dogs sick." Madison lowered her head.

"Sheriff," Franks called on the radio. "Are you there? Did you hear me?"

"Understood. Perry out. The house is doused with kerosene.!"

Rick looked at Madison with a sense of urgency. "Perry, wait a minute."

"Sorry, Rick. I should have told you where it came from," Madison whispered.

"This is my fault. Madison had no idea what she was dealing with. You've had your plate full, Sheriff," Rick said.

"We'll talk later, Agent Malone. Right now, we need to locate Denny and the dogs." He picked up the mike and called Deputy Franks again. "Any sign of Dr. Denson yet?"

"No, not a word. Forestry's helicopter is checking the back roads. The fire is out. Over?"

"Perry out." He put the mike back on its hook.

"I was on the demolition team in the service. I can take care of that fuel. Denny must have some incriminating evidence in that house. We need to preserve the scene before someone else comes along and blows it." Rick opened his door.

Perry stepped from the vehicle. "Sure you want to do that?"

Rick didn't answer; he sprinted to the house.

"It was my fault, Sheriff. I wanted to find out about that stuff myself."

"You know this implicates your aunt."

"Yes, Sheriff! I suspected her when her office burned."

"Mariah, the Melungeon, had a limp, and Denny was the last person to see her."

"You've been holding out on me, Madison. I could arrest you. And that might be the safest way to handle you."

"You don't have anything; besides, Judge Cupp will never let you hold me."

"Will you give me your word that you will stay out of my business and let me do my job?"

She nodded. Rick came around the back of the house. He carried three sticks of dynamite minus the fuses. "I poured baking soda in the kerosene; that way it won't ignite. You need to get someone out here to padlock the doors and clean up the accelerant. Unless you want to search it now?"

"No, we're getting Madison out of here. I might lock *her* up, for her own good."

"Lotta good that'll do. She knows her way out." Rick laughed.

There was silence until the sheriff's car stopped next to Rick's SUV.

"Rick, you're with me. Madison, go home and stay there! Don't say anything to anyone until you hear from me. Call my cell if you hear from Denny. Understand?" He stared at her in his rearview mirror. "I mean what I say!"

Madison nodded and then opened the door. She got in Rick's vehicle and drove back to town. She felt hurt knowing something was amiss on Denny's property. What was going on right under her nose? *Worse still, what does Denny know?* Had she put the clock there to destroy the evidence? Was Denny the one who killed those women? Why else would she have their identifications?

Madison's heart flip-flopped as she realized, *Tina didn't leave town; I just knew she didn't.*

She pulled into the parking lot next to the restaurant and then she went inside to report to her folks. Bud jumped up and spun in circles, showing he was happy to see her. The smoke from the fire had run the customers away, so Jess mopped the main dining room.

"Hey, what did you find out?"

"I'm afraid to even think what's going on. The fire destroyed the Denson woodworking shop. Denny's house and the barn are okay. I guess Denny loaded all the dogs up in the Suburban. There was no sign of any of them."

"What? Did I hear you say the workshop at Denny's burned?" Shirley shoved the swinging door open and stepped into the dining room.

Madison slumped down on one of the stools and put her head on the counter. "I don't know where Denny is. Can't get her on her cell phone. Oh, this is a mess." Madison's voice cracked.

Jess put the mop against a chair and wrapped his arms around her shoulders. "This isn't your problem. That old shop wasn't worth anything. Denny will probably be glad to have that eyesore off the property."

"That's right, listen to your daddy—" Shirley caught her breath. "I mean, Jess knows what he's talking about. There's nothing to fret over. You're just tired. Why don't you go to the house, get a shower and take a nap? You smell like smoke."

"I know, and I could use some sleep." Madison turned to Jess and hugged the tall man.

Shirley walked to the door with her. "If we hear from Denny, I'll let you know. Go on, now, and stop worrying about everybody so much. Take care of *you* for a change."

"I feel that Denny is dangerous. She might have burned her office, and tried to burn her house. Don't let her near you. Don't talk to her if she calls." Madison walked out the door. "And I didn't tell you this!"

Jess called after her. "I'll be over in a minute and bring you something." He went back inside. Madison called Sam, Denny's friend in Alaska.

"Hello, Sam. It's Madison McKenzie."

"Hey Madison, how are you?"

"Fine. I need to know if Aunt Denny talked to you about coming up there recently." She waited for a few seconds. "Are you there, Sam?"

"Yes. She shipped her dogs up this week. Says she wants to train the young ones since we still have so much snow. I'm not sure when she'll be here."

"I need to talk to her. If she comes to you or talks to you, tell her to call me, and *only* me. Okay?"

"What's wrong? She didn't lose another dog, did she?" Sam asked.

"No, there was a fire. The house and barn are fine, but the woodworking shop burned. I want to be the one to tell her. Okay?"

"I understand."

"Thanks, Sam. Keep in touch, will you?"

"I will."

"Bye Sam."

Madison took her cell and house phones with her when she went to shower. There were no calls. She dried her hair and dressed, then she lay on the sofa. Bud lay on the braided rug in front of Madison. She reached down to pet him.

"Let's take a nap, boy."

Bud stretched his legs and then curled into a ball, ready to sleep.

A knock at the door roused her. It was Jess carrying a paper bag.

"Come in, if that's food." She grinned.

"Glad to hear you're hungry."

"Thanks, Jess. You're a dear." She opened the bag and unwrapped a whole-wheat toasted sandwich with turkey slices, fresh tomatoes, and spinach. "My favorite."

"We need to talk. I ran into Jack Kelly at the hardware store, and he said he'd picked you and Bud up down by South Indian Creek. He said you were wet like you'd fallen in." Jess glared.

Madison dropped her head and inhaled deeply. "I should have told you. But things have been hectic."

"What's that about, Madison?"

"Sheriff Perry gave me permission to read some files in the basement of the jail. He's overworked, and can't do his job up on the mountain by day and read through cold case files all night."

"I agree, but why you?" Jess asked.

"I wanted to help, and to read the file on my mother."

"Well, did you find out anything helpful?"

"My hooded jacket. So I can only assume whoever broke into your house put it there. That's when it went missing. I got locked in. I found a tunnel under the jail, a tunnel that leads into a cave. The water from the cave runs out like a geyser, just like you told me when I was a little girl."

"You found it?" Jess was shaken, but not surprised.

"So you believe me?" She studied his face. "You know about the tunnel."

Jess nodded.

Madison saw that it upset him. "I'm okay. It was actually kind of a cool experience."

"Have you mentioned this to anyone else?"

"Not the way out. But the sheriff knows about the tunnel."

"Maybe he's too busy to explore it. Let's hope so." Jess stood. "Don't tell anyone. I'll explain this all later." And then he left.

Jess wasn't surprised. How would he know of the cave and the water if he hadn't seen it, or knew someone who'd been through it? Did someone else escape from that awful cell? Someone he knew a long time ago?

CHAPTER 27

Madison didn't have to look at the clock to know she'd slept all afternoon. The sun had set, and darkness loomed around her. Damp evening air filtered through the screens, so she pulled her windows down and locked them.

I'm hungry. She surveyed the contents of the refrigerator. Before long, she'd fried a pound of bacon, a skillet of hash browns made from leftover baked potatoes, and a half dozen scrambled eggs with cheese. She poured a glass of milk and sat at the table.

There was a slight knock at the door. The way Bud reacted, it had to be Rick. She opened it and was surprised to see Sheriff Perry.

"Sheriff, come in."

"You just opened the door without checking to see who's out here." He stood with hands propped on his hips.

"Only because of the way Bud reacted, I knew it had to be someone he likes."

"You've got a point. Smells good, what are you doing?" The sheriff stepped into the living room.

"Are you hungry?" She asked.

"No, that's okay. I want to apologize for being so sharp earlier."

"Aw, don't worry. We're all a bit testy, with all that's happened. I was just sitting down to eat, and I made plenty. Won't you join me?"

He looked at the pile of bacon. "Would Bud hate me if I had some of that?"

"No, there's plenty." She got another plate from the cabinet and poured a second glass of milk. "Whole wheat or white?" She asked.

His forehead wrinkled.

"Toast?"

"Oh! Wheat, thanks." He spied a ripe tomato sitting on the windowsill above the sink. "Mind if I slice that tomato?"

"Help yourself. Say, that *would* be good with the bacon. You want lettuce?" Madison started to get up.

"No, just the tomato is fine. Thanks. With the restaurant closing early, I didn't think I'd get supper tonight."

"Yeah, I guess the fire scared folks away." Madison took a couple slices of bacon and passed the plate. "About the fire—do you think she did it?"

Perry didn't look at Madison. "Are you sure you can't contact Denny?"

"I tried both numbers; she's not answering anything."

"I have questions for her." Perry finally looked Madison in the eye.

She felt a sting in her gut. "So do I!"

"This is between your aunt and me. Don't even go there."

Madison returned attention to her plate, not feeling so hungry now. Should she confess all she suspected? Would now be the time to come clean with the sheriff? Had Rick disclosed the DNA results?

Madison picked up her milk and drank it. "I have some great peanut butter cookies. You want one?"

"No, thanks. This is good. Thanks for allowing me to barge in on you. You aren't eating. What's the matter?"

"Full of milk." Madison patted her tummy. "You know Shirley deeded this land and cottage to me, right?"

He nodded, still chewing.

"The jail property only goes out fifty feet. After that, my line runs all the way to the top of the ridge."

He nodded again.

"That means the cave is under my property."

"Yeah, we all knew that," he said.

"Not the small one; I mean the big one." She paused.

"You're saying there really is a cave at the end of that tunnel?"

"I told you already! Do you think I'd lie about a thing like that?" Madison leaned forward.

"No; this area is full of mines and tunnels. What makes you think it isn't just another played-out silver mine?" Perry sat up straight.

"This is not manmade. There are rooms; maybe it's even a cavern. I didn't see any stalactites or columns, though, so it has to be a cave. You do know the difference?"

"Not really. But I'm sure you're going to educate me." Perry grinned.

"A cave is just an underground room; a cavern has formations, stalactites and stalagmites and columns. Just between you and me, Jess wasn't surprised when I told him about it."

Perry's eyes narrowed. "What did he say?"

"He asked me not to talk about it to anyone else. His first comment was, 'You found it?' and then he said, 'you found your way out?'"

"Jess knows more about this town than he lets on. I'm going to have to investigate it for myself."

"Not without me." Madison stood abruptly. "And don't tell anyone!"

"I won't. It could be dangerous; you shouldn't go back in there."

"I own the property. You can't stop me."

Perry grinned again.

Madison felt as if she'd won another battle. "You have heard the legend of the Lost Silver Mine of Unaka, haven't you?" she asked.

He nodded, his grin shifting to a laugh.

"Don't laugh. I've heard talk of it all my life. Some old fellow in Erwin knew where it was. He'd slip out of town once in a while, and always returned with silver."

"I talked to a guy who found gold in Cosby, near Gatlinburg. I read about him online and called him. He really believes there is ore in these mountains."

Perry said"I suppose the cave, if that's what it is, could have had silver at one time. But why abandon it?"

"He probably died. That was a long time ago. Others have written about clues they learned from family members. Just look where it is. Hard to believe, but it's right here under our feet. That's why no one else found it."

Perry finished his sandwich quietly, as though processing the conversation.

"Have some more bacon. Bud won't get any of it, I promise!"

"I thought I'd better save a few strips for Rick. He'll be by in a few minutes. He went to shower. I was supposed to tell you he's on his way."

"Okay. I was just about to ask where he was."

Bud stood from his sprawled position on the hardwood floor and walked to the door. Then they heard a knock.

"Come in, Rick. Bud has already announced your arrival." Madison laughed.

"Nobody will sneak up on those ears." Rick scratched Bud's head. "You're still here, Sheriff. I thought you'd be with Nell by now."

"Madison made a tempting offer. You can't blame me for staying, can you?" He waved his hand toward the display of food. "You're lucky I saved you a bite."

"Gee, thanks. I'd hate to go hungry tonight." Rick winked. "I knew I could count on Madison."

"Don't be so sure!" she said.

"Well, I can see it's time for me to hit the road." Perry stood, carried his plate to the sink, and said, "Thanks, I appreciate the handout."

"Don't leave." Madison spun around. "We three need to talk. Besides, Nell went back to Knoxville this afternoon. The things I have to say don't need to be said in front of her. Like it or not, I'm in the middle of this mess, but she doesn't have to be."

Sheriff Perry furrowed his brow and leaned against the counter. He looked toward Rick then back to Madison. "This sounds serious."

"It is." Madison offered tea or milk to Rick.

He sat down and studied the food. "Milk sounds good, for a change."

She poured a tall glass and set it in front of Rick. Then she got the cookies out and put them on the table, too. "Just in case you have a sweet tooth."

"Okay, thanks." Rick raked the bacon onto the remainder of scrambled eggs and hash brown potatoes. He dropped a couple slices of toast in the toaster, and topped it off with the last tomato slice, making one fat sandwich. "This is the way to clean the plates. Okay, I'm all ears."

Perry returned to the table and sat down.

Madison leaned on the sink. "I've wanted to talk to you about some things. Like that room below the basement at the jail."

Perry laughed. "Somehow I knew you'd get 'round to that. This is the way my deputy explained it: The old jail was built over a mineshaft in the eighteen hundreds. That way, if a prisoner was loud or drunk, the townspeople didn't have to listen to him bellow all night. The holding cells were all in the basement. When Franks' grandfather became sheriff, he added new offices and moved the cells above ground, like they are now. He wasn't much at keeping paperwork, so he mostly just threw it down the steps; once or twice he filed them in a strongbox from the old stage. Then Sheriff Franks converted the unfinished basement into the finished file room. We added the file cabinets when I was his deputy. Franks knew where the key was and never thought to mention it to me."

Rick spoke up. "If Deputy Franks' grandfather and dad were sheriffs, why didn't Franks run for the office?"

"Franks is nearly ten years younger than me. He didn't have the experience necessary, so I ran for office after his dad got too sick."

"Besides, Franks is too stupid to be sheriff," Madison added.

"That wasn't nice," Rick said.

"Maybe not, but she's right." Perry grinned. "I can't put my finger on it, but Franks has a dark side. It may just be because I know he was cruel to animals when he was a boy. There's just something about him."

"Yeah, just ask Bud. He can't stand Franks," she said.

"I've noticed. Wonder why?" Rick took a long drink of milk.

"Animals know about people. They sense when someone is shady, you know?" Madison started stacking the empty bowls.

"Don't touch these dishes." Rick caught her hand.

"Okay." She put her hands in her lap and watched Rick clear the table. He filled the sink with hot water and put the few plates and bowls in. He squirted detergent in, and then wiped the stove. In a few minutes he had the kitchen clean and everything put away. "Now, do either of you want a cookie?" he asked.

"Sure, why not?" Perry answered.

Madison shook her head. "Okay, now back to the powwow. I talked to Sam, Denny's friend and guide, who lives in Alaska. He said Denny shipped her dogs out this week and she's going to Alaska to work her team. She didn't tell him when she arrives."

Rick and the sheriff looked at each other.

"You've already thought it, why look so surprised?" she asked.

"I didn't think you'd considered that Dr. Denson was behind both fires," Perry answered.

"It's hard to believe, but when I learned of her personality disorder, ideas ran rampant. I lay many nights awake, just entertaining thoughts of what might be, now that I've learned so much that was hidden." Madison sat forward leaning her elbows on the table. "Denny lied to me about her brother's death; she might have even killed him herself. The sheriff covered it up because they were more than friends. She got pregnant in college; Sheriff Franks might have been the daddy. Anyway, he paid for an abortion."

"And you learned this how?" Perry stared at Madison.

"Old man Franks told me most of it." She leaned back in her chair, "Her roommate told me the rest. I planned to confront my so-called aunt!" She looked at Rick. "Did you tell him?"

Rick took a cookie. "No, I was leaving that up to you."

Again the two men looked at each other.

"According to the DNA test, Denny and I aren't even related." Madison's voice was low and the sheriff leaned in closer.

"What? How's that possible?"

"Danny Denson was not her real father." Rick put his hand on her arm.

Sheriff Perry's eyes locked on Rick. "You have a theory?"

Rick nodded. "I can't prove it yet."

"So, you can't let Denny get away. If she lands in Alaska, you'll never find her." Madison stood. "I researched and discovered Asheville has a large cargo operation, and it ships animals—specifically, sled dogs."

The three talked late into the night. Rick and Sheriff Perry left after midnight, sworn to secrecy. Madison went to bed, relieved that she had aired her feelings.

There was no disputing that Denny was worthy of suspicion. But how could she prove anything? Could Denny's house have the answers?

Whoever set the fire intended everything to burn. She needed to get in there and look for herself. The secrets to unraveling her mysterious life might still be hidden somewhere behind those walls. Madison's untapped character grew stronger with each battle. Feelings of confidence that she enjoyed and determination pulled from within guided her every decision. Like spring blossoms, a new Madison evolved; emerging like the seventeen-year cicadas, her voice will be heard.

Chapter 28

Shirley rested on a stool while Betty served customers. Jess, caught up with grill orders, sat beside his wife when Madison came into the restaurant the next morning.

"That Dr. Baker is pretty smart," Jess said. "She figured out the first bones were buried before 1983. That narrows it down."

Madison poured her own coffee. *That's odd; Rick didn't mention it last night.*

"All they have to do is match the bones to women missing around that time."

"Who did you hear that from, Willy?" Madison asked.

Shirley patted the stool next to her. "He told everyone in the restaurant a few minutes ago. Says there was a fire on the mountain fall of 1983. One skeleton showed traces from intense heat. None of the others had those markings."

Madison sipped her coffee while staring out the window, but did not move to sit down. *I'd love to tell them, but I'll keep my word. My whole life has been a lie. Is there anyone I can trust?*

Just then Rick came through the swinging doors. "Family meeting?"

Jess commented, "I hear Dr. Baker practically broke the case wide open."

"Hardly." He looked toward Madison.

She walked into the kitchen saying, "Got a minute?"

"Sure, what's up?"

She moved in the direction of the back door. "Walk with me?"

When they were by the creek she said, "Rick, Franks told everyone that the first bones were buried before the fire of '83."

Rick stared into the water. "Don't worry, Perry only tells Franks what he *wants* him to know. He's keeping a tight lid on the information you discovered yesterday." They walked along the creek bank for a while. "I'm going to meet Dr. Baker about the DNA. I'd like you to come along."

Madison didn't look at him; she kept walking. "I promised Nell I'd come to Knoxville."

"That's probably for the best, Madison. I'm doing all I can. Trust me."

"I want to take the shooting class where Nell took hers. It's an indoor course. I think I'll feel safer knowing how to shoot, and then get my own pistol. What do you think of that?"

Rick stopped. "That's the smartest thing I've heard you say since we met. It's a great idea."

"I do have a good idea every now and then. I expected you to try and talk me out of it."

"I can surprise you sometimes, too. Call me from Nell's?" Rick asked.

"Okay." They walked back toward Shirley's.

As soon as Rick pulled away, Madison crossed the street, got Bud from the cottage, and left in the Blazer headed to Denny's place.

A Unicoi County Sheriff's Department car sat in the drive. Madison parked and got out, leaving Bud in the car. She walked all the way around the house looking for the deputy. She crossed to the barn and called out. No one answered, so she went inside to have a look.

The dog pens were clean and empty. Denny had been careful not to leave a mess. The tack room displayed harnesses and leashes, and the first sled she'd run the Iditarod, now old style and heavy, hung on the wall like a trophy. Below the sled sat an old wooden trunk with a padlock. Madison looked for something strong enough to pry the lock off. She found a small hatchet and swung it at the rusty lock. At second blow and the old metal broke into two pieces, and clattered across the concrete floor.

The groan of aged hinges mimicked Halloween sounds as she lifted its lid. Blankets that had not seen the light of day in a decade sent up an odor that could rouse the dead. Madison choked and turned away. She stood to increase the distance between her sensitive nose and the reek of the blankets.

She went to a room where fresh straw bales were stacked. There she retrieved a pitchfork and returned to scoop out the offending wool.

"Why would she keep these stinky blankets?" Madison looked up when she heard Bud's toenails tapping on the floor behind her. "How'd you get out?"

Bud wriggled all over and licked her hand.

"I let him out so he'd lead me to you." A familiar voice said.

"Oh, hey, Bobby. I looked for you when we drove up."

"I took a walk into the woods for a—," he cleared his throat.

Madison leaned on the pitchfork.

"You're not supposed to be in here. The sheriff gave me strict orders," Bobby said.

"I'm sorry. I knew the house was off limits. But the sheriff didn't mention the barn." Madison smiled.

"I'm really sorry, but I can't allow you in here."

"I understand."

"I've gotta do a radio check. You'd better leave," he warned.

"Sure. I'll see you another time," Madison said. "I'll just put this pitchfork back, and be right out there."

As soon as he left, she quickly dumped the trunk, spilling out the rest of the blankets. Underneath she discovered a stack of envelopes and some medicine bottles. She stuffed the envelopes into her shirt and the bottles in the pocket of her jacket before she walked out to the car and drove away. She stopped where dense woods blocked the view from the back of the house.

"Stay, Bud!" She hooked his harness to the seatbelt and left the windows down for fresh air. She remembered that the window in Denny's bathroom didn't lock. She had a way in; she only needed to stay out of Bobby's sight.

Quiet as a doe, she crept to the back of Denny's house. As luck would have it, the bathroom window was open. She removed the screen and pulled her weight upward until she sat on the windowsill. Then she swiveled around and dropped to the floor. She avoided windows as she crept carefully to the bedroom so Bobby didn't see her moving through the house.

Common sense told her Denny might have left items out, if she intended for the house to burn. She searched the walls of the closet for a door or secret compartment. She didn't exactly expect to find one, but that's the way they do it in movies. She found nothing.

Next, she slipped into the hall and down to the bathroom. The linen closet had shallow shelves from ceiling to floor, with no door. On the floor, she noticed scuff marks but couldn't recall anything ever sitting in front of the shelves. This made her curious.

She examined the scuffs, which moved from right to left in a half-circle. She was able to fit her fingers between the shelving framework and the wall. Instantly she felt it give, and pulled the shelf toward her like a door.

Behind, she followed stairs to the basement. Her hand slid along the wall, searching for a light switch. When she touched it, she recognized it as the old rotary type, which Jess took out of the cottage a few years back. It was a raised circle, with two buttons in the middle. She pushed the bottom one, and lights came on below her.

A series of three bulbs burned overhead, spaced about ten feet apart with no globes. They illuminated the basement well. She saw dust-covered boxes and totes, obviously newer, all stacked neatly along one side of the room.

She moved to a filing cabinet, the contents of which were strewn about as if one drawer had been rifled through. In the jumbled mess still in the drawer, she read headings that appeared to be from an attorney, addressed to Tina and Danny. They held nothing suspicious, just legal matters referring to the estate of the Senior Daniel Denson. She read until she came to one from a different attorney, addressed only to Tina. She stuffed it into her pocket.

Another drawer held Denny's personal records. She saw medical bills, lab test results, and finally a statement from Smokey Mountain Rehab Facility. That one also went into her pocket.

She walked into the furthermost corner of the basement to examine a heavy wood table. There were dark stains on the top, and a chop-block with a cleaver. Around the edge of the cleaver's handle there were more stains that looked like dried blood. The hair on the back of her neck stood up.

I have to tell the sheriff about this. He's the one who needs to investigate this room!

She slipped up the stairs, careful to turn out the lights. She replaced the shelf-door. *If I tell him, he'll know I went against his orders and snooped unless I just tell him there used to be a basement.*

Back at her car she found Bud undisturbed. "Did you take a nap?" She rubbed his head as she climbed into the seat.

CHAPTER 29

Madison stopped by the restaurant. Jess was talking with a man she didn't recognize. She called the sheriff while she waited.

"I'm checking in so you'll know where I'll be." She listened as he barked orders to someone in the background.

"Sorry, what now?" Perry asked.

"I'm heading to Knoxville in a while. I thought of something Holly told me. She said Denny's house has a basement, but I never knew of one. You might want to look closer for yourself. According to the original floor plan, the old house had a second set of stairs between the kitchen and the hall bathroom."

"You've been to the courthouse?" Perry sounded irritated.

"No, just to my computer. You're so behind the times, Sheriff." She laughed, hoping he wouldn't suspect that she'd been out to the property.

"Rick and I are leaving now, heading to Asheville. When we return we'll stop at Denny's. If there is a hidden basement, we'll find it. Thanks for telling me. I've gotta go."

Madison said, "Yes, me too. Goodbye." Putting her phone in her pocket reminded her of the papers she had taken.

Jess joined her then, so she quickly stuffed them back into the pocket. "Where's Shirley?"

"She went home to rest. She isn't feeling well this week." Jess returned to the grill, and Madison followed him into the kitchen.

"I'm going to Nell's in Knoxville" she said.

"Be careful; I don't like you going alone."

"Bud will be with me." She laughed and went out the back door.

Meanwhile, Rick and Sheriff Perry drove onto the grounds of the VA in Asheville. Old Sheriff Franks wasn't in his room, so they made their way to the dining area. Not finding him there, they stopped by the nurses' station to inquire as to his whereabouts.

Nurse Paige, they read on her lapel, explained. "Mr. Franks is in the intensive care unit by the emergency entrance."

Perry and Rick exchanged looks.

"Thank you," Perry said, and they left the building.

"The ER is in that direction."

"Yep, just down that hill," Rick said.

An ICU nurse informed them that the patient had not regained consciousness.

"What happened?" Perry asked as he showed his ID.

"Possibly his heart; we don't have the lab results yet," she said.

"Can we see him?" Rick asked.

She led the way down a maze of halls to a frail figure with tubes and wires attached to him.

"Five minutes, no more. Doctors' orders."

"Thank you." Perry stepped closer to the old man.

At that moment, a doctor walked into the area with a chart in his hand. Perry introduced himself and inquired about the old man's condition.

The doctor studied the chart for a moment. "Ah, yes. Here are the lab results: poisoned." He looked up. "The man has never had heart trouble. I knew it was something else."

"Have you reported this?" Rick asked.

"Just got the results. So if you'll excuse me, I'll make that call." He walked away.

Rick and Perry looked at each other. "Denny." They said at the same time.

Madison combed through the papers from the lawyer and the rehab center. Her thoughts returned to Sam's comment: "She's shipping her dogs and then she'll arrive later in the week."

Perry can't find her. She'll get away; I know she will. I might be the only person who can reason with her. And now, thanks to the information I just read, I know what happened. She grabbed her phone, talked a few minutes, made notes on a tablet, and made another call.

She petted Bud's head while she laughed and talked.

"You're confused. I can tell." Madison hugged her dog and held him close until he wiggled away. "I have to go, Bud. I'll see if you can stay with Holly." She made one more phone call.

Jess answered his phone, sounding as though he was out of breath. "Madison, I'm glad you called. I called an ambulance for Shirley. They're on the way to Johnson City Med Center. Betty will close down the restaurant. I'm going to the hospital. I'll call you after I see her doctor."

"What happened?" Madison asked.

"Maybe a heart attack. She's been out of breath lately." Jess slammed the truck door.

"I'd noticed." Madison felt tears welling up.

"Honey, I'll call you as soon as I have news."

"I'll help Betty at the restaurant." She disconnected the call.

Madison dressed in jeans and a hooded sweatshirt after throwing some clothes in her suitcase. She lay across her bed, waiting for Jess to call. She dozed off, but her phone woke her. *Jess* showed on the caller ID. "What did you find out?" She asked.

"She's okay; not a heart attack. But they'll have to repair a blocked artery. Thank God, there's only one that's bad. I'm almost home. I left her reading her instructions." Jess sounded as if a weight had been lifted. "I'll go back early in the morning when they do the stint."

"Oh, that's good news. How do you plan to make her eat right?" Madison laughed.

"Take her away from the food." Jess sounded serious. "We need a vacation, so I've come up with a plan that we agree on."

"A plan? You don't mean close down the restaurant?!" She shouted.

"No, but let someone else work it." He answered.

"Ben and Margie? That's a great idea. Have you talked to them yet?"

"No, but I'll see Ben as soon as I get back. We'll have some details to work out. I think it's time." Jess drew in a breath. "When will you be home?"

"Jess, Denny's run off to Alaska, and I'm going after her. So many things have happened that I can't explain, and she's the only person who can answer my questions. Maybe she's running from the law, but maybe she's just running scared. I have to talk to her.

"You do what you feel you have to. Just stay safe."

"I will."

"I'm pulling in the driveway now. Talk to me before you leave."

Madison called Holly next. "I changed my mind about taking Bud to Knoxville. I'd feel better if he could stay at the farm with you, if Henry doesn't mind?"

Holly squealed, "We talked just this morning about getting a dog. I'm excited!"

"If you're sure, then I'll bring him out after I drop by to see Jess. I have some news to tell you, too."

I can't wait to see her face when I tell Holly Momma and Daddy are going on a vacation.

Madison put the phone down and went to the kitchen for Bud's water and food bowls, and got a bag of dog food from the cupboard.

"Okay, Bud. You'll stay with Holly, and you better be good. We want her to have someone for you to play with." She rubbed her hand along Bud's neck.

After a brief visit with Jess, Madison and Bud rode out to the Jacobs Farm. Holly and Henry met them at the steps. Madison got Bud's things from the back seat and turned to Henry.

"Are you sure this is okay, Henry? He'll sleep on the porch. He likes to be outside."

"Nonsense, he can sleep in our room. I've already fixed his bed." Henry whistled for Bud.

"I had an old laundry basket made of straw. Henry got a quilt he used when he was a boy and put it in the basket. And then he put a pillow on top of that." Holly clasped her hands together. "Come in and see, Madison. It's a perfect bed for Buddy."

Madison stayed with Bud as long as she could, but she didn't want to be late checking in with Nell. She felt lonely driving the two hours to Knoxville in the dark. She'd booked a flight out later this evening, with only one stopover in Atlanta. She'd arrive in Anchorage mid-morning tomorrow, so she'd catch up on her sleep on the plane.

If anyone was going to find Denny, it was Sam. With his help, this might be the only way to confirm what Madison feared. *Denny might not be the lone killer, but she certainly had the means to dismember and bury the bodies. Denny won't give up; she'll die first. I have to talk to her before that has a chance to unfold.*

CHAPTER 30

Madison shifted in her seat, allowing a better view of the snow-covered mountains below. Her finger traced the flow of a glacier on the window. The approach to Anchorage was breathtaking, but the inevitable landing spoiled her joy. She really hated landings: the fear of falling, the ground coming up at you, and your total lack of control over the end result. Landings caused an anxious dread in her gut that she could not overlook.

When the captain banked for final approach, she closed her eyes and sunk into the upholstery. Her stomach rose to her throat. She pulled the shade down to block the outside world zooming past.

The captain announced they were ahead of schedule. Sam had been surprised by her phone call, but insisted on meeting her at the airport. She wondered how he'd react when she told him the purpose of her visit.

I feel as if I know Sam, after all the years with Denny talking about their experiences together; he's no stranger to me, not really, but what can I expect in the way of cooperation or information? Will he protect her, even after I tell him all she's accused of?

Her thoughts distracted her sufficiently. The Boeing 767-300 had taxied to the ramp and stopped before she realized the flight had ended. Her heart still in her throat, she waited for most of the passengers to disembark before she stood up. Had she really thought this through? She didn't have an inkling of where to begin, now that she was here.

She followed the remaining passengers through the sky bridge connecting the plane to the terminal. Her body moved without her willing it to, silently and methodically making its way to who knows where. The knot in her throat was growing; the sick feeling didn't go away when she reached the firm footing of the building. Her legs swayed when she stood and gazed at the crowded room. So many hours in the air had given her sea legs; she hoped this would stop soon. Maybe that's why she felt uneasy.

Who am I kidding? I shouldn't even be here. Her world had changed so fast in the past few weeks. Was this the last remnants of Mousey Maddy, coming up inside her? *No, you're gone; I won't allow it. This is my world now, one of my choosing, of my ideas; you're dead to me!*

Sam elected to meet her at the baggage claim area. She looked at all of the surrounding faces for an older man, knowing he was tall and attractive. Would he recognize her with the new hairstyle?

"Welcome to God's country!"

A handsome but young man wrapped his arms around her, lifting her off the floor in a bear hug. *Oh Lord, I think I'm going to vomit.*

"I'm happy you decided to come for a visit." Sam set her back on her feet.

"Sam, I know that voice, but the face is all wrong. You're young?" She spoke without thinking how the words sounded. "I mean, Denny always called you 'grumpy old Sam.'"

"I can be grumpy if that's what you like." He laughed with a broad smile. "First thing we're going to do is get some food in you. You're pale, and thinner than your picture. I approve of the new hair style—or is that a wig?"

"It's me! I got tired of my horse's tail."

"I see." Sam snatched her rolling suitcase.

"I'm sorry this is such short notice. But my life is in danger back in Cold Creek. Besides, I have to talk to Denny."

"Hey, I understand. Nobody will find you here! I'll see to that."

"Food sounds good." Madison smiled. "Thank you for meeting me, Sam. I really appreciate you."

Madison thought of how Denny had once described Sam: "*He's a guide who can take you bear hunting or fishing. He can teach you how to mush a dog team, and flies his own plane. He's in love with the outdoors and the friendliest man you'll ever meet.*" *And a lot younger looking than she led me to believe: she always referred to him as "the old man."* *Just one more of her lies: he doesn't look a day over forty.*

Sam picked up her bag and led her to his waiting truck. She took a deep breath of cool, clean air, much like the mountains of Tennessee in winter. *Sure am thankful he didn't choose to pick me up in his Super Cub. I'd have hurled for sure!*

By the time they reached the restaurant, Madison's insides had calmed and she really did feel hunger pangs.

Dining at the popular Sea Galley proved to be every bit the treat Denny had described after her last visit to Anchorage, right down to the huge polar bear staged behind glass at the entry. Madison enjoyed the grilled Copper Creek salmon, while Sam manhandled Alaskan king crab legs.

After some casual conversation, he asked. "This isn't a friendly visit, is it?" Sam stared straight into Madison's eyes. His dark gaze seemed to penetrate her mind.

She put her fork down, lifted her napkin to her mouth and swallowed carefully, thinking how to answer his challenge. Then she folded her arms across her chest, looking straight into Sam's stare. "No. My purpose for being here is not for fun." She took a sip from her water glass. "Has anyone asked you about Denny?"

"Yep, FBI. Wouldn't say why, but I guess I can fill in the blanks. She told me she'd had a fight with a man friend. He must have gotten the worst end of it."

"A fight?" She rolled her eyes. "Did she mention a name?"

"Nope, and I didn't ask. Not my business." Sam returned to his crab legs. "You won't find her if she's not expecting you."

"Can you help me find her?"

"Depends."

"I need answers, Sam. Answers only she can give." Madison leaned forward, elbows on the table. "Will you help me find her?"

"No." Sam's look was solemn. "If she's done something bad, she had a reason. If it doesn't involve you, you've got no right to pursue it."

"I've got the right!" She raised her voice. Sam reacted with a stiffened frown.

"And, she's done something very bad." Madison leaned back against the heavy wooden booth. "I'll find her, with or without your help. I understand. You're not involved, and she's your friend. I won't hold that against you."

Sam pushed his plate aside and leaned back in his seat. "How bad?"

"Murder, lying, deceit, take your pick. She's not the person we all perceived. Even I can't believe the monster she's turned out to be."

Sam motioned for the waitress. "Check please?" As she withdrew the bill from her pocket, he handed her a fifty and said, "Keep the change." Then he escorted Madison to the front door. "We can talk about this in the truck. We have an hour's drive to my place."

Neither Sam nor Madison spoke as they drove through Anchorage traffic and onto the Glenn Highway. Madison watched the road ahead, hoping to spot a moose. She noticed the sign reading *Give the moose a brake*, and it noted that 322 had been killed along the highway. She saw the Alaskan Railroad shared the flats with the highway and wondered aloud, "Do cars or trains hit more moose?"

"Cars, definitely: speeding along, no notice of nature's beauty. It's quite an impact when they meet, the car and the moose." Sam's focus never strayed from the road.

"I can only imagine." Madison shuddered.

After a while, she said, "I guess you've heard about the bones found near Cold Creek."

"I heard something on the news, didn't know it was in your area."

"Yep, in our backyard, the Appalachian Trail. I discovered the first skeleton."

"Really!" Sam whipped to look at his passenger. "How'd that work out for you?"

"It's been disastrous!" Madison filled him in on the harsh reality of her birthday, and all that had transpired since the onset of the nightmare regarding the dig.

When Sam's truck took the Palmer exit, he finally made a comment. "Geez, Gal, you've got my attention now."

He drove in silence the rest of the way. Madison watched to make sure she could find her way back out. The roads were simple, at least—there weren't that many.

They stopped in front of a large, rustic cabin. With a light brown tin roof. The exterior logs appeared a weathered gray, making the dwelling look old, but well built. Brightly-colored petunias and geraniums spilled over hanging pots on either side of the entrance, a heavy wood door sporting the carved 3-D image of a moose.

Madison's fingers traced the outline. "This is beautiful!"

"Thank you. That door was Dad's last big job. He was famous 'round here for his carvings. There isn't a house or business between here and Talkeetna without some form of his work." Sam's smile brightened his face. "I'll have to show you the life-size bear at the visitor's center. It's so real looking you'll swear he's breathing."

The inside of the house brought a hitch in Madison's breath. She gazed at the rustic but charming old-world interior, looking as though they'd stepped into another time. One wall, all glass, overlooked the valley below, providing a view of the Knick River near the Butte.

Madison stepped closer. "I bet this is amazing in winter. I mean, it's amazing now, but with all the snow, and the river... Oh, I'd love to see that!"

"Have a look around while I check my messages." He left the room.

Madison moved into the kitchen, to the right of the entry. She saw no modern conveniences, only the necessary elements: a wood cook stove, heavy wooden table and four chairs that looked to be homemade, and not much else. A counter along one wall held a bucket with dipper and a deep galvanized sink with a hand-pumped water supply. Below were hand-hewn doors with small bone pulls. A rough cedar shelf above a stacked-rock fireplace displayed matching pottery bowls and a cast iron Dutch oven. There was an Inuit-design rug on the floor under the table. Deep sky blues, brown, and tan patterns woven throughout the rug resembled bears, moose and wolves.

Sam came back and went straight for the coffee pot. "Grab a cup." He said.

She chose a cup and held it toward the pot of steaming liquid which was pitch black and strong smelling. "Smells like a Columbian brew." She inhaled deeply.

"No, just Alaska's winter brew. It's the kind that keeps you awake when the sun goes to bed and you still have things to do: the kind that makes the hairs stand up on your neck. You might not sleep for a week if you have a second cup."

Madison sipped and immediately coughed. "Got milk?" She asked.

"You wimp. It's in the fridge." An empty cup was sitting on the table, and he filled it for himself.

"Where's the fridge?" She scanned the room a second time.

Sam reached for a wooden door with a rope pull, at the end of the counter. It looked somewhat like a barn door, Madison thought. Inside was a 'wide-by-side' refrigerator/freezer.

"You don't think this house is *that* primitive, do you?" He laughed and stepped away, leaving the door open.

"Clever. What else is hiding around here?" Madison spotted a container of half & half, poured a couple splashes, stirred with her finger, and then quickly licked it.

"Come on in here." Sam walked to the next room. "There's the flat-screen TV and Bose radio." He pointed to a blank wall. Or was it?

She detected a couple of doors uniquely arranged into the rich wood-finished wall. A black leather sofa and a recliner faced the wall. Behind them were steps leading to the second floor. Rough-looking unfinished tables sat at both ends of the sofa. Small furs, maybe rabbit or fox, nicely shaped, smooth and clean looking, covered part of the tabletops. Real Native American artifacts, not the tourist shop variety, nestled on the furs. Above the sofa stretched a long shelf with an old muzzleloader mounted above it. The shelf held a powder horn and flask, along with yellowed photos of hunters with their trophies of bears, big-horned sheep, and a wolf.

She pointed to the weapon. "Do you use that?"

"Not so much now, but it was my favorite rifle 'til the day I got these scars." He pulled the neck of his shirt aside, revealing an ugly claw mark. "I was lucky, and haven't used it since." He patted the holster on his side. "This is more effective."

"Oh, my!" She clutched her own throat. "I'm surprised you didn't bleed to death."

"Didn't hit the jugular." He laughed. "He was a young one then; now he's eight feet tall, with an ugly attitude."

"The same bear?" She gasped.

"Heck yeah; he's only got one ear, makes him easy to recognize."

Madison thought Sam's smile showed a distinct satisfaction. "And I'll bet he's angry."

"Getting meaner every year," Sam said. "He's responsible for at least a couple of hikers' deaths. So far no one has been brave enough to track him down."

Sam settled into the recliner, sipped his coffee and motioned for Madison to take a seat on the sofa. "Let's hear the rest. You've got something up your sleeve. I want to know what your plans are."

"Just how close are you and Denny?" Madison asked.

"Let's get something clear. Denny and I aren't any closer than a client relationship. She came here to learn to mush a dog team. That's it, that's all. We don't have a personal relationship. She doesn't confide in me. If she talks, I listen; if not, I don't ask questions."

"Oh, I didn't mean to imply..." Madison said, flustered.

"I didn't take it that way. Doc and I became friends over the past ten, twelve years. I just mean she's very private. I'd like to know more about what's happened in Cold Creek."

Madison nodded, lost in the pain of thought. "I don't really have a plan. I don't know the truth from the lies. All my life, I believed her word as gospel. How can I be sure she isn't lying now? I came here looking for a beginning. Wherever I go from here is pretty much playing it by ear."

"So you don't know she's guilty of anything, except deception."

"Yeah, she's good with deception. She led me to believe you were an older, father-like figure." Madison's brows lifted.

"Really?" He grinned. "Denny's referring to the knowledge she learned from me."

"I have this theory." Madison settled back into the soft leather sofa and sipped her coffee. "It started with her brother, Danny. They argued, and she shoved him into the stripping vat. The sheriff covered for her because they were close—too close. That's probably what the argument was about."

"Why would the authority help her with a cover-up?" Sam stared at Madison.

"It was personal with them. He manipulated Denny for his own needs. I discovered an old jail cell below the basement of his office. Forensics confirmed blood and tissue from the cell, and they're trying to connect the DNA to the skeletons."

"No wonder you have questions," He pushed the footrest out and settled further into the recliner. "Please continue; this is interesting."

"I've done my own research; the law moved too slowly to suit me. I believe one of the skeletons is my birth mother." She fished out the two metal heart pieces on the chain under her shirt. "I found this half of a locket where Bud dug up the skull. I've had the other half all my life. They match."

"What does the law think of your theory?" Sam asked.

"They think I'm nuts. Denny's college roommate shared secrets with me; things that only Denny can answer."

"You told me Denny might not be your blood kin. Do you know the results yet?"

"No, but I have an idea. I'm keeping that under my hat for now."

"Denny's a fugitive from the law. But they didn't move quickly enough. I'm sure she got out of Tennessee with her dogs. I'm surprised she didn't contact you."

"Haven't heard from her, except that one time." Sam finished his coffee. "If she had nothing to hide, she'd have called. No, she's in the wind now."

"That's why I'm here. I want to hire your tracking services." She choked back tears. "I need your help, Sam. If she's done the things that I believe she has, she shouldn't get away with it."

"You've been busy, young lady. You need some rest; I'll show you to your room. We'll talk more later on. You look as though you haven't slept in weeks."

Madison smiled. "Maybe another cup of your coffee will give me a boost."

"No coffee. Rest." He retrieved her suitcase from near the front door. "In this house, my rules apply. You'll be ready for whatever is ahead *only* if you can use your head. First rule of survival: food and rest. No argument, young lady."

She followed her host to the guest room at the top of the stairs. The bed perched high above the oak floor, with a small step stool for easy entry. Walls of western cedar gave a warm glow and pleasing aroma. A white bearskin rug sprawled in front of the dormer window. Madison knelt, digging her fingers into the fur. "I always wondered what these felt like."

She gazed over the Knick River and Chugach Range, breathed in deeply, and then let out a long sigh. "This country is unbelievable: lush and beautiful in every direction. No wonder she came here to hide."

"Everything you'll need is in the bath, next door on the right. Make yourself at home."

Sam placed her bag on a stand next to a wingback chair, and then disappeared into the hallway.

Madison heard his boots on the stairs as she took in the ambiance of the room. There was a dressing table with a bench, a tall chest of drawers, a full-length mirror along one wall, and a cedar chest at the foot of the bed. "Thanks, Sam." She called out as she pushed the door closed.

The weight of her emotions brought her to the chair, strategically angled toward the window. She sat, mesmerized by views of enormous beauty. She noticed how the snow-covered peaks glistened in the afternoon sun. Blue-green streaks hinted of glaciers draping their gaps. The melt had begun early this year, swelling the river to swift and muddy, like her feelings welling up inside. Tears pooled in the corners of her eyes as her lids drooped.

CHAPTER 31

A tap at the door aroused Madison. She glanced at her watch. "Oh, my!" She gasped, seeing that the sky was still bright. It reminded her of the time difference. Her long legs took the steps two at a time, as she followed her nose to the kitchen.

Sam greeted her, saying, "Sorry to disturb you, but I didn't want you to sleep through supper." He dished up a bowl of stew. "Sit there."

She sat down where he had pointed, and her host sat across from her at the rugged table. "Your advice was right on. I needed to rest."

"Hope you like elk stew; a buddy of mine got it over on Kodiak."

"It smells good." Her senses awakened as she tasted it. "This is delicious."

Sam gave her a weather update. "Got a front moving in; might get snow tonight, so I need to split some firewood. It's always good to have plenty on hand."

Madison didn't look up from her stew as she said, "I'll help."

"You can come along, but don't plan on swinging an ax." His laughter filled the room.

"You'd better get used to the idea of me helping out. I'll clean up our dishes while you chop the wood, and *then* we can carry it in together." Madison stared at the robust man.

His face took on a puzzled expression. "You're certainly not the meek little whiff Denny talked about. Guess she lied to me, too."

"No doubt." she nodded, "Are you through?"

"Yeah, leave the dishes, I'll get 'em after while." He stood, six and a half feet of muscular man eyeing her. "Denny refers to you as a church mouse, and yet here you are, taking on Alaska—and now me. And all to confront the toughest woman I've ever met. You're no mouse. You're a tiger! Must be your Southern Appalachian roots. You gals have guts." He snatched a biscuit as he went out the door.

Madison felt her face burn. A *tiger, huh?* She plunged their bowls, utensils, and cups into the hot soapy water and returned to dip the remaining stew into a refrigerator storage container. The warm biscuits went into a zip-bag, left on the table to cool before she sealed it. Back to the sink for the bowls, quickly clean, rinsed and laid out on a towel to dry.

Stepping out the back door, Madison zipped her hooded sweatshirt to ward off the cool evening air. She marveled at how with one blow of the ax Sam split the largest of logs.

"Is it okay if I meet your dogs?" she asked.

"Sure, they love attention." Sam cracked the ax through another log.

As she approached, the alpha male stood, stretched his back legs, and wagged his tail. The other dogs stayed on the ground until they sensed a signal from the alpha, and then they all stood, gathering around the unfamiliar human. She spent a few minutes petting each one before she returned to where Sam loaded his arms with split wood.

"They're beautiful." She stooped to load her arms and followed Sam to the porch. She waited while he stacked the kindling and larger pieces in separate bins near the door.

"You really take good care of your dogs. I'm sure they love you tremendously."

"Love and a mutual respect."

Madison thought Sam's smile could melt an iceberg.

"We can visit some of the local sights, since we still have plenty of daylight." Sam brushed loose dirt off his shirt.

"Sure, I'd love to—but I don't want to interfere with your schedule."

"I don't have a schedule, really. I like spontaneous, you know?"

Madison's smile dropped from her face. "Spontaneous, I like that; compared to my life, which is more of a reflex. So many unpredictable events, espe-cially where Denny is concerned. She's like Jekyll and Hyde, lately. I don't know who she is anymore—or me either, for that matter."

"Madison, don't underestimate yourself. It doesn't matter what you were told growing up, you're the same amazing woman and no one can quench your spirit."

"Thank you, Sam." She breathed deeply and let out a sigh. "Over the years, through your calls to the dental office and all Denny said about you, I just knew you were the person I needed to turn to." Sam gave her a secure feeling.

Howling wind in the wee hours of the morning brought Madison to the window, where she watched a whiteout blocking the view. She dressed and rushed down the steps, nearly smacking into Sam.

"Good morning." He stepped to one side as she slid to a stop in stocking feet.

"Is it? I heard the wind."

"I fed the dogs and they were completely relaxed. So I guess it's going to stop soon. Nature's creatures know these things," he said and walked into the kitchen.

Madison stepped up to the blazing fireplace. "Have you had breakfast?"

"I waited for you," he said.

"I could eat a horse." She wrapped her arms around her thin shirt. "Coffee ready?"

"Are you kidding? I nearly drank it all waiting for you." He reached for the pot ,and poured her a fresh cup. "I even warmed the milk."

"Aw, you're a dear; thank you."

As soon as breakfast was over, Madison went upstairs to dress warmer. She dug new hiking boots out of her bag. Sam was outside by the time she was bun-dled up and tied in. The temperature had dropped from yesterday, and a stiff wind blew in her face.

"I had a hunting trip scheduled, but the wind is too strong for flying. They chose to drive: smart move."

"Now what will you do?" Madison felt guilty for hoping he'd spend time with her.

"Show you more of our local sights, I suppose." Sam leaned against a porch post.

Madison looked at the mountain. "So we can't go up at all today?"

"Maybe in the afternoon, if the wind dies down. Last time we talked, Denny asked about rules for Hatcher's pass."

"I saw on a map that's not too far from here." Madison rubbed her hands together.

"The pass is rough territory, not accessible by wheelers until later in the spring."

She lowered her head. Her heart sank. Everything was out of her control: the weather, the strange territory... She felt small and insignificant.

The next morning Madison was roused from a deep sleep by a hand on her arm. "What's wrong?"

"Nothing. I just couldn't wake you by knocking. Sorry I startled you." Sam disappeared out the door.

She pulled herself out of bed and stumbled to the shower, hoping the water would revive her. She looked through the small bottles of shampoo and chose a conditioning green apple scent, compliments of a fine hotel.

She dressed in jeans and sweatshirt, then tossed her hair while drying it with the blow dryer. Then she bounced downstairs, feeling hopeful but guarded.

"Sorry I overslept," she said.

Sam sipped from a large mug. "No worries. I thought you'd like to get an early start since we don't have any wind today."

"You mean we can fly? Why didn't you say so?"

"I've been up since five. I thought surely you'd wake before noon," Sam teased.

"What am I paying you for?" Madison threw a dishcloth at him.

"Okay, from now on, I'll roll you out in the floor when I get up."

"Deal!" Madison cringed, knowing he'd keep his word.

With breakfast behind them, she ran upstairs to grab her sunglasses. When she returned, Sam was ready. "The plane is tied down at the Palmer Airport, a twenty-minute drive."

They loaded a small pack each and climbed into the close interior. Madison was surprised the seating was tandem, but she had only flown in a 727. This was a Super Cub on wheel-skis. Sam explained that the wheels were down for hard surface landings, and could be cranked up to use skis on snow.

The taxiing was effortless. She couldn't help but grin, because she'd imagined it would feel bumpy. Their slow speed at liftoff caused her to wonder if they were actually flying, until the airport grew small below her window. Sam circled over his house, making a low pass. The dogs jumped up and barked, obviously familiar with the engine sound.

The view was endless, and Madison was so taken in she lost her sense of direction. Sam pointed to Hatcher's Pass. The long road looked short from the air.

Sam reduced their airspeed, flying lower as he scouted the valley. "You keep a watchful eye out the right side, and I'll watch the left." He shouted over the engine noise.

Madison couldn't help but look every which way. *Why did I dread flying in a small plane? I like this better than the big ones.*

She asked, "What am I looking for, some kind of tent?"

"It's called a wall tent, made for frigid temperatures: lightweight, easy to set up, even with just one person. They use wood-burning stoves for heat. It will be hard to spot in the snow because their canvas is often off white."

"Sounds simple enough. Guess I was expecting a teepee." Madison laughed.

"Just below that rock face, you can make out a square shape. That's an old abandoned gold mine. You usually can't see it this time of year."

Madison thought the mine didn't look like much from the air. She spotted the remnants of a wooden pipeline, which Sam explained had carried water down to the miners. Because the water in the mines was toxic, they had to pipe in fresh drinking water from further up the valley.

North of the rock face, the valley widened. A turquoise stream meandered like a snake through its center. Madison saw a beaver dam, but no humans or signs of a camp. The snow was mostly melted except in the heavier drifts.

Sam flew beyond to the next valley and the next. Seeing no signs of humans or a dog team, they returned to Palmer.

Madison tried to hide her disappointment when Sam walked with his arm around her as they went to the truck.

"Is it because there wasn't much snow in the pass?" she asked.

"Could be. Denny hoped to keep the dogs on snow to make the load easier. I'll have to give her that; she cares about those dogs. She's higher in the mountains by now. No way of knowing which direction she's gone. We'll look toward Matanuska Glacier tomorrow. There's snow on those mountains year round. That's the kind of terrain she wants."

CHAPTER 32

Another morning dawned before her body was ready. Madison sat on the back porch deep in thought about how vast Alaska really was. It had seemed like a perfect plan, to locate Denny with Sam's guidance. Now that she was here, she had the feeling it was a futile effort. Sam, the professional guide, wasn't even sure where to look for Denny. How could she hope to accomplish this overwhelming task?

She jumped up when heavy footfalls on the boards jarred her back to the present.

"You ready?" Sam asked.

"Whenever you are." She stopped short of asking about the wind. He'd never fly if conditions were not right.

The small plane climbed towards the mountain where the Glenn Highway snaked its way toward Toke. The nose of the plane was angled at a slight incline, causing Madison's ears to muffle and then clear when she swallowed. She watched as the ground grew increasingly whiter. "Are we going to some specific area?"

"Last night, I remembered a place Denny talked a lot about. It's north of Chickaloon, toward the upper Big Sus River. She discovered a lake full of fish in a valley surrounded by steep mountains. If I can spot the lake, we might find a place to land."

Madison settled back into her seat. As much as she hated landings, the idea of landing without a runway was almost unimaginable. She'd cross that bridge when they came to it. For now, she concentrated her attention below, looking for any sign of life.

Miles passed quickly as she watched the tiny community of Chickaloon pass, far below them. Sam banked the plane left into a north-northwest direction, bringing mountain peaks closer to the plane. This made Madison feel uneasy, until the slope dropped away as quickly as it had risen. She noticed the slight bump when air currents rose beneath them.

The higher the sun rose, the more unsettled the air became. Just when Sam was about to turn back, she pointed over his left shoulder.

"Is that a lake?"

"You've got good eyes. Let's look closer." He circled in a wide pattern, analyzing the terrain around the lake. "Cottonwood trees and lots of spruce grew right up to the edge of the water. We'll look further up the valley." He pointed to a plateau at the end of the valley, made a quick pass, and then circled back. "Hold on."

"You've got to be kidding," Madison mumbled. She closed her eyes and sunk into the seat cushion. *Sam does this all the time,* she repeated in her mind, over and over.

When the skis touched down, she was surprised by the white, powdery snow flying up to block her view, but the ride was not bumpy, as she feared. The plane glided over the snow and then slowed to a stop, making a crunching sound as it settled.

Madison let out a huff. "That was quite a surprise."

Sam laughed. "Outside air temperature is thirty-two degrees. I'll see how deep the drifts are. We might need snowshoes to make our way to the lake."

He climbed out in his shirtsleeves, and walked a short distance from the plane. He returned with a smile. "The ground is solid. We got lucky today; I smell a campfire."

"Why didn't we see it?" Madison climbed out from the backseat.

"Your eyes were shut, and I was busy watching the ground coming up at us." He laughed and pushed her backward.

"I hate landings!" She snapped.

"You ready to hike?" He pulled out a pack from the compartment behind her seat.

"I'm with you."

"There are prospectors in these parts, and grizzlies don't build campfires. Let's hope the welcome party is friendly."

They followed the smell of smoke for nearly an hour before spotting a cabin nestled in the thick spruce. Sam said, "She never mentioned a cabin."

"So this isn't the place?" Madison felt like crying.

"Probably not. We'll see if anyone will talk to us." He pushed through the snowy path. "Hello in the cabin," he called.

A dog bark was his only answer.

Madison caught his arm. "Only one dog? Let's go; she's not here."

"It's okay. If they were going to shoot we'd be dead by now."

"Howdy!" A voice caused Madison to spin around.

"Seen your plane come in low; not in trouble, are ya?" An old man, looking a bit tattered with a full beard, approached from another trail. He leaned heavily on a staff. A husky heeled close to his side. "Name's Roscoe." He shoved his hand toward Sam.

"Sam Hornburg, and this is Madison. We're up from Palmer. Glad to meet you." Sam shook the ol' timer's hand, then petted the husky.

"Howdy, Ms. Madison. Don't see many pretty ladies here. What can I do fer you folks?"

"Nice to meet you, Roscoe. What's your friend's name?" Madison knelt to pet the dog.

"That's Rufus. Been my companion going on fifteen years."

"We landed on the plateau." Sam pointed the direction they'd walked. "No trouble, just a beautiful day to check out fishing sites."

"It is that! Don't see many in the spring. We're having warm weather early. How is it down in the flats?" Roscoe rested both hands on his staff and spit into a snowdrift.

"Warm, unusually warm," Sam said. "How's fishing in that lake?"

"Shadow Lake, it's purty fair. Got lake trout, some good burbot."

"What's burbot?" Madison asked.

"Just the best whitefish you ever put in your mouth." Roscoe scratched his head. "Funny, the other day I run into a feller asking the same question."

"Are you sure it was a fellow?" Madison asked.

He grinned. "Unless women figured a way to grow beards, it was a man." Roscoe made a step toward his cabin. "Where's my manners? You all come and sit a spell. Don't get much company. I got a good moose stew simmerin'. Be more'n happy to share with you. Used the last of my coffee a while back, though."

"I have coffee in my pack. Be a fair trade, coffee for a taste of stew," Sam said.

After a long conversation over lunch, Sam asked. "Is there anything I can bring you from the flats next time I'm up this way?"

The old man wrinkled his forehead. "Don't reckon so, but you can always trade coffee for a meal." He raked the scraps off the metal plates onto a flat rock for Rufus. "He loves moose stew." They all laughed, watching Rufus lap it up so eagerly.

"A friend of mine told me about this lake. She comes here with a dog team. Ever seen her?" Sam asked.

"A woman musher?" Roscoe dunked the plates into a wash pan.

Sam nodded.

"Been a while back: a couple years. Ain't seen her this year. But I don't go on the other side of the lake anymore, since I got this bum leg."

"Well, we better be going before the weather changes. It's nice to meet you, Roscoe, and thanks for lunch. You keep the coffee, and I'll bring you more from time to time." Sam patted the old man's shoulder. Then he bent to stroke Rufus's head. "Good boy. Take care of things here."

"Thanks, Roscoe, I loved your stew." Madison gave the man a hug. Rufus followed them a ways from the cabin then turned and went back.

When they reached the plane, Sam made his outside inspection, checking the flaps, pitot tube, cables, tail section, and the skis.

Madison turned away from the panoramic scene and looked hopelessly into Sam's eyes. "I'll never find her, will I?"

"No, Madison. Not you nor anyone else, unless she wants to be found."

"She had a dog named Rufus. He's the one that died."

"Yeah, I picked up on that too. I'd say she's met this one."

After a while, Madison reluctantly turned and got into the back seat.

"We'll make a low pass on the other side of the lake. Maybe we'll spot some sign."

Madison sighed, feeling that wasn't realistic. But she wasn't willing to give up, either. She'd come too far to go home empty-handed, no matter how hopeless it might seem. In her experience, she'd learned her lesson about "things are always darkest just before dawn"—unlike Denny, who said, "Things are always darkest just before they go completely black!"

CHAPTER 33

Thursday morning when Madison came downstairs she found a note in the kitchen:

Be back by the time you fix your own breakfast... sorry about that! Will you feed the dogs? Then we'll look at the area around that lake again. I have a feeling about Roscoe; he lied!

Sam

Madison quickly swallowed toast and scrambled eggs. Next, she fed the dogs. Soon after she returned to the house, Sam walked in carrying a shopping bag from Three Bears, a local grocery.

"What's in the bag?"

"Coffee, for one thing." Sam grinned.

The flight over snow-covered ground seemed longer today. Her heartbeat quickened when she spotted their reflection passing over Shadow Lake.

"That direction." Sam banked the wing. "I'll bet you we'll find a campsite." He made a spiral turn and eyed the ground with a trained hunter's eyes.

Eager as she was to look, she also had that fear creeping up: the fear that sooner or later, they'd land down there. Madison stiffened and stared forward; a fixed spot on the windshield *should* settle her stomach; it wasn't working.

"Sam, I don't feel good."

"Sorry, I wasn't thinking." He quickly returned to level flight. "The sky is totally clear; we should spot any smoke."

"Like that?" Madison said, pointing.

"Exactly like that," Sam shouted.

He circled the lake, took his bearings, and then began his descent for landing where they had previously. He'd deliver the coffee first.

The approach felt too fast to her, but what did she know? Madison tried to find a cloud to focus on, but there were none. She pulled her seatbelt tighter, sinking as low as she could. She felt her neck muscles tighten along with the belt. Something felt very awkward today. The plane was going faster than when these same trees streaked past yesterday. They weren't floating softly toward the ground; they were gaining speed and losing altitude.

The stick in front of her was jerky, like Sam was fighting the plane. There was no time to ask questions. She heard Sam say, "The wind shifted."

The end of the valley was nearing too quickly. Madison didn't have to ask what would happen if they reached the trees at this speed. She felt it. The sudden lunge of the fuselage as trees ripped off the wings, made it seem they went faster still. Branches beat the windshield into Sam's face. He groaned. She ducked, but a branch slapped hard across her shoulders.

Their forward movement jerked sideways and slammed to a stop. Losing all sense of feeling, she heard branches scraping as they settled around the plane, a whooshing sound, and then silence.

Madison was aroused by water dripping on her face, and she tasted blood. Her left eye was blinded. She tried to move, but her head was wedged against the front seat by the shoulder harness. The blood came from above her. *Sam!* She called his name, but there was no response.

She slid one hand along the seatbelt, searching out the buckle. She lifted the clasp and immediately screamed from the pain. Her body had dropped hard, onto the roof of the plane. They were inverted! Sam was above her. Her legs felt numb, and her left hand fell limp when she tried to use it. Then she found her knees still worked, and crawled out into the snow.

She lay there taking inventory of her limbs. They all hurt, a good sign—she hoped. She couldn't stand, so she slid herself along a few inches at a time, backing away from the plane. "Sam!" she cried. "Sam, can you hear me?"

Still no response. She was sure she smelled smoke. She rolled onto her side. Her right eye watched flames spew into the air from one wing. She was glad they were surrounded by snow. *At least snow won't burn.*

The cold was only rivaled by her pain when she realized she had blacked out. *I've got to get to Sam.* Again she tried to move. Her knees held this time, and she stood. Her left arm had no feeling. She shuffled toward the mangled fuselage, which was not only upside down, it teetered on a large bolder—thus the sudden stop.

She couldn't climb back inside or it might fall, but she needed to know Sam's condition. Then a twig snapped behind her. Slowly she turned to her right, afraid of what might be there. Her good eye combed the scene. Nothing moved. *Maybe it was just the trees settling in.* Airplane parts littered the path of torn up trees and gouged snowpack along the ground. She turned back to Sam. Were her ears playing tricks on her? Had the sound come from inside the plane?

"Sam?" Still, there was no sound from her pilot.

Madison was dizzy, and suddenly felt like throwing up. She dropped to her knees, vomiting profusely. The movement was more excruciating than she could stand. She felt herself falling forward, and couldn't stop her motion.

The next thing Madison felt was warmth and the weight of a blanket. Nothing made sense to her; she heard a crackling sound and smelled smoke: wood smoke, not the plane's burning fuel.

A blanket? She tried to open her eyes. One didn't work at all. Then she remembered the crash. "Sam!" she cried, and then wished she hadn't moved.

She felt something wet on her face. A dog. "Bud?" Madison tried to roll over so her right eye faced up. It hurt too much. *It smells like a dog. Does a bear smell like a dog? No way.*

Her movement was limited. Even her right arm felt restricted. At least she could feel her left arm now. But it didn't make sense; her wrists were together. *Oh my God, I'm tied up.*

The licking continued. *Shep?* She hadn't found Denny, but apparently Denny had found her.

Madison felt someone rolling her over. With her one good eye, she saw Denny standing above her, with a long barrel rifle pointed at her face. Her eyes looked like marbles of coal, full of black, stone-cold anger. Her teeth were clenched tightly enough to make her neck muscles bulge.

Madison's heart felt like it would burst from fear. *I can't let her see that I'm terrified.* "You lying witch. Now what do you plan to do?"

"You watch your mouth! Don't forget who you're talking to." Denny's head shook as she spoke through clenched teeth. "You've got no right to talk to me that way."

Denny's voice echoed in the inner chambers of Madison's ears. She could barely understand the words. "I have the right after all the *lies* you've told me! Where's Sam?" She demanded.

"He's out there in that wreckage. He's dead." Denny turned her face away.

"I'm hurting all over. You've got me hog-tied. Do you really need that rifle?"

Denny set the gun against a box on the floor. "Sam caught the brunt of the windshield."

"Can't you untie my hands? What am I going to do?"

"Why are you here?" Denny said.

Her demeanor sent chilling signals through Madison. "Let me go so I can check on Sam. You've lied so much."

Denny was Sam's friend. If he were dead, wouldn't she be more disturbed? Maybe not this Denny; this was a cold even her niece had not witnessed.

"I guess you aren't going to run. Where would you go?" Denny picked up a ULU knife and cut the ropes.

Madison felt the release and struggled to right herself. Her left arm hung limp. "My arm is broken."

"No, it's just a bad bruise." Denny showed no sympathy. "What do you expect to learn from this visit?" Denny held the ULU knife in a threatening manner.

"No! We don't talk until I know about Sam." Madison turned her face away.

"Where do you think all the blood came from? You have bumps and bruises, but not a cut anywhere." Denny pulled Madison's chin toward her, offering a better look at her eye. "You must have hit the back of his seat."

Madison remembered the blood dripping onto her face. Denny was right, she didn't have a cut. It was Sam's blood and that much blood meant he was hurt bad. "Did you even *try* to help him?"

"There was nothing I could do. He's gone. You dragged him into this mess; I didn't. You got him killed. I didn't." Denny's voice wavered, softer than previously.

At least now she's showing some emotion. Sam must be dead. Madison felt guilt tugging at her heart. Her eyes felt moist, but she couldn't let Denny see.

Denny paced back and forth. "What do I do with you?"

"You owe me. I want to know what happened to Tina. It's that simple."

"There's nothing simple about that! I did what I had to do." Denny grabbed the rifle, then walked outside. Madison limped in excruciating pain as she followed her aunt to the campfire.

Denny bent to pick up the coffee pot. She offered Madison a cup. "This will warm you."

Madison took the enamel mug. Denny filled it and one for herself. Then she sat on a log, propping the rifle next to her. Madison settled on a stump not far away, and sipped the strong black coffee while Denny talked.

"You know I lived with Danny and Tina after our folks died. When I was still in high school, Tina told me that I should have died along with them. She hated me."

The look on Denny's face gave Madison a creepy feeling. *She's talking about Tina as if she was nothing.*

"After that, I never turned my back on her. As soon as I graduated, I went off to college, only coming home when Danny begged me."

"Why didn't you tell Danny what you suspected?" Madison pretended sympathy.

"He thought the sun rose and set in Tina. I was his baby sister, and always giving him grief. My brother was a weak man. I got all the backbone in our family. That's the only reason Tina hung on so long. She completely controlled him." Denny stood, pacing between the fire and the tent.

Madison kept her eye on the rifle. "Tell me what happened the day Tina died." She shifted, edging closer toward the weapon.

Denny sat again refilling her coffee mug. "The week Danny died, he told me Tina wanted a baby, but they hadn't been successful. The next week, she told him she was pregnant. He didn't believe it was his, and he cried. She played him for the fool he was!" Denny kicked at a stone.

Madison stood and stretched her legs. "You argued?"

"Mm," Denny nodded. "I went home over the next weekend. It broke my heart when I watched him fall. I knew he was dead." Denny stared into the flames of the fire.

"You saw Danny fall, yet you couldn't help him?" Madison's voice rose to almost a shout.

Denny was oblivious to her words. "After you were born, I tried to tell Tina what happened with Danny. At first, she wouldn't listen. Then she came at me with a look like she could kill. She fell and her head hit an ax." Denny turned up the mug and drank several gulps.

Madison dropped onto the stump. "I see." She rested her elbows on both knees. She looked up, dry-eyed and angry. "How could you just drop out of my life and expect me to not follow you? You knew I'd show up here, didn't you?"

"Maybe. I didn't give you much thought. I knew I didn't stand a chance in Cold Creek." Denny took a deep breath. "I thought you'd give up when Bud went missing. No, you had to go all detective on me, and find him yourself!" Denny stood, pacing again.

"You did that? I thought it was Franks," Madison said.

"Separating you from the thing you loved best should have worked. What's with all your sudden changes?" Denny's eyes appeared black as coal once again; her words cut the air like a blade. The more she talked, the more her features hardened.

Madison swallowed hard. She had to fight back. "Get used to it. Nobody is telling me how to live my life ever again." She straightened her back and sat as tall as she could. Her heart pounded. Denny's next comment surprised her.

She said, "Good for you."

Then Denny settled into the most astonishing testament. "When I was a child, I watched Dad put our pet dog into the chemicals used to strip wood. He'd discovered it also cleaned away flesh, soft tissue, and muscles from the bones. Decomposition was quicker, and there was no smell."

Madison sensed Denny's voice had changed.

Denny continued. "Couple of days later, he retrieved the bones and we hiked up in the forest. He built a wood cross with Topper's name across it. I carried my little shovel and helped." Denny paused to drink her coffee. "Topper died because he was old. I guess burying the bones was supposed to make me feel better." She was still for a moment. "All I knew was my best friend was gone, and that chemical was to blame."

Denny shook her head as though to clear the image of Topper. "When I saw Tina's body sprawled on the floor, the memory came back to me. It made perfect sense. Nobody liked Tina, and they'd never miss her. My problems were solved. I had only to bury her bones far from the house, and forget about her. Why not? Dad got away with it, and Tina was not as dear as a dog."

Madison sat quietly, letting Denny relive her story.

"I was friends with Sheriff Will Franks. He confided in me about his most private thoughts. I disclosed the details about Tina. He understood."

"He already knew about the effects of the chemicals because of Danny's state when he pulled his body out," Madison argued.

Denny whirled around. For a moment, Madison thought she was going to pick up the rifle, but then her look softened.

"You're not going to leave this alone, are you?" Denny asked.

"No! You might as well tell me the truth." Madison stood and stared her down. She knew her only chance was to convince Denny she wasn't scared. "No doubt, all those women deserved to be punished. You were a vigilante team, you and the sheriff."

"You want the truth? He came to me to ask what I knew of Tina. She'd escaped from his jail. She was a tramp, and he didn't like tramps in his town."

"And there were others, after her," Madison said.

"Sheriff Franks brought their bodies to the workshop. I couldn't say anything. I had no choice but to dispose of them. He threatened to arrest me for Danny and Tina's murders. He was ruthless." Denny said. "Franks was a killer, not me."

"The letters in your basement, they were from Sheriff Franks?"

"Oh, you've been snooping around. So, my house didn't burn with the workshop?" Denny put a small log on the campfire. "What else did you find?" There was that gruff voice again.

Madison shrugged her shoulders. "Not enough to answer all my questions. What about Mariah? Did you kill her?"

"Mariah was awful sick when I got back from Alaska. She tried herbs, but they poisoned her. I moved her baby and buried them together."

"It was the decent thing to do." Madison made her tone sincere. "Dr. Baker says Mariah had a knife wound."

Denny nodded, "Yeah, the pain from the poison must have been so bad she tried to shorten the time. The knife was still wedged in between her ribs, just here." Denny placed her fingers under her breastbone. "I had a hard time pulling it out. She'd been dead a day or two, I estimated."

Madison guessed that since she knew where the knife had been, maybe she was telling the truth about that part. Poison was painful, she'd always heard.

"I never planned to hurt anyone. It was all circumstances beyond my control. I'm not the villain here." Denny looked into Madison's eyes. "You don't hate me, do you?"

Madison tried to shake her head. The pain blocked her thoughts. "I don't know...I—"

Behind Denny, there was movement, high over her head and broad as two of her. Madison's mouth felt dry as cotton, and she couldn't make a sound. She lunged for the rifle.

Denny stepped backward, stumbling over a stone. "You don't have to worry. I only really loved two people in my life, Dad and you."

Madison managed a shrill scream, just as Shep lunged for the bear. Old One-Ear swatted the dog like a fly. Shep rolled across the ground, yelping. Denny whirled around to see the next swat of his paw bearing down on her. She raised the rifle. He was too close, and dislodged the weapon from her hands with one paw; the other landed a blow to her chin.

Madison rolled away from the bear and snatched the rifle off the ground. She raised it and sighted down the barrel. Through her good eye, she saw the grizzly turn and leap toward her. She squeezed the trigger. The sound reverberated her head. He kept closing on her. Another crack of a rifle shot and Old One-Ear crashed forward, landing inches from Madison's feet. The hot rush of his final foul breath gagged her and turned her stomach.

Movement caught her eye. She threw the rifle barrel up and pulled the trigger. The hammer made a click sound. Denny's rifle was empty. *Thank God for that!*

Sam lowered his arm and stepped toward her. A wide, white bandage encircled his head. Madison turned her stare at Denny's lifeless body. Her spine was severed, her body barely attached to her head at the back of her hairline.

Then she remembered Shep. His tail flayed the ground, but he couldn't stand. She crawled to him. His neck gaped open, and blood melted the snow as it pooled. She pulled the scarf from her neck and pressed it into the wound. "Sam, help me."

Sam was already at her side. He pulled off his jacket and ripped the sleeve from his flannel shirt. He tied it snugly around the dog's neck. "We need a first aid kit. Look in the tent."

Madison hobbled inside to where she'd seen the ULU knife. She returned with the kit and a canteen of water. Sam instructed her to hold pressure until he was ready. Then he sutured the dog's neck to stop the bleeding.

Madison held Shep's head, but he gave no fight. He was smart enough to realize they were trying to help him. With the suturing completed and the bleeding stopped, Madison trickled water into Shep's mouth.

Sam sat next to her. "When the old man found me, I couldn't figure out what happened to you. My head was hurting so bad I thought I'd die. Something that old-timer put on it made the difference. It doesn't even hurt now."

"Denny told me you were dead." She leaned against Sam with her head on his shoulder. "Thank goodness the old man came along before she went back. Or, I don't know, maybe she really *did* believe you were dead. I had a lot of your blood on me."

"Blood mixed with water looks much worse, and head wounds bleed a lot anyway. You know that. As soon as I saw the tracks, I knew Denny had you."

They sat quietly for a while, in disbelief about what had just happened. A nearly beheaded corpse and a one-eared grizzly sprawled on the ground at their feet.

Sam wrapped his arm around Madison. "I'm sorry for Denny. She didn't deserve to die like that, no matter what she's done."

Madison wiped tears off her face. "How ironic that you're the one who finally brought Old One-Ear down." She tried to smile, but her face was too swollen. "I'm sorry about your airplane."

"Ah, I've wanted a different one for a while. Now I don't have to justify getting an Otter, or even a Beaver. It's only money. Either one of those will pay for itself in a couple of seasons," he said.

Sam rigged a sling to carry Shep. Then he hitched Denny's team to her sled and placed her blanket-wrapped body on it.

"The emergency locator transmitter was engaged, so a chopper should be at the crash site by now. They'll take you and Shep to Palmer, and then return for Denny. I'm sure Roscoe will keep her team." Sam's voice penetrated Madison's ears, but she didn't fully understand what he'd said.

"We're at the chopper," he said gently.

Madison looked at the crash scene. The chopper's bright red color stood out in the snow like a big pool of blood. Madison felt her legs turn to mush as she sunk toward the ground. Then she became aware of blue uniforms all around her, and she was lifted into the belly of the helo. She saw the friendly face of a young woman kneeling over her. Her lips moved, but Madison couldn't hear or focus. She closed her eyes and could not gather the strength to reopen them.

CHAPTER 34

A rescue squad and state trooper met the Coast Guard helo at Palmer Airport. A second helicopter returned for Denny's remains. Old One-Ear had taken his last victim.

An EMT put Madison's arm in a sling. He thought the ulna was broken. Then he wrapped Shep's neck with clean gauze, and gave him a shot to guard against infection. Madison was still unaware of what was happening. An ambulance took her to Wasilla hospital for an x-ray. Indeed, she did have a hairline fracture of the ulna, near the wrist. The ER doctor was concerned she had a concussion, so to rule out any skull fractures he ordered a CT scan.

Sam delivered Shep to a nearby friend, a retired veterinarian who agreed to watch out for him through the night so he could stay by Madison's side. She was released after the scan showed no concussion or fractures.

The trooper, one of Sam's friends, showed up at the cabin the next evening to take their statements. The veterinarian stopped by to deliver Shep. He was getting along fine.

The Division of Wildlife sent another team of men in by helicopter for the bear. Old One-Ear was famous in these parts, and would make a great display at the Alaska Museum of Science and Nature in Anchorage.

The trooper explained that Denny's body could be released anytime. No autopsy was necessary. Madison wrote down the name of the funeral home in Erwin, where Denny was to go for her final appearance in Tennessee.

Then she immediately crumpled the paper. "You know, as much as she loved Alaska, I think she belongs here." Madison looked at Sam. "What do you say?"

He nodded and said, "You're right. She wanted this to be her resting place. She once told me she'd like to be cremated and spread across the mountain tops from a plane." Sam draped his arm along Madison's shoulders. "Good call. I'd be happy to take charge of that."

"Somewhere along the Iditarod Trail," Madison said.

"I know just the place." Sam pulled her into a gentle bear hug. He held her for a while and then excused himself to feed his dogs.

Madison trudged upstairs to shower. The ER doctor had given her an oversized rubber glove that extended to her elbow to shield her cast from water. It was not easy to wash her hair with one hand.

She dressed in comfy sweats, and brought her pillow and a blanket down to the couch. She slept there to be near Shep. Sam patted her as he passed, going to his room.

"If that sofa gets too cold, come lay on my bed."

"Good night, Sam." Madison said firmly.

The next day, Madison took Shep out in the yard for some exercise and sun. He acted happier laying on the porch than inside, so she left him and went to her room for a nap.

The afternoon shadows were lengthening when she found her way outside again.

Sam met her with good news. "The vet was pleased to see Shep walking so well. He suggests you leave him here when you return to Tennessee."

"That's fine, if you don't mind." Madison stroked Shep gently.

The dog responded by licking her hand below the cast, as though he understood she was hurt too.

"You haven't eaten anything today. Inside, young lady," Sam barked, and Madison obeyed.

"I'll wash up."

"I've ordered catering service." Sam caught her arm, leading her to his bathroom. "Don't go up the stairs unnecessarily; use mine." Then he left the room.

Dinner arrived with a flurry of people. The table was set with dishes of food arranged in a buffet. Then they retreated, as quickly as they had come in. An attractive red-haired lady in tight jeans carried three bottles of wine into the kitchen. "Break out the real glasses, Sam. Let's eat!"

"Rebecca, sweet of you to join us." Sam wrapped his arms around the shapely lady. "That better be from your private stock."

"Only the best for you and your friends. You know that." She pulled from his grasp and set the wine on the counter as Madison entered. "Becky Loren." She extended her hand. "Madison, I'm relieved you and Sam weren't hurt worse. That was an awful crash."

"Thank you, Ms. Loren. I'm sorry Sam lost his plane." They shook hands.

"No Ms., young lady, just Becky," she said.

The doorbell sounded and Sam left the kitchen returning with a surprise guest. "Look who I found."

"Rick!" Madison ignored her pain and rushed into his arms. "I'm so happy to see you."

"Now that's a welcome sound," Rick said.

"Agent Malone, this is Rebecca Loren, my dear friend."

"Rick, it's nice to meet you." She shook Rick's hand aggressively. "Call me Becky. Sam, where's your corkscrew?"

Dinner and the private stock wine were magnificent. Madison's eyelids tried to close more times than she could count.

"Rick, I'm done for." She laughed. "Will you help me up the stairs?"

"I'm pretty exhausted too." Rick stood and pulled out her chair.

"I can't believe this bad dream is over." Madison stood. "Thank you, Becky, for this delicious meal. I hope I'm not too rude going to my room, now."

"I understand, Madison. We'll see each other at breakfast. You get a good night's sleep." Rebecca smiled and patted Madison's hand.

Rick took hold of Madison's arm.

Sam said, "Rick, your room is at the end of the hall. I've already taken your bag up."

"Thank you, Sam. Good night, Becky, and thank you, too." Rick and Madison left the room.

Madison turned to Rick. "Thanks for coming. I don't mind admitting I need you."

"Now, that's a first!"

They climbed the stairs together. Rick pulled the coverlet back and knelt to remove her shoes. She fell back onto the soft pillows. "Think I'll just sleep in my clothes..."

"You know, I *should* be angry with you. Bad as this is, it could have been much worse, young lady."

Madison opened her one good eye. Then it closed again. She was instantly asleep.

Rick turned out the light. "I can't be mad at you. You've been through so much." He gently kissed her forehead and then slipped her door closed, and located his room further down the hall.

In the quiet of dwindling daylight, he sat on the side of his bed, pulled his phone from his pocket and pushed some keys. "Hello, Sheriff, just wanted to let you know she's okay. Got some bad bangs and a broken arm, but our girl is going to be fine."

He ended the call after Sheriff Perry agreed to walk to Jess and Shirley's to tell them personally of the outcome in Alaska. Rick lay back onto the pillows, thinking how glad he was not to be the one delivering the news to her folks.

Her folks. He laughed aloud. *Will she be surprised when I break that news to her!*

CHAPTER 35

A familiar aroma swirled around Madison's nose. She opened her eyes and met Rick's stare. She breathed a sigh of relief and said, "I thought I was dreaming."

"Of coffee, or me?" He fluttered his eyelashes at her.

"I smelled coffee, not you." She reached for the mug.

"I was going to offer you breakfast in bed, but just for that remark, I'm leaving you to fend for yourself." He kissed her forehead softly.

"Thanks for the coffee." She sipped, and then nearly spilled it on herself setting it down on the nightstand. "My eye! It's open. I can see out of both my eyes this morning!"

"That's great!" Rick leaned in closer, "Still has a lot of swelling, and it's pretty bloodshot, but I can see the green again." Rebecca knocked on the open door facing. "Need any help, Madison?"

"Thanks. I could use your assistance." Madison looked to Rick. "Meet you downstairs."

"I'm out of here." He disappeared into the hall.

"I need to cut the arm of a sweater open to fit over my cast."

"Let me do that. It can be hand sewn back after the arm heals, if it's done right." Rebecca reached for the sweater in the top of Madison's suitcase.

"Oh, that's a good idea. I love this sweater. Denny gave it to me for Christmas..."

"You'll have a lot of pleasant memories. Don't push them aside. Let them flow; talk about her whenever you feel like it." Rebecca pulled one thread and unraveled the seam of the sleeve. She helped slip it over Madison's head and threaded her arm through carefully. "Now, I'll get a needle and tack it in place. This is an expensive garment, and now it's repairable."

Madison watched the bouncy red-haired lady disappear out the door. *Hmmm, she sounds like a psychologist or something. I wondered why Sam brought her here.*

In a few minutes, Rebecca returned. She made a few stitches at the edge of the cast and then rolled the sleeve and tacked the roll into place. "How does it feel?"

"It's great." Madison studied her face and then asked, "Rebecca, what do you do?"

Her smile widened. "I'm a psychologist who knits as a hobby. Don't worry. I haven't found any cracks in you, and don't expect to. It's traumatic to see someone die, and you'll relive the nightmare. But you're okay, Madison. I'd tell you if I saw any hint of trouble," she said.

Madison took a deep breath letting it out slowly. "I hope you're right."

Madison and Rebecca joined the men for breakfast, then they all drove to the Palmer Airport. The medical examiner met them with a small urn.

"I wanted to deliver this personally, and meet the strong lady from Tennessee."

"Thank you." She accepted the ashes and they all loaded into an airplane.

Sam directed the pilot to the spot he'd chosen, and they landed on a dry riverbed close by. Madison, Rick, Sam, and Rebecca disembarked and walked a short distance up the beautiful valley.

"Denny stopped here during her last race because it was so peaceful. It was snow covered then, and she fell in love with the view. It seemed a fitting place to put her to rest." Sam said.

Madison handed the urn to Rick and pulled a small piece of paper from her pocket. She read, "Sometimes we learn things we don't want to know. Sometimes we know things we don't want to admit." She looked up at the endless blue overhead. "It's all part of a plan we don't control. We're not expected to understand, but if we listen, God shows the path to choose, faith gives us strength to get there, and our hearts tell us it's right." She nodded to Rick.

He removed the lid and let the breeze carry the ashes. Some floated down into the riverbed, while others blew to the bare branches of the shrubs along the shore. A songbird whistled a melody from somewhere unseen, and an eagle soared high above them. Denny was at home in her beloved Alaska; pain was over, for her.

Madison elected to remain in Alaska the rest of the week, allowing the swelling to leave her eye. She didn't want Shirley and Jess to see her bruises from the crash. It was going to take years for the damage on the inside to heal.

She reasoned that because she forced the hand of evil, Denise Denson was dead. Dr. Rebecca Loren suggested she weigh the evidence.

Denny may have caused her own brother, her sister-in-law, and possibly her parent's death. As for Old Sheriff Franks, he killed at least six women. I brought life to the tragedy, but Ol' One-Ear handed down the punishment.

"I understand what you're saying, Becky, and because I am optimistic, I'd like to think the souls of the women from the mountain can rest in peace, now that their story was told."

"Please call me if you have anything you want to talk about, Madison." Becky gave her a business card. "You can reach me at any of these numbers, day or night."

"Thank you. I'll be all right," Madison said, as she took the card.

CHAPTER 36

Rick and Madison boarded their flight to Tri-Cities via Atlanta. The nine-hour flight gave them time to talk about what lay ahead.

Madison started the conversation as soon as the plane leveled out. "I knew you'd stop me from going to Alaska. I had to slip away, and I'm not sorry. Denny would have killed you. She was so mixed up at the last; it's like she had a split personality."

Rick nodded. "Actually, she did. I got a text about documentation at the Knoxville Clinic. Since she's deceased, they had to release her records. But that's not the biggest surprise. Franks knew his dad was the killer, and he was blackmailing Denny."

"The fact that Denny was telling the truth is the surprise, not that Franks had a hand in it."

"Franks knew from a young age that his Dad had a thing for, shall I say, wild women? He held them in that cell, where no one could hear their screams when he tortured them. He left them down there to die, and then took their bodies to the workshop, leaving Denny to clean up his mess. He knew that's what she'd done with Tina's body."

"How did things get so out of hand?" Madison shook her head. "Denny said Sheriff Franks was not as forgetful as he wanted us to believe. Deputy Franks had to know. Will he be charged?"

"Not necessarily; he cooperated after Sheriff Perry and I questioned him.

He can't be charged with what he learned as a child. We do have him on shooting Perry and blackmail at the very least. And get this—he admitted to killing Bud's siblings."

"That's why Bud hates him!" Madison sat up tall. "Oh, Bud. I put him in a hurtful situation."

"That cut on Bud's tongue? He nearly died too. He managed to get away from Franks, but he sure enough remembered him."

"When did you learn the truth about Deputy Franks' dad being the killer?"

Rick looked away. A frown replaced the tenderness of his face. "We were suspicious for a while. Mr. Olsen gave us some incriminating clues. We set Franks up, hoping he'd confirm our worst fears. And he did."

Madison unhooked her seat belt and turned toward Rick.

"Tina and Danny suspected Denny set the fire that killed their parents. She resented the love between her mom and dad; when she thought her dad was away on business, Denny meant to only kill her mother. At the time, the sheriff didn't believe she was guilty. Danny had her committed for observation. She was released after a short stay, and nothing more was done. She had been abused, and Danny felt sorry for her. Tina was scared of her."

"And how did you learn all this?" Rick asked.

"From papers and letters I found in Denny's basement." She held up her hand, "Don't even ask, Agent Malone!"

"I don't think you should tell me this..."

"Get over it. I'm a good detective. Anyway, later, when Danny died, Sheriff Franks asked Denny about the relationship with her dad. Denny was afraid of Sheriff Franks at first, but then she became involved with him, too. He replaced her daddy, a twisted father figure. She got pregnant, and the Old Sheriff paid for the abortion."

"He told you all of this?" Rick was on the edge of his seat. "Why didn't you tell me?"

"I didn't know who to trust. Besides, it was my family secret to investigate and bring to light, or bury forever."

"Maybe not." Rick leaned back in his seat with a wide smile.

"What do you mean?"

"We didn't get around to discussing the DNA results," Rick said.

"That's right. But I already know Tina is one of the skeletons."

"Yeah, but you don't know *why* your DNA didn't match Denny's." Rick leaned close and smiled.

"She wasn't really my aunt. I know that much. Was she adopted?"

"I can't tell you yet." Rick clammed up.

Rick put his thumb and finger to his lips and drew it across as if it were a zipper.

"You can't do that!" She raised her voice.

He put one finger on her lips and whispered, "Shush, we're not talking about this subject anymore."

Madison spotted Shirley and Jess in the corridor at the Tri-Cities Airport. She ran to hug them. "Are you feeling any better, Shirley?"

"I'm going to be better than ever, if I live through this diet the doctor has me on."

Madison turned to Jess. "Did you bring Bud?"

"He's in the car." Jess pulled Madison into his arms. "Please give me a chance to explain before you judge me or Tina."

Madison looked into her father's eyes with tears streaming down her face. "I'd never judge you. You're the kindest most loving man I know. I've always wanted you to be my real dad."

The three walked toward the car, Agent Malone following with the two rolling suitcases.

Bud clawed at the glass as soon as he saw Madison. Jess opened the door, and the dog leaped into her arms. He licked every inch of her face before he noticed the cast. He whined like he didn't want it there.

Madison held on to him as she climbed into the back seat. Bud barely moved for her to fasten her seatbelt. His trembling body told her he'd missed her.

"Denny coerced Willy Franks into kidnapping Bud. He admitted to her he shot Sheriff Perry. We knew he framed Henry, we just didn't tell you." Rick smiled in the rear view mirror.

"Did you know he broke into Jess and Shirley's house?" Madison asked.

"How do you know that?" Rick asked.

"My hooded running jacket disappeared, and I knew I'd locked the deadbolt. Bud sniffed his scent and led me to the back door of the jail. That's what he used to make Bud follow him to the cave. When I was locked in the jail, I found it laying in a box."

"What? Locked in the jail?" Shirley shouted.

"Oh, yeah. I need to explain that, don't I?" Madison gave her mom a glance.

"I know it was Franks. He didn't expect me to escape, but I found the old mine shaft that led into the cave—which is under my property, by the way."

"That's how Tina escaped," Jess said.

"Tina was Sheriff Franks' prisoner, and you found her by the river, wet and bruised from the beating. She's the one who told you about the stream running underground. Remember, when you took me fishing, you told me about the water coming up in the creek above the river." Madison put her hand on Jess's shoulder. "I figured it out."

Jess nodded. "I told Shirley the entire story. She was already suspicious. I'm thankful she's a forgiving soul."

"So, did you ever go into the cave yourself?" Madison held tight to Jess.

"No. I guess I didn't want to believe the awful things that took place there."

When they drove onto Main Street in Cold Creek, Madison noticed a dozen or more cars next to the restaurant. "Looks like Ben and Margie are drawing a crowd."

"Oh, yes. Ben added some new items to the menu," Shirley said.

Rick parked in Madison's driveway. Taking her suitcase inside, he said, "I'll meet you all at the restaurant. I'm starved."

Madison waved as she and Bud walked across the street with Shirley and Jess. When she entered, everyone clapped and cheered. She was overwhelmed, seeing her lifelong friends and neighbors as they gathered around her.

"Speech!" someone called out.

Madison laughed. "What can I say? I'm happy to be home, and have such great friends. Thank you for the welcome." She wiped her eyes.

"We're happy to have you back." Mrs. Olsen hugged Madison gently. "Are you all right?"

"I am. It was sad, but it's over and I'm relieved to be home."

"Yeah, we're sorry for the loss of our Denny. Part of her was good. She did a good job of hiding the other Denny," Mr. Olsen said.

Holly couldn't wait any longer; she rushed to Madison and enveloped her. Henry pulled her back and said, "Watch her arm, Holly. You don't want to hurt her, do you?"

"Its okay, Henry. I won't break." Madison hugged Holly again. "Thanks for keeping Bud. I hope he was a good dog."

Henry answered, "He was! And I want one just like him."

Shirley drew Madison's attention to the table in front of the window. "Margie decorated this lovely cake. Isn't it pretty?"

Madison read the inscription *Welcome Home Madison*, in bright green lettering over white frosting on the top layer. The sides of the three-layer cake were decorated with yellow daisies and fresh blueberries. "That is beautiful, Margie. Thank you."

Beside the cake sat trays of finger sandwiches, fresh vegetables and dips, a tray of fruit cut into flower shapes, and a display of hard cheeses and soft Brie.

Madison sniffed the air. "I smell...seafood?" She turned to look at the bar. There stood a large bowl of steaming Alaskan king crab legs, with a card that read:

Complements of Rebecca and Sam.

Enjoy! We love you, Madison.

"Now that *is* a first! Seafood in Shirley's Restaurant," Madison laughed.

"A first, yes, but more to come. Bring it out, Betty," Ben called.

Betty entered with a large tray, filled with fresh, grilled salmon. "It's Copper River salmon," she said. "Your friend Sam must really love you!"

"Oh, my!" Madison snatched a small bite. "Let's eat while it's hot!"

Nell and Dr. Baker made their way to Madison.

"Since you two have not actually met, Dr Gerre baker, meet Madison McKenzie."

Madison said, "It's nice of you to come."

"I wouldn't have missed your homecoming," Baker said. "I hear you like my line of work, so I'm here to recruit you. I need more inquisitive students like you."

"Has Rick been talking to you?" Madison laughed.

"Well, if it's true I want you on my team." Dr. Baker shook Madison's hand.

"Dr. Baker, following in your footsteps is exactly where I want to be." And then she hugged the doctor. "I'm ready."

The crowd thinned as the food dwindled. The sun set on the sleepy town as Madison and Jess sat side by side on the back steps of the restaurant, listening to the croak of frogs from the creek.

"How well did you know my real mom?"

"Tina?" He shook his head. "About as well as anyone. She was young when she married Danny."

"What was she like?" Madison hungered for information about her birth mother.

"She was a nice person, but she was scared of something or someone."

"Why have you never talked about her?" his daughter pleaded.

"I respected and loved Shirley, so I kept quiet." Jess put his head in his hands and rested on his knees. "I guess you're old enough to make decisions about her. She was your mother."

Jess stretched his long legs down the steps toward the ground. Madison noticed how lanky they were. His torso was long, too. No wonder he dwarfed Shirley, even with her heavy weight. Jess was a big man. *And no wonder I'm tall and thin; Jess is my real father.*

Madison had always felt close to Jess. Somehow, talking to him now felt different. He knew Tina and was willing to talk about her. All of Madison's life, she knew she could count on Jess. He never lied, as far as she knew.

"The first time I saw Tina, I thought she was the prettiest woman I'd ever seen. She was smart, flirty, and demanded attention. The guys at the sawmill said she was married, but I didn't care. She was drawn to my shyness, I suppose. No woman ever looked at me the way Tina could." Jess looked over his shoulder.

"I found her crying that evening down by the river. She had cuts and bruises all over, and she was soaked to the skin. I thought she'd fallen in the river. I took her home with me and patched her up with my first aid kit."

"Who did that to her?"

"She wouldn't say, but now I believe it was Sheriff Franks. Danny was nothing like Denny. He couldn't see the bad in Tina, or he just didn't care. He and I both loved the woman she *could* be, not the woman she actually *was*."

"You *loved* my mom?" Madison stared at Jess.

"Yes, I did. She stayed that night. We slept on the porch, wrapped in a blanket. She loved the open air and the night skies. I begged her to divorce Danny, but she said she couldn't. She stayed with me for three days; after that, I never saw her again. I'd say she was scared of Denny and the sheriff. That's why it was easy for me to believe she left town."

Madison took a deep breath and blew it out. "Did Denny know?"

"No one knew. Don't hate Tina; she was a disturbed, frightened woman. Sometimes she could be an angel. Those are the times I see her in you, the angel side." Jess wrapped his arm around Madison.

She said, "I could never hate her or you, Jess. Thanks for being honest. It's nice to know who I am, at last."

"You have your mom's beautiful face."

"I do?"

He nodded. They sat quietly for a while before Rick joined them.

"We have one more thing to clear up," Rick suggested.

"What do you mean?" Madison asked.

"Well, we need to explore the cave," Jess answered.

"Great idea!" She jumped to her feet. Jess and Rick followed her into the restaurant.

"Nell, how would you like to end this story on an upbeat note?" Madison asked.

Nell looked puzzled. "Well, I already am, because of what you did in Alaska."

"There's more; round up Perry, and a bright flashlight." She turned to Dr. Baker. "Want to see the Lost Silver Mine of Unaka Mountain?"

"You bet!"

"Momma, do you want to go?"

"No Honey, I think I'll go home," Shirley said. "I'll take Bud with me."

"I'll walk to the house with you, Shirley. I'm bushed," Margie said.

The treasure hunters, believers and non-believers trekked to the sheriff's office, down the steps with flashlights, and into the tunnel. Perry and Madison led the way, followed by Jess and Rick, and then Baker and Nell. They heard a voice calling from upstairs.

"Wait for me!" It was Mr. Olsen. "I've always wanted to see that cave. I never dreamed it was under my feet all my life!"

When they came to the collapsed tunnel, each stepped carefully around the edge, hugging the wall tightly. At the fork, Madison pointed to the left passage. In moments the LED flashlights illuminated the enormous natural cavern. The river cutting through it ran fast due to recent rains.

Mr. Olsen spoke first. "This is really it, just like the Indians described. They said that when the water ran swift, the silver room could not be seen. It's there." He walked to the slippery slope that Madison had slipped down.

"Be careful, Mr. Olsen. It's very slippery there." She moved quickly to his side.

"You were in it? And you didn't see the silver?" Perry asked.

"Remember, my penlight battery was nearly dead. I was scared that I couldn't get Bud out. The silver didn't cross my mind."

"The passage where the water runs under the wall can't be seen either," Jess said.

"That's right. The room drops down about fifteen or twenty feet, and then you go up a narrow path to the final room, much smaller than this one. I was lucky the water wasn't high. I don't know if I could have found my way back with so little light." She shivered. "I could have lost Bud."

Perry shined his light down the slope. Well, it's too flooded to go out that way now." He shined the light to a higher part of the room and then walked closer. "And here's the smelting pot the Natives used. I knew it was stone. Not much to look at, but they knew how to utilize it. "

"We'll have to wait for the water level to drop to know for sure. But Madison, I'd say you own the Lost Silver Mine of Unaka." Perry placed his hand on her shoulder.

"No, the town of Cold Creek owns it. I would have never found it if it had not been for wanting to bring our town back to normal. And it's funny, in a way, because Cold Creek will never be the same again." Madison smiled at Jess.

"And you'll never be the same, either. My little girl has grown into a lovely, ambitious woman," Jess said.

"This time the choices are all mine, and I have the faith to trust my own decisions."

Madison felt she'd won the battle outwardly. The war within had only just begun. She'd left Denny behind in her beloved Alaska. Cold Creek was rid of its evil influence. Her birth mother had not abandoned her; *I am worthy of love.* And best of all, in her heart she knew that her strength was sent from God, who watches over her and all who will listen to His word.

The End

ABOUT THE AUTHOR

Bev Freeman was born in Virginia, living in the Appalachian Mountains until her teens when her family relocated to Florida. Missing the mountains, the tumbling streams and changing seasons birthed a love for writing, giving her an escape, for at least short stays.

After high school, life and a career in the dental field got in the way of returning to the mountains. She married a Floridian and raised a son.

However, the year 1993 brought shattered dreams and a divorce, so she followed her family back to the Appalachian region. In 1996, she married a local, God-fearing man and ever since, life is beautiful in Tennessee with two spirited grandsons living close by.

Retirement offers days free for writing stories of unique characters set in her beloved mountains, making local history and legends come to life. A member of The Lost State Writers Guild, Bev attends yearly writing conferences and workshops surrounding herself with authors and writers.

She and her husband, Bill, enjoy weekends touring the backroads of the beautiful Blue Ridge and Great Smoky Mountains on their motorcycle, with similar cycle-loving friends.

You can find Bev on Facebook and the fun world of Pinterest.

COMING SOON

Where Lady Slippers Grow is the second in the trilogy of Madison's life in the Southern Appalachian Mountains.

It begins five years later, as Madison McKenzie takes a break from year-round classes at the University of Tennessee to spend a summer volunteering with the Division of Forestry and the Tennessee Bureau of Investigation looking for a lost hiker. During the search she learns she wants to give back to her hometown in a big way when Sheriff Perry is injured. Will she return to college? Or let her heart lead her in an unexpected direction?

CPSIA information can be obtained
at www.ICGtesting.com
Printed in the USA
LVOW08s0839291116
514856LV00006B/6/P